I Know Your Secret

?

Question Mark Press

Jess Roy

First published in 2021 by Question Mark Press

?

Question Mark Press

I Know Your Secret/ Michael Scanlon. – 1st edition
ISBN: 9798753591562
Cover design by: Elli Toney
Blog Tours by: Zooloo's Book Tours

Chapter 1

Thursday September 5, 2019, 4.32 p.m.

Doctor Amanda Brody emerged from the revolving doors of the White Rock Medical Clinic and walked quickly towards the private hospital's car park. It was just after four thirty, but the early September sun was still hot in a clear blue sky. In a corner of the car park, where a sign said "Staff Only", she pointed her key-fob, and a lime green Mercedes in the second row of vehicles made a squelching noise in return, and blinked twice.

She crossed to it and got in, pulled off her high heeled leather shoes and threw them into the passenger foot well, took a deep breath, held it, closed her eyes, and exhaled slowly before repeating the process. She did her potato sack routine, imagining on each exhale potatoes, which represented thoughts from her busy day, running out of a bag. When the bag was empty, in theory, her mind should be empty too, leaving her to refill it with happier thoughts. It usually worked.

With her eyes still closed she pressed her feet and rubbed them across the hard rubber grooved pedals, the rough sensation soothing in a way, further removing her from her head. Then she imagined pouring herself a gin and tonic when she got home, plopping a slice of lemon into it, raising it to her lips, taking a sip... *hmm.* That was better.

She opened her eyes and placed the key in the ignition, turned it, fired the engine into life, flicked the car into gear and was about to move off when she saw it. Tucked beneath the driver's windscreen wiper directly in front of her. It was a white envelope.

Didn't whoever had placed it there know that unsolicited material was strictly forbidden within the hospital and its grounds? Even staff members couldn't promote anything, not even charity events. She thought of nurse King, with her lucrative side-line business selling expectant mums and dads coloured images of their babies in the womb. Even she wasn't allowed to advertise.

Amanda cursed under her breath, tempted to activate the wipers and try and brush the damn thing away. But she was a little curious too. Because who went to the trouble of placing a flyer inside an envelope? It didn't make much sense.

She opened the door and stretched out a hand. The thing was just beyond her reach so she was forced to get out, feeling the gritty tarmac through her nylons. She snapped the envelope out from under the wiper with a thumb and index finger, and held it gingerly, like a sample just taken from a patient. She got back into the car and threw it onto the dash. She noticed it was sealed shut too. She leaned forward and picked it up again, turned it over, like a curiosity in an antique shop. There was nothing written on it. Carefully, she lifted the edge of the seal and peeled it back just enough to place a finger inside and tear it open.

It was not a flyer, she could see that straight away, but a sheet of plain white paper. As she touched it, it felt thicker than standard copy paper, but not quite board paper either. It felt somewhere in between, like a type of card paper maybe. Amanda pried it from the envelope - it had been neatly folded in three - and opened it out. As she stared, her mind scrambled for meaning.

Was this a joke?

But as she read, her blood ran cold.

No. This was not a joke.

Chapter 2

I KNOW YOUR SECRET

She stared at the words printed on the sheet of paper in her hands, her eyes going over each letter, noting the curve of the "S", the squat bluntness of the "I". Fifteen letters in total, combining into four words, combining into one sickening belly punch.

She released it and watched it float down, coming to rest on her lap, touching her like a burning ember. But she ignored it, because at that moment a memory came crashing into her consciousness, sweeping all else before it...

Of a sliver of grey light seeping around the edges of a large curtained window next to a bed she was lying on.

And a smell, of wood polish and soap, mixed with alcohol and sweat - male sweat. She was petrified, too petrified to move or to make any sound, to even breath. From outside, she could hear the occasional swoosh of a passing vehicle. The air against her skin was sharp and cold. She realised then she had no clothes on, and her arms, painful and heavy, were like lead weights. She forced herself to try and move them. But she could not, and immediately she understood why. Her wrists were tied to the headboard. She opened her mouth, heard the loud shrill noise and realised it was that of her screaming.

I KNOW YOUR SECRET

Amanda clutched the steering wheel, tighter and tighter, a low croaking noise coming from her throat, her breathing rapid. She could feel her nails digging into her palms. But she welcomed the pain, because it diverted her attention from her rising panic.

I KNOW YOUR SECRET

Who knew her secret?
Her mind whirled.
Who?
She looked ahead, completely still, a tsunami of fear devouring her.

Chapter 3

S he drove home in a blur, her hands shaking on the wheel. Once or twice she felt tempted to pull in, that she couldn't go on, her mind churning the words over and over: I know your secret, I know your secret...

Oh, Jesus!

She slammed on the brakes at an intersection as she noticed almost too late the traffic lights had turned to red in front. The driver behind her honked his horn. She dropped her head into her hands in desperation. What was she going to do?

Tell Edward. Of course! He'd know. He'd know what to do... well, wouldn't he? Her husband was a doctor too, a consultant at one of the largest public hospitals in the country. Yes, Edward would know. Calm, practical, completely unflappable, her Edward... oh, get a grip, who the hell are you bloody well kidding? Edward...? I don't think so. The driver behind honked again, longer this time, more insistent. She glanced in the rear-view mirror, saw him gesturing wildly with his hands as he pointed. She looked and saw the traffic lights had turned to green. She moved off quickly, keeping her eyes straight ahead as the car behind shot into the next lane and overtook her.

As she continued, she realised she'd been fooling herself for so long. Long enough that the reality had almost escaped her. She mulled it over, a large white colossus looming up out of the corner of her vision. She glanced across, saw that there was a huge juggernaut alongside and she was too close for comfort. She yanked on the steering wheel, the car wobbling momentarily as it righted itself.

Okay, she told herself, relax, before you kill yourself. Take a breath, nice and slow...

When she got home to Ocean View House she made herself a stiff gin and tonic and gulped it down, made another and sat in the drawing room sipping on it, staring across the room through the French windows of the big old house to the garden outside, but seeing absolutely nothing at all. Her mind began to reach back through the years, dredging through time, trying to make sense of it all, trying to find an answer to that one question: who? Who knows my secret?

'There you are.'

She looked up, startled.

'Is everything alright?' Her husband was standing in the doorway. 'You look like you've seen a ghost. Really.'

Is everything alright? A thought sprang to mind, of being asked the very same question by someone many years before.

'What time is it?' She glanced at her watch. 'Oh, I didn't realise... I'll get something on... are you hungry?'

Edward Brody dropped his case. 'Maybe later.' He came and sat next to her.   'Tell me, how was your day?'

She felt his hand on hers and looked down at it. It was such a slender hand, a pianist's, or a surgeon's, and there was a time when its touch could have made her scream, could have sent her wild. But not anymore. She looked up into his face, such a handsome face. One time she'd thought he might be everything she had ever dreamed of. A horrible

9

sense of shame and self-loathing crawled through her as she stared at him silently, unable to speak.

'Well,' he said, tapping his knee, 'I'm going to get one of those, pointing to her glass. 'I don't think you need another, you've already had your quota for the day in that one I'd safely say.'

The warm glow from that first drink was now wearing off, leaving her feeling even more hopeless than before. She would like another gin and tonic, and maybe another one after that too, enough to send her to sleep and not to have to think about any of this until morning. But Edward would *tut tut,* and *tut tut,* and *tut tut* about it for days. It was better just to go along and keep him happy. Anyway, he was right. She'd reached her daily alcohol quota in the first glass, so it was probably all for the best.

'Really,' he said, 'you don't look so good.' He smiled. 'I should know. I'm a doctor.' It was an attempt at humour, about the limit to his grasp of the subject. Normally, Amanda might force a chuckle at a time like this, instead she sat there stony faced, as Edward placed a palm against her forehead. 'No temperature,' he said, his expression earnest, and added, 'Seriously, darling, is everything alright?'

It was all a charade of course. This polite, happy domesticity that usually passed unnoticed and invisible between them. Now she felt she couldn't take it any longer. She wanted to curse and scream, to jump up and shake this man and reveal to him her terrible, dark secret. She wanted him to come and protect her, to rescue her, to be her knight in shining armour.

But she knew that was impossible.

'How was your day?' she asked instead.

'How was my day?' looking at her strangely. 'You wouldn't be trying to change the subject now, would you?'

This time she forced a chuckle. 'Of course not.'

They were silent, a silence she felt would suffocate her, would drown her within it, a silence that had a sound all of its own, like a feral scream.

'I'm going to lie down for a little while,' she said. 'I won't be long. There's some lasagne in the fridge, just pop it in the microwave.'

His expression changed, and she realised her mistake. She might as well have mentioned one of the ten best ways to catch the bubonic plague as mention the microwave. The only reason the appliance was even in the house was because it had come free with a kitchen refit. While Amanda used it occasionally, she was always careful to clean it afterwards and have it look pristine, like it had never been used in the first place.

'The microwave?' Edward said. 'The microwave? Tell me you're not using that.'

'No, well, very rarely…sometimes, if I'm in a rush.'

He pursed his lips.

'Please, Edward, don't give out, not now. I don't feel so well.'

She could tell he was debating whether or not he would. He opened his mouth, and closed it again. For a moment he said nothing, then: 'You go and have a rest. I'll check on you in a little while.'

She smiled, a genuine smile, one of relief this time.

'But what's brought all this on?' he asked. 'I know something's up.'

She leaned forward and kissed his lips.

'Nothing's brought this on. Don't you ever have a bad day?'

11

He arched an eyebrow, an expression she found irritating.

'Well yes, of course, everybody does.'

'A lie down,' she said, 'that's all I need.'

'A good night's sleep is what you need,' he answered. 'Really, I think you should stay in bed until morning.'

She nodded. 'Yes, maybe I will.'

She left the room, feeling his eyes following her every move. She went quickly up the stairs to their bedroom, into the en-suite, locked the door and crossed to the toilet bowl, crouched over it, and vomited.

Chapter 4

Before...

She screamed until she could not scream any longer, and once, when she opened her eyes, wondered if it hadn't all been a nightmare, that she really wasn't tied to a bed, this bed, and that she had not been screaming. But then she tugged on her arms and realised she was wrong, she really was tied to the bed. She ran her tongue over her dry lips and swallowed, her throat so sore and raw the effort made her wince, as she realised that yes, she really had been screaming. Her fear morphed into an altered state of reality, one in which she was both apart of but separate from at the same time. The swooshing sounds of traffic were more frequent, and once or twice she could hear voices, loud voices from somewhere outside, somewhere below, bringing with them a reassuring sense of normalcy, blunting her fear just enough for her to think rationally for the first time.

Her mind became filled with images, a jigsaw of random memories, frozen snapshots without any order or logic. She forced herself to concentrate, picking up a piece of jigsaw and peering at it, picking up another, trying to put the two together, discarding it again when they didn't fit, picking up yet one more, and starting all over again until eventually... Click, a piece finally fitted with the one she was holding, snapping into place. She looked at the two images newly joined together, smiling faces, hers and Fiona's...

Of course. Yes, she and Fiona.

She quickly selected other pieces, knowing what she was searching for now, found them and pushed them together, click, click, click...

She considered the enlarged image. It was of the flat, she and Fiona's. Okay... they were in the flat. She ran her eyes over the remaining pieces of jigsaw. What now? She picked up some more but nothing would fit this time. She picked up more still, becoming frantic, trying to force them together, desperate to find meaning, but nothing was making sense, her memories were even more confused... then, click, as two more pieces fitted together. She stared, her breath quickening, a hollow sensation in the centre of her chest. Two dull orbs floating on a brown sea beneath a diffusion of coloured lights. She concentrated on them, bringing them into sharper focus, everything crystallising, becoming familiar, the orbs - brass handles; the brown sea - wood panelling; the diffusion of colours - an abstract of coloured glass... Yes, yes, that was it. The door to the pub. The Merchants. She and Fiona had gone there. Yes, yes, yes. She remembered, a complete section of the jigsaw coming together all by itself. The image came to life. Stepping in from the cold, from the miserable night outside, a wave of heat washing over her, as they began to push through the thick forest of people, the band on stage tuning up, 'testing, one two three...' reaching the bar and Amanda leaning over, her eyes sweeping across the faces of the serving staff, catching the eye of a barmaid, a girl with a crew cut and huge doe eyes that reminded her of Goldie Hawn.

'Two bottles of Pils,' having to shout because the band had suddenly launched into their first song, "Dirty Old Town".

As if by magic it continued, the jigsaw pieces moving of their own accord through the air, criss-crossing, seeking each other out in correct order. Everything came back to her until there were no jigsaw pieces left. But yet, but yet, the puzzle was not complete. There was still a section blank, like a great big bite had been taken out of her consciousness, her reality tapering to the jagged edges of a black void.

Panic began to rise in her again, she realised she was never going to make sense of this. Of how she had come here, had ended up in this way. And where was Fiona? Where the fuck was Fiona?

She opened her mouth to scream again, but all that came from it was a muffled croaking sound.

Chapter 5

Friday, September 6, 2019, 8.43 a.m.

She did indeed stay in bed as Edward had urged, sleeping initially, but then waking up, lying as still as possible so as not to wake her husband. He hated being woken, but yet still insisted they sleep together in the same bed. At the very least, twin beds would suit Amanda much better, but as with everything, she went along with it because she felt she had to. So for much of the night she had lain still, her mind churning, as she fought against her thoughts, not allowing any to fully develop and consume her, which they would do, an endless battle against half formed images, many too shocking even to contemplate. When the dawn light finally seeped through the curtains, she slipped out of bed and went to the en-suite, turned on the shower to full power and stepped in, hoping she could wash her exhaustion away. But when she stepped out again and wiped the condensation from the mirror to look at herself, she knew it would take much more than that, much more. 'I look dreadful,' she muttered, two bloodshot, black-ringed eyes staring back at her.

I Know Your Secret

This was bound to happen. She'd been fooling herself to think her past would just go away, disappear. Even after all this time, all these years. She thought of Edward. She really wanted to love him, but the man made it just so damn near impossible. 'The microwave,' she mimicked. 'Tell me you don't use that.' She covered her mouth. My God. Had she really just mimicked her husband like that? What did that say? Was she coming to hate him now?

She shook her head. Focus, she told herself, and opened the cabinet above the sink. Make-up and eye-drops, that's what she'd need, plenty of both to get her through this day.

When she went into the bedroom again, Edward was sitting on the side of the bed, naked. One time she might have taken this as an invitation, but not now.

'Are you feeling better?' he asked.

'Yes,' she lied, 'I didn't sleep very well, but apart from that, I feel fine now.'

He stood, gave her one of his searching looks. 'It's hard to feel good when you don't get a good night's sleep, I know.' He passed her, heading for the bathroom and added, a crust to his tone, 'You have far too much bloody make-up on, by the way, it doesn't suit you, makes you look cheap.' Then she heard the door bang shut.

But she could not compromise on her make-up, and it would remain. They ate breakfast - wholemeal bread, boiled eggs and avocadoes, in near silence, Amanda merely picking at her food. When she rose to take her plate and clear it into the sink disposal unit, Edward stared at it, then looked up and stared at her with an expression she considered to be one of disgust. She felt an almost irresistible urge to fling the plate at him. How would he like that? That would shatter the charade between them once and for all. But then she thought of her secret - her secrets - her

17

past like a great monster that had suddenly reappeared, trailing along behind her, growling, snarling, full of menace. She felt sullen and dirty. What man would have bothered with her had he known the truth? She cleared the plate into the sink, turned, told Edward she was sorry for upsetting him, lowered her head and left the kitchen quickly, denying him any opportunity to reply. Because she had to be first to leave this house, she couldn't risk another note being left on her car, and worse still, Edward finding it before she did.

She stepped out of the house and stood on the porch. The day was cloudy, but the breeze was light and cool on her face. She looked down towards her car, parked a short distance away next to Edward's big, staid, Volvo. She put a hand to her mouth, felt like throwing up again, took a deep breath and swallowed, felt a little better. She stepped onto the gravel driveway and it crunched beneath her feet as she walked towards the Mercedes. And with it a weakness came over her, and she began to stumble, just getting to her car in time to reach out and lean against it and stop herself from falling. A tall privet hedge shielded her from the house, so she knew if Edward was standing by a window looking out he would be unable to see her. She closed her eyes tightly, waited a moment, then slowly opened them again, took a couple of tentative steps forward until she had a view of the windscreen. She stared at it, and blinked...

*

'You have a full schedule,' Amanda's secretary said when she got to her surgery, handing her a clipboard with a print-out of names, times and other details on it.

18

Amanda looked it over quickly and turned away, started walking towards her surgery on the other side of the reception area.

Doctor Brody.'

She turned. 'Yes.'

Her secretary pointed to the fawn leather handbag with its gleaming brass buckles resting on the counter.

'Your handbag.'

'Oh,' Amanda felt herself blush, but knew this couldn't be seen under all the make-up she had on. There was an awkward silence as she stepped back and reached for the handbag, meeting the questioning gaze of her secretary. Amanda took great pains to present an image of professional, efficient detachment - at all times. She was not the type to forget a €5,000 Pierre Zuzo handbag. And she knew her young secretary knew this too.

'Thank you, Layla,' she said, picking it up.

She walked across the plush carpeted reception once more, feeling the eyes of Layla burning a hole into her back.

For the most part, her surgery did not look like a surgery, being predominately all dark wood panelling and soft lighting, with a large bay window to one side looking out onto the car park and the green area behind it and off in the distance, Galway Bay. To maintain the relaxing aesthetic of the office area, the actual surgery was hidden behind a remotely controlled privacy screen that divided the room in two. Her surgery, or medical suite as it was known, was one of a number at the White Rock Medical Clinic, all offering a particular speciality. Hers dealt mainly with referrals from insurance companies for long-term illnesses and injuries, as well as interactions with corporations, usually via Skype or Zoom, on health and safety policy.

Jess Roy

Amanda dropped the clipboard and her handbag onto her desk, went and stood by the window, folding her arms and staring out, her mind churning again like a rough sea, but just that little bit calmer now. Because there had been nothing there, on the windscreen. She had circled the car, making sure there was nothing lying on the ground either. Which there wasn't. Then she had thought, what about under the car? She had hitched up her skirt with one hand and had been about to get down onto her knees to have a look, but had realised the pebbles would probably tear her tights. She had unlocked the car instead, sat in and started the engine, moved it forward a short distance, got out again and inspected the ground it had been parked on. If Edward had seen her, he would have come out demanding to know what she was up to. But she didn't care. Because it didn't matter. Because there was nothing there.

There was nothing there.

She could have whooped for joy. Because if there had been a note there, it would have meant, of course, that someone had breached her world, not just the physical high walls of her home with its automatic gates, but also the immanent world, someone had violated *her*. With no new note today, it allowed her to think, maybe this had all gone away?

Now, standing by the window of her surgery, she allowed herself another thought - what if this was all a coincidence? A crazy, unlikely coincidence for sure, but that's what coincidences are? Definition of coincidence - a remarkable occurrence of events or circumstances without apparent causal connection. Of course, even taking that into account, this one was an extreme freak... but nonetheless possible. Well, wasn't it? Yes, she decided. Yes it was. That note, could be anything. She relaxed. But then another voice

20

spoke - no, no, no, it's not possible, it couldn't be anything, that would be too much, way too much of any kind of coincidence, you're just trying to fool yourself, couldn't happen, couldn't possibly...

Or could it?

She refused to discard that hope, clinging to it, holding it close, willing it to be possible, willing it to be a way-too-much-couldn't-possibly-happen-freakish-coincidence. It was possible. It was. She gave a nervous laugh, then laughed some more, a little harder this time, and was soon doubled over, clasping her hand tightly over her mouth trying to stifle the sounds. If Layla heard her, she would definitely think something was not quite right with her for sure.

The landline phone sounded on her desk. 'Doctor Brody,' Layla's voice through the intercom, 'your first patient has arrived. Shall I send Mr Henderson in?'

Amanda quickly gathered herself. She hadn't even looked at her list properly, but there was nothing she could do about that now. When she spoke, her voice was surprisingly bright and cheerful. Hopeful.

'Yes, Layla. Send Mr Henderson in, please. Thank you.'

By lunch-time, she was ravenous. Her two o'clock client had cancelled. It was a pet hate of hers when a client cancelled without giving the required twenty-four hours' notice – unless the situation was completely unavoidable, of course. But today, when Layla told her that her two o'clock appointment had cancelled, she just thought, Thank God. With the extra time, she pondered going into town for lunch. But as she did, it came back again, the fear, her belly tightening, her anxiety levels rising. That would mean taking the car. And now she could picture it, walking to the Mercedes, her heart pounding, and flickering in the wind beneath the windscreen wiper there it would be – another note. She hadn't thought about it until now, she'd been too busy. But here it was again. Oh, God.

The hospital had an excellent canteen, she'd eat there instead, sit in a corner, her back to the door, no one would notice her; she didn't want to talk to anyone, didn't want to see anybody. 'A coincidence, that's all,' she muttered to herself, 'just as you said earlier.' Go into town, because you can't live in fear like this, with your imagination running wild, go down to your car, there's nothing under that windscreen wiper, you'll see, that's never going to happen again, a coincidence, that's all, go on, go into town, go...

She left the hospital. People she knew passed her by, they spoke to her in greeting, her reply a robotic drone. Outside the wind was strong, scattering her hair about her face, but she scarcely noticed. She was aware of a sensation inside her chest, like the galloping of horses, and a loud cascading sound in her ears. She knew it was an adrenaline rush, causing her heart to beat faster, increasing the blood flow...

Her hand was clammy as she raised the key-fob, and pressed it. The car made its familiar squelching sound and blinked twice, just as it always did. She realised she had unconsciously lowered her gaze, so that she could not see above the line of the car's headlights. Slowly she raised her head to take in the windscreen.

Oh God, please, please, don't let there be another note.

Know Your Secret

Chapter 6

S he stood frozen, staring. Beneath the windscreen was... nothing.
Nothing!

She giggled, and remembering her laughing fit earlier and thought, don't start that again.

She took a slow, tentative step forward, then another, and when she reached the car, slowly began to walk around it.

'Did you lose something, doctor?'

She was at the driver's door now, and looked towards the sound of the voice.

The security officer was standing a few feet away, in his uniform: blue jacket, flannel pants and shiny brown shoes. Amanda thought it required only the addition of shoulder tassels and a bicorn hat to complete the parody of a naval officer. In the White Rock staff bulletin the head of security had boasted the uniform represented both a sense of chic and understated authority. To Amanda, she thought the uniform looked silly, like something out of a fancy dress shop.

Jess Roy

'No, Bill, just checking my tyres, it felt like one might have been a bit flat on the drive in this morning.'

Now, just toddle off and mind your own bloody business, will you, Rear Admiral?

But she realised her answer had not been the correct one to achieve this goal.

'Let me have a look at it for you,' he said instead, stepping forward.

'No. It's fine, Bill. Thank you. I know a flat tyre when I see one.'

He stopped.

'I'm sure you do, Doctor Brody. Aye, I'm sure you do. Sorry.'

'But thank you anyway,' she said, softening her tone. 'I appreciate it, it's very thoughtful of you. Now, I'd best be on my way.'

She opened the door and was about to get in, but could see from the corner of her eye that he was lingering.

'You know,' he said, 'there was someone at your car yesterday...'

Her body tensed, and with it an invisible hand reached inside her chest and squeezed - hard.

'What?' she said, suddenly breathless.

'I saw them from the main door. The policy is strict, doctor, as you know, no flyers or promotional material of any kind. So, of course, I rushed over immediately, but they were gone before I got here. I noticed an envelope under the wiper, didn't know what to think, so thought I'd best leave well alone, didn't consider it an emergency, said to myself I'd tell you when I saw you. I hope that's alright. Is it?'

She was silent, her mind spinning, cogs engaging, trying to work it out. *Someone was at my car.*

'Who?' she demanded. 'Who? I mean. A man? A
woman? Them? You said 'them'. Who's them?'

She could hear the frightened urgency in her words.

'No, not them,' he said, 'it was a man, looked like.'

'A man,' she repeated, 'young, old, what?'

The security man looked uncomfortable.

'I dunno, Doctor Brody, too far away to tell.'

'What was he like? Old, young, slim, fat, black haired...
what? Tell me.'

'He had a hat on, I didn't...'

'What type of hat?'

'Red. A beanie hat. That's all I know. I'm sorry. He was
too far away to tell anything else.'

'Okay. Okay. His build, surely...'

'Tall, okay doctor? Really, that's all I can say.'

'Then how do you know it was a bloody man...?'

She realised she'd gone too far.

'Sorry. Sorry, Bill. That was uncalled for. Totally
uncalled for. Really. I'm sorry.'

His expression hardened, and he said nothing for a
moment, like he was calculating his best response. Then a
trace of a smile cracked his thin lips.

'And I know a man when I see one,' he said, savouring
the retort. 'What I'd like to know is: what should I do if it
happens again? Call the police? I mean, we have CCTV. I
could give it to them. The hospital takes this seriously, the
thin edge of the wedge and all that.'

'No!' She practically shouted the answer. 'I mean, from
what you tell me, sounds like a, well...' her mind scrambled
for words, 'a former patient, yes, it's why I was so insistent
on a description, sorry, because it's a very delicate matter,
um, this person, this former patient has... issues, that's all.'

His expression became earnest as he nodded.

'I don't want to take any action if at all possible,' she added. 'It's just a difficult period for, um, him, one that needs my complete understanding. So, we need to keep this discreet. Between the two of us. Yes?'

He nodded again, energetically this time. She took this as confirmation of his complicity in keeping this grave professional matter secret.

But he would have a different opinion if he knew the truth, a very different opinion indeed.

She summoned up a wide smile.

'Would there be any chance,' she asked sweetly, 'if you could let me look at that CCTV?'

His expression gave nothing away, but then the Rear Admiral nodded slowly, and she promised herself never to call him by that name again.

The security office was just inside the main door to the hospital. Another officer was sitting at a desk, watching a bank of monitors. He turned as they entered.

'Everything alright?' he enquired, looking at her.

'Yes,' she said, glancing to his name tag, 'everything is fine, Peter, thanks.'

Peter was older than his colleague, bespectacled, with white hair.

Bill spoke. 'Doctor Brody just wants to look at some CCTV. See if she can identify the person who left an envelope on her car yesterday.'

'Someone did that, did they?' Peter said, 'and what was that about? Everything alright I hope?'

'A delicate matter,' Bill added, lowering his voice, the holder of a great secret.

He had not closed the office door. Amanda could see out to the busy foyer. She turned her back in the hope that anyone looking in wouldn't recognise her.

'Can you bring up yesterday, Pete..? Now, what time was it 'bout..? Four o'clock I'd say, ya, four, I was just coming back from the canteen then... bring up the staff car park, Pete, about four o'clock, ya?'

'Righteo.'

Peter pressed on a keyboard and indicated with a nod of his head to a monitor a little further along the desk. 'Monitor three, Bill.'

They stepped over to it, images of a hospital corridor flickering and disappearing, replaced by those from the car park outside. They stood silently watching for what to Amanda seemed like forever but was in fact mere minutes, before a person appeared, striding in from the bottom of the screen towards the rows of vehicles.

'Freeze it, Pete,' Bill said. 'There, Doctor Brody. That's the person, right there.'

Amanda stared at the screen, her belly tightening. She leaned in for a closer look. The person was too far away to see very much, but the gait and posture told her it was probably a male, tall, wearing a red hat – a beanie – and dark clothing, possibly navy blue jeans and a fleece.

'Can you get in close, Pete, thanks,' Bill said.

The images on the screen magnified.

'A couple of cameras are down for maintenance, Bill,' Peter said, 'this is the best I can do. Not great.'

The images continued to magnify until they eventually pixelated, the person in the beanie hat becoming a mess of charcoal strokes against a lighter bubble wrap background.

'Whooo,' Bill said, 'hold it, zoom out again, Pete, play it once more, normal resolution please.'

The screen reverted to normal resolution and began to play. Amanda watched as the person walked, a little hesitatingly to begin with she considered, by the first row of

27

vehicles, almost to the end, where he stopped, walked down between two cars to the second row. There, she was surprised to see, he walked away from her car, but only for a couple of paces, before he stopped and retraced his steps, stopped next to the one alongside hers. There, he reached into a pocket and took out the envelope, his head turning both ways before settling on the Mercedes, like he was inspecting it, finally stepping over to her car and placing the envelope beneath the wiper. Something about his gait and stature seemed vaguely familiar to her.

'The car alarm should have gone off,' Bill said, 'you'd think, though he seemed very light of touch about it... Now, and as you can see, he's walking away, heading for the short-cut through the bushes onto the road outside. No cameras out there I'm afraid.'

'He knows the area then,' Amanda said, 'would you think?'

Bill shook his head.

'Everyone knows that shortcut, it's no secret.'

'No, it's not,' Amanda agreed.

She straightened and felt, well, strangely relieved. The person she had just witnessed didn't seem very threatening to her. Indeed, she had the feeling they didn't know exactly what they were doing, seemed uncertain of the car they were looking for.

'Sorry? What did you say?' realising Bill was speaking to her.

'Anything else we can do for you, Doctor Brody?'

'No, Bill,' following up with another radiant smile, 'except to apologise for my being a little off hand with you earlier.'

He waved a hand through the air.

'Don't mention it, pressures of the job and all that. I understand. Anything any of us can do here at security for you in the future, don't hesitate to ask.'

'Thank you,' she said turning, 'to both of you. And I won't. You've been very kind.'

She left the security office and walked away quickly, realising she was sweating, emerging through the revolving doors into the daylight, the breeze like a soothing balm against her skin.

Her mood lightened, and she suddenly felt like some company. Who was available at such short notice for lunch?

Chapter 7

S he parked in a multi-storey at the rear of Shop Street close to the heart of Galway City, having played out everything in her mind on the short drive in. Now that she had witnessed the person actually place the envelope on her car, she felt both the relief of earlier but also a reassurance. Because someone had to have placed it there, it couldn't have gotten beneath the wiper all by itself. And now that she had seen this person, she felt again as she had before too, that everything was still the same, what she thought about this whole business, that it was merely a coincidence. It could be anything, a prank, a joke, someone just happened to place the envelope onto the wrong car, that's all. Well, it could. She didn't know why. Whatever the reason was for it. She didn't care, just so long as she was left alone in the future. Matter resolved, stamped "Coincidence" and filed away for incineration. Yes, it was a coincidence, because she needed it to be a coincidence. She would not start dwelling on this again. It was over.

But while Amanda would be the first to call out someone who was simply fooling themselves, she couldn't see this in herself now.

But was she fooling herself?

She'd soon find out.

*

The day felt more like one in July than it did September. Normally, she enjoyed walking through the old, narrow streets of Galway City, at this time of year still packed with locals and tourists alike. But not today, today it just didn't feel the same.

Pri was waiting in the small fish restaurant just off Shop Street, at a corner table towards the rear.

'Thanks for meeting me,' Amanda said to her friend, taking a seat, 'I didn't think you'd be able to.'

'Well, you know me,' Pri said with a laugh, 'any excuse for a good lunch with a good friend...you had a cancellation, right?'

'Right, Pri, I had... Look, I really need to talk.'

Her friend's expression became earnest. 'What's up?' lowering her voice.

Amanda felt her eyes start to well up, and she blinked back the tears, her positive conviction of just a little earlier deserting her. 'Oh, Pri.'

The waiter appeared, stood for a moment by the table, before silently withdrawing again.

Pri reached for Amanda's hand and held it in hers. 'Come on,' she said, 'tell me. What's up?'

Amanda took a breath, steadying herself. She looked at her friend, and considered that she looked tired, drawn. Was it fair to burden Pri with her problems?

She hesitated.

'Go on,' Pri prompted, 'tell me.'

'A note,' she replied flatly. 'On my car. I know your secret, that's what it said. Pri, my secret. *Someone knows my secret.*'

31

'Amy, you're not making much sense. A note? On your car? I know your secret. What secret? You never told me. Anyway, we all have secrets, don't we?'

'Yes,' Amanda agreed, fumbling in her handbag and taking out a tissue, dabbing her eyes with it, 'but not like this.'

Pri raised her eyebrows. 'Really? Come on, Amy, how bad can it be? Have you spoken to anyone else about it? A problem shared is a problem halved you know.'

Amanda shook her head. 'No. I haven't.'

'When did you get this note, by the way?'

'Does it matter? Yesterday, when I was leaving work.'

Pri's eyes widened.

'Yesterday. Why didn't you ring me before now? You could have come round. I had the house to myself. We could have talked.'

Amanda took a breath.

'I couldn't. I was in shock. Anyway, Edward likes me to be home when he gets in, you know...'

'Yes, I know...'

Pri's tone said it all.

There was silence for a moment.

'Do you want to talk about it?' Pri asked.

Amanda considered the question for the first time.

'Yes. Of course I do. Not now, that's all. Not just yet. I'm not ready. What I need right now, Pri,' she could feel tears welling up again, 'is to know that someone is there for me, that's all, someone I can trust, that's what I need. Right now.'

Pri smiled. 'Oh, Amy, you know I'm here for you. I'll always be here for you...' Her voice dropped, as she added. 'You were there for me, remember?'

Amanda remembered. Outwardly Pri was the polar opposite to Amanda, gregarious and with a wide circle of friends, yet it was to Amanda she had turned that time.

'God. I nearly left my husband for him,' Pri said, before pausing, glancing over her shoulder, then continuing, 'like, really? That'd never have worked out. Thank God you talked me out of it. I mean... ugh.' She squeezed Amanda's hand. 'That's it for me. I'm never having an affair again.'

Amanda couldn't help but smile.

'Really,' Pri said, 'I'm not. But maybe...'

'But maybe what?'

Pri gave her a long, searching, look.

'But maybe you should.'

Amanda felt a jolt. 'What?' she spluttered. 'I couldn't. I love Edward.' A silence descended again, heavy this time, a silence that she couldn't stand, that she needed to banish. A kaleidoscope of thoughts flashed through her mind, each one separate and distinct, of her father, past boyfriends, of crying alone, abandoned, unloved, unwanted. 'You see,' she said, quietly, the words escaping as if of their own accord, without any conscious effort on her part. 'I could never please my father. All my life I sought acceptance, approval, attention... from men. This may sound strange Pri, but when I got it, and I did get it, I felt unworthy, undeserving, and then I moved on.' She paused, took a deep breath before continuing, the words tumbling out. 'It was when I found a man who didn't give me what I wanted, what I thought I wanted, attention I mean, well, I stayed in that relationship, because then I had to strive to convince him that I was worthy, just as I had with my father, and I'm an only child, so everything was magnified, but if I could convince a man to treat me how I wanted to be treated, if I could change him, then in my mind, I might have been able to change my father too…'

Pri cocked her head to one side, like she was trying to make sense of what she was hearing.

'… to have him love me,' Amanda added, her voice faltering. 'Of course, I never could convince a man to change… pathetic really, that I thought I could, and it's a mistake many women make I think, which is also why I'm in this situation, with my marriage I mean. I know it, but I don't want to change it. Edward loves me, I know he does… in his own way.'

'In his own way?'

'Yes. I know that sounds stupid, and I feel stupid too for saying it.'

Pri smiled. 'You shouldn't be so hard on yourself,' her voice soothing. 'And you, stupid? Come on. You're one of the smartest people I know. How can you even think like that? Please, don't think like that, I forbid it you beautiful, intelligent person you.' Pri stretched her hand out onto the table, peering down at it, looked up again as she asked, 'How long is your dad dead now, Amy?'

'Twenty years, almost. Mother three. She was a drinker, as you know, which didn't help matters.'

'No,' Pri said, a sudden vacant look in her eyes, 'it never does, does it? Now. Come on, let's eat.'

As they sipped on coffees afterwards, everything seemed to have melted away, and Amanda felt renewed. The conversation while they ate, after the initial heaviness, was light and distracting, with nothing more serious mentioned than the axing of the Jeremy Kyle show. Amanda forgot about the note. She sat back in her seat and watched over Pri's shoulder the pedestrians streaming past the window outside, the constant movement almost hypnotic, her mind

34

blissfully empty. She saw someone stop, but didn't really pay attention until they approached the window, cupping their hands about their face, and pressed it against the pane, peering into the restaurant. She blinked. It was a man, tall, dressed in dark clothes, wearing a red hat, a red *beanie* hat. Her coffee cup clattered against the saucer as she put it down and it toppled onto its side. She dropped her gaze to it, saw it was empty, and took a gulp of air.

'What's the matter, Amy?' Pri said, 'you look like you've seen a ghost.'

Amanda said nothing for a moment, glancing up to the window again, staring at it. But now there was no one there. She wondered: had there been anyone there at that window in the first place? Or had she just imagined it? She continued to stare, but couldn't be sure, she couldn't be sure of anything.

'One minute,' she said, rising. She walked quickly through the restaurant to the door and stepped out onto the busy street, looking up and down. She couldn't see the person.

She suddenly felt very foolish. The mind can play tricks, she knew, as if it had a mind of its own.

She went back inside, catching the wary side long glances of some of the other diners.

'I thought I saw someone,' she said at the table again, but she didn't sit down. She needed to get back to work. 'The person who left the note on my car. I had to go and look.'

'That again,' Pri said. 'And was there anybody there?'

Amanda shook her head. 'No,' she said sheepishly.

'Okay then,' Pri said, getting to her feet too, 'I think we need to talk, so I can judge just how bad this secret is. In the

35

meantime, can you let it go, please? This is doing you no good, no good at all.'

Amanda nodded. 'Yes,' determined that she would. 'Let me go and get the bill.'

'I've already looked after it,' Pri said.

'You didn't.'

'I did.'

'That's naughty, Pri, it was me who invited you, remember?'

Her friend adopted a deep, husky voice, batted her long eyelashes.

'Moi? Naughty? Well, heaven forbid.'

They laughed and left the restaurant.

On the drive back to work, she looked in the rear-view mirror and imagined the envelope and note floating on the air behind her, and as she continued, she imagined that she was leaving both further and further way back in her past, until eventually there was nothing there, both had simply vanished. There hadn't been someone outside the restaurant window she decided, well, not *that* person. What, in a red beanie hat and dark clothes just like the one on the CCTV? That would be too much of a coincidence. How would they even know she was there for God's sake? It wasn't possible. And then just disappear again like that? What was the point? Yes, it was all a result of that over active, anxious, imagination of hers. Had to be.

She spent five minutes back at the surgery going through her list for the remainder of the day. All thoughts of the freakish coincidence had gone. She placed the clipboard onto her desk and realised that she was humming a song. She smiled just as the intercom sounded.

'Doctor Brody,' Layla said, 'your three o'clock appointment is here. Shall I send Mrs Clooney in?'

'Of course, Layla,' she replied brightly. 'I'm waiting, send her in.'

At the end of the day, as she returned to her car, parked in its usual spot, it returned - the dread, as her heart began to beat faster, fear tickling the back of her neck. But this time when she looked at the Mercedes her gaze did not flinch, rather it was steely, almost defiant. She walked up and looked it over carefully. All was exactly as it should be, with nothing on it that shouldn't be there. No note. Nothing. She began to hum again, scarcely even aware of it, as she pointed the key fob and – *squelch, blink, blink.* She smiled, and got into the car.

At home, she went into the drawing room and made herself a gin and tonic. A small one, mind, and deciding there would be no topper uppers slipped in before Edward got home, even if it was a Friday. And tonight, with a bit of luck, she would sleep until morning, when she would awake refreshed with her life having returned to normal.

She wasn't hungry, not after the hearty lunch she'd had. When Edward got home, she'd cook him something. She liked to do that, and she would be extra nice to him too, because she couldn't help but feel the tension between them was her fault. In the meantime, she had the house to herself, and she loved that. She noted fresh flowers in a vase on the bog oak coffee table she'd had specially commissioned from a craftsman down in Clare some years ago, and on the chest of drawers against the end wall was another set within a half circle of family photos. Of course, she'd forgotten. Today was one of the two days her part-time housekeeper came in. Bridie used to work Monday to Friday when the kids were young, but now two days a week were sufficient.

Yes, she thought, I need a good night's sleep. Tomorrow, everything will be back to the way it should be.

Jess Roy

She must have dozed. When she opened her eyes again, she was staring into a large dark patch on her skirt. She looked to her glass of gin and tonic and saw it was lying empty on its side in her lap.

'Shit,' she said, jumping to her feet.

The glass fell from her lap and shattered on the hardwood floor.

'Christ.'

There was a noise from the hallway.

She glanced to the antique grandfather clock. Yes, of course too, it was that time, just gone six. A familiar voice sounded.

'Darling. I'm home.'

Amanda froze. She heard Edward's footsteps crossing the hall and then he was standing in the doorway. He stopped, looking at her, noting the stain on her skirt, the shattered glass on the floor.

'I fell asleep,' she blurted. 'I woke up with a start. It just fell to the floor. I'll clean it up, it's no big deal.'

His eyes became hooded and she could see his five o'clock shadow was deep and pronounced, like black polish on his skin. He always looked like that when in a foul mood.

'This,' he said, 'is what I come home to. Really? This.'

She stood there, her hands by her sides, feeling helpless, dejected, useless. I deserve this, she thought, I deserve everything that happens to me. She began to sob, and this sparked something in Edward, a look of pity crossing his face. But she didn't want pity, she wanted something other than pity. Why did he only feel either anger or pity for her? Why? She needed something, anything, to escape from this moment, one that would make Edward happy, make them both happy. In a flurry she ran to him and wrapped her arms around his neck, causing them both to lose balance and stumble against the wall. She didn't care, she pressed her lips hard against his. 'Please,' she said, 'please, take me to bed, make love to me, I want you, I need you, pleeease.'

Edward pulled his head back and peered at her. If he rejected her it was over, she would leave this house immediately, and she would never return. He stared at her, she couldn't work out the emotion, but one thing was certain, his blue eyes were twinkling.

Doctor Amanda Brody, she of the cool, professional, clinical, detached demeanour, made love frantically. Desperately, escaping into that blissful world of sensual pleasure, a screaming, grunting rollercoaster escape that left her panting and exhausted when it was over. She had heard a term for it: survivor sex. Crazy or not, but that's how it felt.

As she lay there afterwards, her head resting against Edward's chest, floating on a sea of calm, her husband's gentle breathing signalling that he had fallen asleep, she was reassured that all was not lost with her marriage, that underneath everything, there was still something strong holding it together. She had never begged Edward to come to bed with her before, but she could tell that he had liked it. What she couldn't be certain of, however, was whether it was the offer of sex that had turned him on, or the control he felt from having her beg him for it. With a pang she realised that maybe she was fooling herself after all, maybe there was nothing strong about her marriage, but rather, something rotten to its very core. She closed her eyes against this thought, hoping that she was wrong, but knowing too that probably she was right. She desperately sought and needed her husband's approval, thus giving him the power to dictate how she felt. Tears began to gather in her eyes, and she squeezed them shut. All I want is love, she thought, both to give love and to be loved in return. Nothing more. Nothing less. That's all. A pure love, untainted by cruel emotions. Did it even exist?

Her mobile phone on top of the bedside locker suddenly pinged an incoming text alert, the noise loud and sharp in the silence of the room. She stiffened, expecting it to wake Edward, but her husband didn't stir. She reached out, fumbling about until she'd located it, bringing it close to her face as she brought up the message and peered at it.

And then, as if a chasm had suddenly opened beneath her, as she and her world tumbled through it into a great black void, she read the words:

BITCH. WHORE. I KNOW YOUR SECRET. DID YOU THINK I HAD GONE AWAY? HA HA HA. NO I HAVEN'T. HA HA HA. YOU BITCH!!!!!

She dropped the phone as if scalded by it and it fell onto the bed. She began to cry, her body shaking silently as she tried desperately not to make a sound. It had not gone away, none of it, she had been fooling herself all along, all her life in fact, about everything, and not only this.

Who, she wondered, could hate her so much to do this now, after all these years? Who?

That was the burning question.

Who?

Chapter 8

Before...

Four empty Pils bottles sat on the ledge of the wall next to them. There was no space on the table to put them down, it being taken up by too many elbows, other glasses and an overflowing black ashtray with the letters JPS written in gold lettering along the sides. Beyond the table was another, and beyond that another, with the spaces in between standing room only, and in such a way was the pub completely filled, with the band visible on a low stage above it all under neon lights that flashed in sequence to the beat of the bass guitar.

Amanda sat on the edge of her stool, sharing it with Fiona. They'd decided not to bother fighting their way to the bar again for another drink. The air pulsed with the sounds of music and laughter, shimmering the curtain of cigarette smoke.

The band started up another song, 'Living Next Door to Alice', with the addition of the unofficial extra chorus, 'Alice, Who the F*** is Alice', Amanda and Fiona scrambling to their feet like everybody else, laughing, belting out the extra chorus. Their glasses were half full, and they held them in their hands. Someone pushed into Amanda from behind and she turned, but all she could see was a swaying sea of faces. She turned back to look at the stage, unaware that her flat beer was suddenly effervescent.

'Hi, Amy.'

The sound of the greeting was nothing more than an audio scratch against the mountain of noise. Amanda wasn't sure she'd even heard it. She looked to the side, recognised the person.

'Ah, Christopher,' shouting to be heard, but at that moment the band fell silent, as she added, still shouting, 'it's you.' She laughed. 'Sorry.'

He smiled. She wondered if he thought she was not shouting but rather unable to contain her exuberance at seeing him. Christopher fancied himself, but she considered he was one of those people who looked much better when they didn't smile. When he didn't smile he looked broody and handsome, but when he smiled, it pulled down one side of his face, the lip drooping in a corner, making him, well, look odd. Amanda thought: if only he didn't smile, then maybe...'

'I'm here with a couple of the boys,' he nodded, 'they're over there. And you?'

Amanda placed her free arm around Fiona and pulled her in close.

'I'm with Fiona, my amigo.' She laughed, the almost two bottles of Pils she'd had just enough to loosen her knots.

'Want to join us?' Christopher's eyes widening. She could see a little pulse beginning to throb on the side of his forehead.

She felt a discreet nudge into her side from Fiona.

'Um, sure, we'll follow,' she said.

Christopher pointed. 'We're over...' a screaming guitar riff drown out his voice.

Amanda mimed the words 'We'll find you,' and
Christopher gave another of his lopsided smiles that
probably he considered was his most irresistible feature. He
pointed to her glass and made a drinking motion, telling her
he was going to get more drinks.

Amanda nodded, draining her glass, before scrunching
up her face and smacking her lips, poking her tongue out.

'Ugh, tastes a bit off.'

Fiona leaned in.

'What did you say?'

'Nothing. Let's go over to them.'

Fiona ran a hand through her hair and opened an extra
button on her blouse.

'Christopher, really?' Amanda said. 'You fancy him?'

Fiona smiled. 'Maybe...and it's not Christopher?
Everyone calls him Chris. I could say the same about
Edward, you know.'

Amanda pursed her lips.

'Ya,' she said, 'and you'd probably be right.'

They both laughed.

'Then why the hell are you with him?' Fiona asked.

Amanda looked around.

'I'm not with him, am I? I don't see Edward anywhere
here, do you?'

'You know what I mean.'

'Ya, I know what you mean. I'm not with Edward, it's
strictly casual, okay? I'm not with anyone, okay? I'm just
out to enjoy myself, nothing else. And I've told Edward the
same. But he's persistent.'

Fiona nudged her again. 'Then get a move on, girl,
before all the good ones are gone... I bet you like the
attention though, don't you, just a little bit, go on, admit it,
don't you?'

Amanda shook her head. 'Actually. No. I don't,' but couldn't help give a slight smile, 'well, okay, maybe just a teensy bit.'

Fiona laughed, as Amanda suddenly stumbled, bumping into the woman behind her, spilling some of her drink.

'Hey,' the woman called, 'look where you're going, for God's sake.'

'Amy, you alright?'

The sound of Fiona's voice was distant, muffled, fading, other sounds too, as the lights dimmed, like everything was being sucked out of the world, disappearing into a black hole, becoming smaller and smaller...

She suddenly felt like she was about to get sick.

'I don't feel so good,' her voice sounding distant, feeble.

She stumbled forward, then everything went black.

Chapter 9

S he didn't know how she got through that evening and the long night that followed. But somehow she had. They had gotten up after a couple of hours and, without consulting her, Edward had ordered in a take-away meal for two from a new organic Thai restaurant everyone was raving about. They had sat in the kitchen eating straight out of the cardboard take-away containers - unusual for Edward - and sharing a bottle of wine, because Edward decided that that was okay too. He had mellowed, cracking terrible jokes to his usual standard, and she had laughed uproariously at each, masking the torture she was going through – because that's what it was, torture. At the first opportunity she yawned, feigning tiredness, adding with a cheeky grin that a certain work-out had left her feeling exhausted. But the truth was she craved the darkness of the night so she could hide within it, so she wouldn't have to pretend, where no one could see her, where no one could find her. It was taking every ounce of her energy just to pretend, and she couldn't continue. It was then she had decided she needed to get away. If only for this weekend. Because it would be impossible to stay here. She would literally fall apart if she had to keep this pretence up, and, she knew, with a new day, and a slight hangover, Edward

45

would be impossible to be around. He would notice, he would ask questions, he would keep scratching, scratch, scratch, to get to the bottom of what was wrong with her. No, she had to leave. There was no alternative. None. A couple of days away would buy her time... but for what, exactly? To help her decide how to deal with this, surely? Because to stay was to live inside a pressure cooker, the pressure building and building, requiring more and more lies in order to release enough steam so that it didn't explode. But what if it did explode, what then? She had shuddered at the thought, and the bile had begun to build at the back of her throat again. She had kissed Edward goodnight and gone to bed, and as before, made it to the en-suite just in time before getting sick.

The next morning, she knew Edward would be playing golf just as he did every Saturday morning. She waited in bed until she heard him leaving for the club, then got up. She had a tentative, sketchy plan in mind, but nothing more. She had turned her mobile phone off after receiving the text message the evening before, and would not turn it on again until she had left the house. She had decided to go stay with Danny until Monday. She would travel back Monday morning. Her son lived in a student apartment in Trinity College. At the weekends, most students went home, but Danny had been determined to assert his independence and decided to limit his visits home to once a month. It was a four bedroom apartment with a large communal area. She'd take his bedroom and Danny could sleep on the sofa bed in the communal area. After all, it was she and Edward who were paying for the place. She reckoned at least a couple of his flatmates would have gone home over Saturday and Sunday. And Danny was so engrossed in his own life, and was at an age where he liked his party lifestyle, he would take little, if any, notice of her, she felt certain. He wouldn't like her staying, of course, but he had no choice. And she needed to be around someone at the same time. Danny would be perfect. Also, the student apartment complex was within the walls of Trinity College, and was a secure area. The gates were shut at night and the area patrolled. She would be safe.

As she packed her bag, she felt a little better. But what would she tell Edward? Should she ring Pri, discuss it with her? She decided against that. Because there was a fine line between discussing something and procrastinating over it. Ultimately, this was her problem, not Pri's, and this was something she needed to do herself.

When she was ready to leave, she sat at the kitchen table, a pen poised over a blank sheet of paper. She still didn't know what to say, but began to write anyway: *Darling, I feel dreadful, so have decided to take myself off to Dublin and have booked myself into a wellness centre, you know the one, on Dawson street, I went there before...* No, that wouldn't do. What if Edward were to ring the place and ask for her. So she took another piece of paper and started again: *Darling, I feel dreadful, so have decided to go to Dublin and take a couple of sessions in a new holistic centre I heard about. They had a last minute cancellation and can fit me in. Sorry about doing this without any notice but I'm sure you understand. It's only for a couple of days. Please don't be mad. I didn't ring to tell you because I know you're playing golf. Will talk later. Love you. Hope to be back early Monday morning... oh, I'm going to stay with Danny, and no, he doesn't know I'm coming, I'll tell him on the way. Amanda, XXX.*

She knew he would blow a gasket, but there was no alternative. And anyway, she wouldn't be around to see it, and by the time they spoke again, hopefully he would have calmed down.

Now, as she drove along the motorway to Dublin, she rang Danny on the Bluetooth via the steering wheel

47

controller. No surprise when there was no reply, which suited her just fine, so she left a message instead.

And then, as she drove in silence, with all the frantic activity over, which had served to act as a huge diversion, now that she was actually driving to Dublin, it returned. She could not ignore it. Could not keep it at bay. The fear. The numbing fear. As images from the past flashed across her mind, bringing her back there, to everything that had happened...

There was a sound, a piercing scream, that wretched her back into the present, with it an explosion of white, intense light. It came again, and again. The motorway lane stretched ahead of her, strangely empty. She realised she was in the fast-lane, but that her speed was so slow she was crawling along. The screaming sounds and the explosions of light were the flashing of headlamps and the honking of horns of the vehicles behind her. She checked her mirror and moved into the far lane, staring ahead, avoiding the glares and gestures she was certain she was receiving from those passing her by.

In the rear-view mirror a flashing blue strobe light appeared suddenly and with it the alternating wailing sound of a siren. She took a deep breath, gripped the steering wheel tighter, glanced in the mirror again. The police car was much closer now, barrelling along the fast lane, the vehicles before it scampering out of its way – heading straight for her.

Chapter 10

Before...

S he felt something, like a brush stroke against her naked flesh, and realised it was a draught of cold air. She swung her head to the side towards it, her eyes discerning shapes in the murky light, of furniture, and a door, slightly ajar, that same grey light that seeped around the edges of the curtains seeping through here too.

She took a breath and held it, realised that someone had to have opened that door. She peered ahead, taking in a contoured shape, set in relief within the gloom, like a cardboard cut-out.

And knew.

Someone was standing here, in the room.

She watched. And waited, could hear the sound of her own breathing, like the winds of a hurricane, filling her ears, filling the room, filling everything. She watched, not daring to blink, every image in the room scorching onto her memory, objects identifiable only by their shapes: the outline of a TV fixed high up on the wall, that of a long low dresser, and beside it a wardrobe, in a corner a curved back chair and a small circular table before it. Her eyes took them all in.

And the contoured shape, that began to move now, her body juddering in response, an involuntary movement. Amanda began to shake with fear. The shape had a strange fluidity about it as it moved, like a shadow within a shadow, a shape shifter. It approached the window and stopped, the edges that were rimmed in that grey syrupy light. But it was enough to discern it as a male, the hairy thigh and lower leg like an animal that was standing on its hind legs, the edge of a belly, a milky white arm, the corner of a neck...

She stopped herself from looking up. To the face. Because she knew to see it, or part of it, would carry grave risk. From somewhere her mind flung out a headline for her to ponder, a warming: Accused said he killed the victim because she had seen his face and could later identify him.

No, she could not look at his face.

As if he had read her mind, he reassured her: 'It's alright. You can look.'

She knew she shouldn't, and everything screamed for her not to, but her head raised itself anyway and she stared with fatalistic resignation. To him. To his face.

Chapter 11

Saturday, 7 September, 2019

'No parking on campus, ma'am'

'What?' Amanda said. She had turned off the busy city street into a Trinity College entranceway. She hadn't expected to meet a security guard and a closed barrier gate. 'You mean there's no parking on the college campus?' she added.

'Staff and designated visitors only, ma'am,' he said, glancing behind her to a van that had pulled up. 'Now. I'll have to ask you to move. You're holding up deliveries.'

'Where can I park then?'

The security man gestured to the van driver, indicating with hand motions for him to reverse.

'There's a parking area further along Pearse Street,' he said with a gruff, distracted air, 'turn left, right again at the lights, you'll see it.'

'You mean left after I reverse out of the...'

'Please, Mrs, will you reverse? Now. I've been polite. You'll have the whole area clogged if you don't get a move on sharpish. Come on now, reverse, please.'

She began to do so. The van behind her was holding up traffic on the roadway outside so she was able to swing out without difficulty. A police car travelling in the other direction passed by without showing any interest. She thought of earlier, on the motorway, the police car that had been barrelling along behind her. She'd felt certain it was coming for her. It wasn't. It simply zoomed by, on its way to some emergency or other. Fear wrapped its cloak tightly about her as she thought of it, as she thought of all that had been happening to her lately. She shook her head, clearing her mind, for a short time at least.

She found the parking area; it was little more than a strip of derelict waste ground with a billboard above it announcing that construction of a new office block would commence early the following year. In the meantime, a stooped man with a money bag slung from his shoulder was collecting €20 for a day's parking. Amanda was grateful to pay it and so be free of her car.

A blast of warm air suddenly pushed against her and the ground vibrated, with it a loud rumbling noise. She found she was standing at the intersection of the busy street without having any recollection of having walked there. The tips of her shoes were over the edge, her body dangerously close to the passing traffic. The warm air and the rumbling noise she had heard had come from a passing box truck. She stepped back, catching the looks of those around her. When the lights changed she hurried across the road and went through the gates onto the Trinity College campus.

A strong gust of wind suddenly stirred, pushing before it an empty coke can that tinkled over the ground as it was swept along. Why couldn't the lazy so and so who had thrown it there have placed it into a rubbish bin instead? Was that so difficult? Maybe it was her own son who was responsible? Would he do such a thing? She forced herself to consider the matter, seeking any diversion from her thoughts she could find.

But then she heard a sound, something other than the clumping of footsteps all around her because Trinity College was also a busy pedestrian thoroughfare too. She turned her head as she walked, cocking an ear. She listened, filtering out all other sounds, waiting for whatever it was to come again. But it didn't, so she continued, dismissing it once again as the work of her imagination. But just as she did, there it was, unmistakeable this time, drifting on the air...

'I know your secret.'

She froze, stopping in her tracks, as she spun around, the person walking behind crashing into her with a loud *ooomph*. It was a young woman dressed in a red floral pattern dress. The woman glared at Amanda, and Amanda could not help but glare back. The young woman patted herself down and walked around her, giving Amanda a wide berth, no longer staring, as if having decided that she was simply a crazy person and so best avoided. The young woman hurried away, glancing over her shoulder a couple of times, probably to make sure Amanda was not following her.

Amanda wondered: is this the person who left me that note and text message, who's begun to make my life a misery? And who has just whispered those words? She was tempted to follow, but instead simply stood and watched, the distinctive red dress fading until it disappeared.

To secure student accommodation on campus required luck and perseverance. In her son's case, it was mainly luck. Amanda always considered that if only he had to actually work for something, then Danny might appreciate it, but he never had.

She pressed the button labelled 15A in the panel by the door of the student hall. The building was a long three storey red brick affair with lime stone columns, in keeping with the general architectural style of the college.

There was no reply, so she pressed the button again, longer this time, more insistent.

An electronic crackling sound followed, then a disjointed voice came through the intercom, unmistakeably her son's: 'Ya.'

'Danny. It's your mother. Let me in.'

'One sec.' He sounded sleepy. There was a buzzing sound and a loud click as the door unlocked. She pushed it open and stepped into the foyer.

The apartment was on the second floor. When she went in she saw that it was surprisingly clean. Not spotless, and not exactly clean, but *surprisingly* clean. Danny was dressed in flip flops, grey sweat shorts and a green T-shirt that had a prominent stain on its front below the neck. He needed a haircut too, and was unshaven, his blue eyes bleary. She got the distinct impression he had hurriedly cleaned the place up just before she'd arrived. For a moment, as she observed her son, she completely forgot the reason she had come here, her mind blank, as if she had passed through into the eye of a storm. But just as quickly it was gone, and the great weight pressed down again on her shoulders, threatening to crush her beneath it, and as it did she felt her knees begin to buckle. She reached out, but there was nothing to hold onto. Then, just in time, Danny rushed over and scooped her in his arms as she began to fall.

'Mum... What's wrong? Are you okay?'

He led her to a sofa and sat her down.

'Mum?' he said.

She forced a smile.

'It's nothing. I just felt a bit lightheaded. I'm fine.'

'No, you're not. You almost fainted for God's sake. And where's Dad? Why are you here anyway? On your own? You look terrible. Have you and Dad had a row? Is that it?'

She laughed aloud. She and Edward hardly ever rowed. She could count on two hands the number of times they had, and that was with a couple of fingers surplus. Edward didn't need to have a row to get his point across, and she knew better than to provoke him.

'No,' she said, 'of course not.'

'Why then? Tell me.'

She stared at her son, her beautiful, young, impetuous, gregarious, and in many ways still innocent as a child, son. As she thought this she caught a movement in the corner of her eye. She turned. Standing in the doorway of her son's bedroom was a girl, dressed in nothing but a bra and knickers.

Maybe her son wasn't so innocent after all.

Chapter 12

'Danny,' the girl said, 'have you seen my clothes anywhere?' And looking at Amanda, raised a hand, wriggling the fingers in greeting. 'Hi.'

'This is my mother, Sally,' Danny said.

'Hi,' Sally answered, displaying not the slightest hint of embarrassment. 'Oh, I see them, it's okay.'

She crossed the room and stepped behind the kitchen counter. Amanda didn't want to think of how her clothes had ended up there. She pulled on jeans and sweatshirt and caught Amanda's look again.

'Oh, don't ask,' stepping out from behind the counter, pulling on a pair of Ugg boots. She went and kissed Danny and walked to the door. 'Dan, catch you later, ya? Nine o'clock, ya?'

'Ya,' Danny said, 'see you there.'

She raised her hand and wriggled her fingers again. Amanda was beginning to find this irritating.

'Bye,' she said and left the apartment, the door closing gently behind her.

Danny ran a hand through his thick hair, and looked to the floor, seemingly waiting for his mother to say something about Sally.

'I'm staying a couple of nights,' she said instead, quickly forgetting all about the girl. 'Tell me you have clean sheets for your bed.'

He looked up, surprised. 'A couple of nights. You never said you were staying a couple of nights.'

'I did, Daniel, it's in my texts. Didn't you read them?'

'I didn't study them, if that's what you mean. Anyway, I can't find my phone. It's around here somewhere. Sal tried to ring it, but the battery must be dead. Mum, I have some friends coming round later. Can't you book a hotel instead?'

'Christ, I pay for this place, you know, your father and I both. The least you can do is allow me stay over on the very odd occasion when I want to... sorry, Daniel, I'm not in a very good mood, and I don't feel so well.'

'Yes, I can see that. Well what's wrong then? Tell me.'

She suddenly remembered she had not turned her phone back on. She fumbled in her handbag, found it and pressed it to life.

'I'll be fine. I have an appointment at a wellness centre, I've been overworking, the usual, that'll sort me out.'

'Wellness centre? I never heard you mention one of those before.'

'That's because you probably weren't listening.'

Danny gave her a look. 'In the linen cupboard,' he said. 'What?'

'The sheets. Clean sheets. There's a stack of them in there.'

She saw on her phone she had seven missed calls. All from Edward. Her belly heaved. Suddenly it rang again, giving her a start, Edward's name flashing across the screen. She took a deep breath, answered it, pressing it to her ear. 'Edward, I'm...'

'Amanda, what the hell? Where are you? You're not answering your phone. And you just took off li...'

'Please, Edward, I'm not feeling very well, not now, I don't need it.'

'You never told me,' he exploded, ignoring her plea, 'you never mentioned. Not one word. And for what? A holistic centre? You don't need a bloody holistic centre, you're a doctor for God's sake, we both are.' His breathing sounded like small explosions in her ear.

'Sorry,' she said softly, knowing to do anything else was useless. You can tell him the truth, can't you? Because, whatever else, he's your husband after all.

'Is there something you want to tell me?' he demanded, as if reading her mind.

'No,' she said, alarmed, shocked that she could even contemplate telling him. She would tell, could tell, Edward nothing.

'Are you having an affair?' he asked, his tone low, blunt.

'What?' spluttering. 'Is that what you think?'

'It crossed my mind, but then I thought that if you were, you wouldn't draw attention to yourself the way you're doing now. I don't want to be made a fool of, Amanda, I don't want to be cuckolded... God, what a word.'

'I...I...'she began, and fell silent. Then: 'I have never been unfaithful to you. How could you even think such a thing? Especially after...' She glanced at Daniel, who was standing by the breakfast counter out of earshot. 'After last night. Can't you tell?'

'What, at how desperate you are, is that it?'

His words hit her like a punch to the stomach.

58

'I'm sorry,' he said, but he didn't sound it, 'that was uncalled for.'

'Yes it was. But what's new? You know how to hurt, don't you, really hurt I mean? Those little comments of yours, sharp and pointed, you know how to twist them in, right in.'

'What?'

'You know what I mean. An affair you say. Maybe you're the one having the affair? Why mention it? You think I feel good enough about myself to have an affair with anybody? Do you?'

'So, you've thought of it, have you? Amanda, don't turn this onto me now.'

'Just answer, Edward.'

'No. Of course not.'

'But you would say that, wouldn't you?'

Again, he fell silent. There was only the sound of those little explosions in her ear. Then he spoke, slowly.

'I'm worried about you. I'm beginning to think you need...'

'You're beginning to think I need what?' she snapped, cutting him off. She rarely, if ever, snapped at Edward.

'To talk to someone for God's sake, a counsellor maybe.'

'A shrink, that what you mean?'

'Yes, if that's what you want to call it. A counsellor. Why not?'

'I told you, Edward. I don't feel so well. A session at the holistic centre should help. Please, can't you just understand that?'

'I'm trying. But you're not making it easy. In fact, you don't make anything easy, you know that, don't you?

Yes, I do, she thought.

Edward laughed softly, the sound almost bordering on a sneer. 'You come home when you want to, Amanda, okay. You do whatever you want.'

'I'll be home Monday morning.'

'Fine. Whenever. We'll talk then. See if we can work this out. But I'm tired of it all. Very tired. In fact, I think I might have had enough.'

He hung up. She took the phone from her ear and looked at it, at the same time noticed that Daniel was standing much closer to her than she had thought.

'An affair,' he said. 'Mum...?'

Amanda couldn't help it, she burst out laughing, opening her arms wide.

'Come here and give your mother a hug. What do you think? An affair?'

She was surprised when Daniel came to her without hesitation and squeezed her in a tight embrace.

'I know what Dad's like, Mum. It's not your fault. I know you're not having an affair.'

'Not my fault?' she repeated, as if she had never considered that before. 'You mean that?'

'Yes Mum, I do. Dad's a pain in the arse, everyone knows it. And he's said before he was going to leave, but he never does. Truth is, I don't know how you put up with him, I don't know why you don't just leave.'

'You don't?' she said.

'I love Dad an' all, but no, I don't. I told you this before.'

'You did, Daniel, yes, you did.'

'But you need to be reminded of that, don't you? You're the best, Mum, you really are.'

And with that comment it all returned. Her secret. The calamity. *You're the best, Mum.*

60

Oh no. I'm not the best. I'm the worst. I'm evil.

Chapter 13

I t was still bright outside when she went to bed, feeling utterly exhausted. The flimsy curtains did little to block the light from filtering through. Still, she mercifully fell into a deep, dreamless sleep.

She awoke abruptly, her eyes snapping open. The room was dark. For a moment she was confused, reaching out to the other side of the bed for Edward, but it was cold and empty. She sat bolt upright, looked at the ribbon of light framing the door that was the light from the communal area outside. An eruption of sound followed: *boom, boom, boom,* which she recognised as the pulsating bass line of some song or other being played at a very loud volume, and then the sound of a girl giggling, then a male voice shouting, *'Knock it back. Knock it back. Knock it back,'* each shout accompanied by a chorus of grunting noises, getting louder and louder each time.

Amanda jumped out of bed, threw on her dressing-gown, went to the door and yanked it open. She stood looking out at a crowd of youngsters gathered round a sofa, someone standing on the armrest, pouring the contents of a bottle of wine from a height down she guessed into the mouth of someone else lying unseen there. None of them noticed her, she doubted they noticed anything. She spotted Daniel, swaying at the edge of the group, a bottle held haphazardly in one hand, foaming beer dripping onto the floor. She stormed over as the last of the wine trickled from the bottle and there was the sound of spluttered coughing. The group erupted into wild laughter and then, as if on cue, turned and looked at her. They fell silent. The lad nearest - he was wearing a Trilby hat pushed back on his head, and jeans so low they revealed half his Calvin Klein underwear - staggered in her direction.

'Hi there,' he slurred, 'w-where've you been hiding, g-gorgeous?'

Gorgeous, had he really just said that?

'P-personally, I've always liked the o-o-older woman myself. You know w-w-what they say? The older the f-f-fiddle, the sweeter the t-tune.'

'What?' She looked at the lad, and then towards her son. 'Daniel. Come here. Now!'

He strode over to his mother, suddenly appearing very sober, lowered his voice as he hissed. 'Mum, what are you doing here?' He placed a hand on her back and nudged her towards the bedroom.

'Hey, Danny, why n-not introduce us?' Trilby Hat said. 'Age is o-o-only a number, right.' And then the whole group broke into drunken laughter.

Daniel led her into the bedroom and closed the door. He glared at his mother.

'What?' he demanded. 'Are you doing? What?'

'What am I...? I'm trying to get some sleep, that's what I'm trying to do. What time is it anyway? No one could put up with this racket. No one.'

'Well, we can, and Mother, you have no right...'

'No right,' she cut him off, 'just you remember your father and I pay for this place, like I told you, we pay for everything, your education, don't you forget that, we're paying for the whole lot, my laddie.'

'Ya, ya, ya,' Daniel shot back, 'I've heard it all before. But these are my friends, and so what if we're drunk and stupid. So what? I'm twenty years old, I'm supposed to get drunk and act stupid sometimes. But I rarely miss lectures, none of us do. Can't you just leave us alone, this is our world, okay? Let us be stupid. Weren't you ever stupid? And Dad too? Come on...'

She opened her mouth to say something but closed it again. She took a step and wobbled as she thought of it, her secret, reached out to hold onto something, but there was nothing. Danny rushed to her, reaching just in time once again to stop her from falling to the floor.

'Christ, mother. I'm worried about you. I really am. I'm going to ring Dad, sorry, but I have to.'

'You won't need to,' she said. 'Because I'm leaving. Right now.'

'What? You can't. You almost fainted.'

'I can, and I will.'

'Where'll you stay?'

'In a hotel, in my car, on the bloody street, who cares? Just give me my bag.'

'Wait a minute, Mum, okay,' Daniel said, leading her to the bed, sitting her down. He then left the room, and there was a clicking sound. What, he hasn't? she thought. She stood, slowly crossed to the door and tried the handle. She couldn't believe it. He had. He had locked the door.

Locked the door! He can't lock the door. He can't. And right then she was back there. Her breathing came in short gasps as she closed her eyes tight against the sensory onslaught, the nightmare memories. But it was too late. She could feel the ropes again that tethered her to the bed, chafing against her skin, drawing blood. She could feel the dark cloak of fear pressing in on her. Her eyes opened and she stared at her wrists, as if seeing them for the first time. There was nothing there; no rope, nothing. She looked about, in a daze, began moving, half staggering, half stumbling, towards the bed. Before she reached it she fell to her knees, sobbing, drowning beneath the memories.

Chapter 14

Before...

The side of his face was like it had been sprinkled in fine dust, or ash, with a metallic sheen to it that brought to mind a robot. She was no longer shivering, the room had become so suddenly very hot, the air thick and clammy. Her mind felt limp and heavy, but her body seemed to have detached itself and floated off, was separate, she no longer could feel even her arms. He took a step towards the bed, and she registered it with little more than a twitch of her eyes. She felt like an observer, watching from somewhere far off, and she felt strangely unafraid; rather, she felt resigned. Still, his face fascinated her. The light had softened, not only was it visible along the edges of the curtains, but through them too, like they had been dipped into a pool of light and taken out again, leaving them soggy and dripping with it. Without taking her eyes from him, she could see in the periphery of her vision the shapes taking on colour, as if being painted by an unseen hand, all bland beiges and browns, except for the curve-backed chair, that was a series of bright swirls and hexagonals, like it was demanding, shouting out to her for attention. Instead, now that she could see it, she completely ignored it. And her complete focus centred on him, totally on him.

He reached the foot of the bed and stood there, the strangeness of the face giving way before the increasing light its secret. A mask. He was wearing a mask. She wondered at her calmness. Why was she not frightened? Was it because the mask was not so much scary as odd? It stretched over his face, cling wrapping his ears and nose, buttressing his lips, cobwebbing his eyes behind a fine mesh.

She shook her head, trying to shake away the heaviness there, the movement as if in slow motion and seeming to continue even when she'd stopped. He was standing just a little down from her when she peered again. There was a creaking noise, and she saw that he was sitting on the bed. She felt something on her leg, soft and warm, and she shifted, trying to push whatever it was away, the same slow motion sluggishness as before, the movement seeming to flicker and continue even after her leg had stopped moving. It started to crawl up her, and she narrowed her eyes and looked at it, saw it was a hand, his hand, as it turned and went over the crest of her thigh, disappearing into the crevice between her legs.

She spoke, a slow, slurred, rasping sound.

'You bastard. Fuck off. Bastard. Fuck off.'

Chapter 15

Sunday, 8 September, 2019, 9:20 a.m.

When she opened her eyes again she felt like she had a filthy hangover, her head hurt, she was nauseous, but more than anything, she had absolutely no recollection of how she had gotten... well, where, exactly?

She looked about the room. A mirror on the lilac wallpapered wall reflected the sunlight through the window as did the mini chandelier that sent dancing orbs around the ceiling.

She recognised it now. It was one of the spare bedrooms in her house.

'You're awake.'

Her head spun round, sending a bolt of pain through it. She winced, then blinked twice.

'Lauren,' she said.

Her daughter rose from the chair by the bed and smiled, then leaned down and hugged her mother.

'It's okay,' she said sweetly, 'just let me do this first, Mum.' She reached for Amanda's wrist with one hand to check her pulse. 'Much better,' she said as she rested her hand back onto the bed.

'Lauren, darling... shouldn't you be at the hospital, your internship?'

'Don't worry about anything Mother. I took a couple of days off, nothing happens for the first few days anyway. I've just started. I can catch up later, no problem. The first module is genomics and stuff like that. No big deal.'

'But,' Amanda said, 'what happened? And where's your dad? Lauren, your studies. Genomics and *stuff,* as you call it, are important. I don't like this. I-I...'

'Please, Mum,' Lauren said, resting her hand gently against her mother's cheek. 'It's okay, we all need a little help sometimes. You were always there for me, remember. Now it's my turn.'

'I'm your mother, Lauren, I'm supposed to be there for you.'

'And I'm your daughter, I'm supposed to be there for you too. Okay?'

Amanda smiled. 'You've turned out to be a fine young woman. I'm proud of you. And Danny... God, Danny, I have some explaining...'

'Shhh,' her daughter said again, 'don't agitate yourself, Mother, everything is fine with Danny.'

'Really?'

'Really.'

'What day is it?'

'Sunday evening, Mother.'

Amanda processed this information. The pain in her head had subsided. She felt unusually calm. She glanced to the bedside locker, saw a container of pills.

'Dad prescribed you something Mum, it's really helped.'

'It's given me a hangover,' Amanda answered. 'Sunday. I've lost a whole day. My God. Tomorrow. My patients...'

'I've told Layla that you've come down with something. I rang her at home, there's no problem, she's contacted all the patients on your list. I told her to do it for Tuesday too. Yes, mother, you're going to need a couple of days' rest. You haven't been a day off sick in years. So, no work until Wednesday, okay?'

Amanda smiled. 'Thank you, and Lauren?'

'Yes, Mum?'

'Am I losing it? I mean, really.'

Lauren was silent. Then, 'I think you need a little rest, Mum, that's all, afterwards you'll be fine, really.'

Amanda tried to sit up, but slumped back against the pillows as a stab of pain cut through her head again.

'Mum, take it easy, please, come on, don't move now.'

'Okay,' Amanda whispered, 'but for God's sake, tell me what happened, please. Sunday evening, I can't believe it.'

Lauren took a breath. 'Dad went up to Dublin to get you. He left here straight after Danny rang, got there about five o'clock in the morning.'

'Edward,' Amanda muttered.

'You were...'

'I was what, Lauren,' when her daughter didn't finish. 'Tell me.'

'You were crying when he got there, rambling, stuff... you don't remember anything?'

'No, sweetheart, I don't... and Lauren?'

'Yes, Mum?'

'I'm sorry, from the bottom of my heart, for all this. You understand that, don't you?'

'Of course I do. You're my mother, and we're family. This is what it means to be family. This is what we do. Dad put you in the car and brought you home. He's been thinking about contacting Andrew.'

Andrew O'Shaughnessy, clinical psychologist at Galway University Hospital and a golfing buddy of Edward. His wife Emily moved in the same circles as Amanda. She felt a ripple of anxiety run through her. She didn't want that woman knowing anything about this.

'He didn't, did he? Ring Andrew? Tell me he didn't.'

'No, Mum, he thought you wouldn't like that. He prescribed something himself instead, hoping that would help.'

Amanda sighed. Thank God.

'I think he called it right,' Lauren said. 'By the way, Pri rang. I told her what happened. I hope that's alright, Mum. It's Pri after all.'

Amanda smiled. 'That's alright. Pri, I don't mind, you know I don't mind. I was going to tell her myself.'

They were silent then.

'Is that it?' Amanda asked her daughter. She had the feeling Lauren wasn't telling her the whole story. 'What about Danny? How is he?'

'He's been surprisingly mature about all this. Dad said everyone else at that party was wasted, except him. Danny was concerned solely with looking after you. I'm quite proud of him actually.'

'And me too,' Amanda said.

'No one much even noticed what happened. But Mum, now you have to tell me. What did happen? Are you going through something? Do you need to talk about it? I need to know. We need to know. You understand that, don't you?'

Amanda nodded. 'Of course I understand, sweetheart.'
She paused, because she hated having to lie to her daughter,
to her family. 'I'm not going through anything. I was a little
unwell, probably had a temperature, that's all, but I'm fine
now. You know, I had a patient one time who had a
temperature of a hundred and three degrees, thought he was
Superman, absolutely off his rocker. That's what it can do.
I'm sorry, but I'm fine now. '

Lauren looked at her gravely.

'Are you sure, Mum, there's nothing else? You would
tell me, wouldn't you?'

'Of course, Lauren, sweetheart, and I'm sure, there's
nothing else.'

Lauren bit her lip. 'You were sobbing, saying you were
sorry. What were you being sorry for?'

Amanda closed her eyes. 'I don't feel so good, darling,
can we talk about this later?'

She could feel her daughter's eyes on her, could sense
her debating what to do. Despite the medication, Amanda's
heart began to gallop, as the dark cloak of fear tightened
about her again, each breath catching in her throat. She
needed to change the subject.

'How is your father taking all this?'

'Well, you know Dad.'

Yes, Amanda thought, I do.

'He's concerned, Mother, like we all are.'

Lauren's relationship with her father was much closer
than Danny's, and Amanda was always careful not to be
seen to criticise Edward when around her.

She said with a forced laugh, 'I have no clue what I was
rambling about. Now, I'd like to rest a little while, darling,
okay?'

'Of course, Mother.'

72

'You can go if you want.'

'No. I like sitting with you, if that's alright?'

'Of course... and Lauren?'

'Yes, Mother?'

'Your dad. I don't want to, I mean, I couldn't face... Just, don't tell him I was awake. I'll talk with him in the morning, can you do that?'

Lauren did not reply for a moment. 'I understand, Mother,' she said. 'Have some rest. Don't worry about Dad.'

Amanda closed her eyes, and lay still, hearing the sounds as Lauren sat back in her chair by the bed. Never in her life had she felt so hopeless.

What am I going to do?

Chapter 16

Before...

The shower had been running for ages, the grinding noise of the motor piercing her brain, a pounding pain beginning to build behind her eyes. The silence that followed amplified her confusion and so too her hopelessness. She stared through an open door to the right of the bed, a vista of a toilet bowl, empty shelves above it, the corner of a window high up on the wall, all shrouded in steam. There was a raw wetness to her crotch. She knew without remembering, she knew, and felt disgust, but more than anything, fear.

She listened. There was the soft padding sound of feet from behind the door, then a buzzing, like a swarm of bees, she recognised it as that of an electric razor. The normal sounds of a morning, but there was nothing normal about this. It was morning after all, well, wasn't it? The light through the windows told her so. A bright, hard, cold light, not the waning glow of evening.

There was another sound, like a brush across a floor, as she saw the door move, opening wider. She took a breath, held it, forgetting all about the growing pain in her wrists and arms, waiting...

A hand appeared around the corner of the door, and a man stepped out from behind it, shrouded in the swirling mist from the shower, a malevolent apparition, transfixing her with fear, the mask that cling wrapped his head glistening. And she wondered: is this the end?

His feet made a squelching sound as he walked across the room towards her. Her sense of vulnerability was acute, and she crossed her legs, pressing her thighs tightly together. The rawness in her crotch became a burning sensation, but she ignored it, squeezed even tighter.

He reached the bed and his hands hovered over her face, and she felt a pressure on her nose, knew it was his fingers squeezing her nostrils closed, forcing her to open her mouth, dropping a pill into it when she did, sealing it shut again with his hand and pinching her nostrils once more, forcing her to swallow. Then he released her and she gagged, listening to the sounds of his footsteps retreat from the room. She didn't know how long it was – could have been an hour, could have been a day - before she heard footsteps returning, and the side of the mattress sagged, and she turned, saw him climbing onto the bed beside her.

'No,' her voice a garbled muffle, squeezing her thighs, ignoring the pain, but her strength was ebbing, and she was beginning to feel numb and sleepy. She looked on, a mere observer again, as he nudged her legs apart with one hand, rising up momentarily before her, before coming down and settling.

She tried to turn her body away, to shift him off her, but it was no use, he was much too strong, as everything started to dim again, fading, fading, then gone.

Chapter 17

Monday 9 September, 2019.

It was late afternoon; Amanda and Lauren were sitting in the conservatory, the sun streaming through the glass panels making it very warm.

'You're not cold, Mother, are you?'

'No, sweetheart.'

'I just saw you shiver,' Lauren said. 'I hope you're not getting another fever.'

'No, I'm sure I'm not, a bodily reflex, nothing more, as it returns to normal. My headache is gone, and I don't feel groggy. Yes, I'm much better.'

'If you're sure.'

'I'm sure.'

Amanda stood, rearranged her dressing gown, securing the cord tightly around herself. 'I'm going into the garden for a breath of fresh air.'

Lauren was about to get up.

'No,' Amanda said, 'on my own, if you don't mind. I want to get my head in order.' At least that part was true.

'Of course, Mum, whatever.'

'And Lauren, I want you to go back to your hospital placement tomorrow. Please. Will you promise me?'

'I can't promise you anything, Mum. Let me talk to Dad, first. Okay? He needs to be involved.'

She nodded. 'If you think. But it's what I would prefer, I don't want to disrupt your studies any more than I already have. You understand that?'

'Of course.'

'Good. Then let me get some fresh air. We'll talk later. Have you seen your father?'

'This morning, at breakfast, before he went to work.'

Amanda said nothing. It was obvious Edward was avoiding her, which suited her just fine.

'I told him you were doing well,' Lauren said. 'He asked.'

Amanda nodded, standing up shakily. 'It's okay,' she said, noting Lauren's look of concern. 'I can manage.'

She went outside, and the air was fresh and bracing, holding she detected, the first chill of the approaching autumn. At the end of the garden was a shaded nook between two old Spruce trees. From a branch of one hung a wicker egg chair. It was one of Amanda's favourite spots. The house was not visible from here, it was her own little corner of the world. But what she had said was true, she did feel much better. Because she had a realisation, like the first time as a junior doctor when she had encountered an emergency and had looked around to find nobody was there to help. That she was on her own, the life of someone depended on her and her alone and no one else. So, she had learned to cope, to deal with whatever was thrown her way. And now she had to deal with this too. She took a breath, for the first time rationally considering her options.

When she went back into the house she was taken by surprise. Because she could hear voices from the drawing room, one of which was Edward's, but he was supposed to be at work. The other was the unmistakeable booming tones of Andrew O'Shaughnessy. She didn't want to speak with either of them, because she knew Edward sought to test her mental stability. She wanted nothing to do with it, because she wasn't certain of what the answer would be. As a doctor, she knew all it sometimes took was a signature on a piece of paper to have someone locked away for their own good. Perhaps she was a little paranoid, but much had happened – was happening – to give her cause to be this way. She crossed the hallway quickly, heading for the staircase, planning to go back to bed, lock the door, stay there until...

'Amanda,' Edward's voice sharp as it echoed across the hallway.

She turned. He was standing in the doorway to the drawing room. She considered he had been standing there all along, out of sight, waiting for her. 'Andrew is here. Come on in and have a word, won't you?'

She hesitated.

'Well, won't you? You don't mind surely?'

His voice was pleasant, which it wouldn't have been if his eminent friend hadn't been there. However, there was a hardness in his eyes as he stared at her. For a fleeting moment she considered feigning a headache and going to her bedroom anyway.

'No, of course not,' she said meekly instead, walking towards him.

Andrew O'Shaughnessy was standing in the centre of the drawing room, hands casually in his pockets. He was wearing a crumpled linen suit and she guessed he had come directly from his practice. She felt guilty at the inconvenience she was causing both the psychiatrist and Edward who would have had to juggle his own work schedule too to be home this early. She picked up immediately on a sense of forced relaxation about both men, especially her husband.

'Amanda, how are you?' Andrew said casually.

She was aware that she looked dreadful, without any make-up, her hair a mess. She ran a hand through it self-consciously.

'How's Emily?' she said, because it was all she could think of. She heard the door close and looked around, saw that Edward had left the room. It was just herself and Andrew now.

'I'd like to talk to you, Amanda, if I could. And don't you worry about Emily, I promise this will be strictly between ourselves. I won't say anything to her, nothing, you have my professional word on that. Shall we sit down?'

His tone was sombre. She stood silent, staring, as a fleeting thought crossed her mind. Could she tell him, could she tell him, *everything?* Because this was her chance, perhaps her only one. And then it was gone just as quickly again.

No. She couldn't tell him. Of course not. She couldn't tell anyone. The thought of what would happen if she did, chilled her to the bone. No, she could not take that chance. Ever.

'Yes, let's sit,' she said, walking to an armchair and sitting, indicating to the one opposite, smiling, determined, desperate even, to convince this man, and everyone else, that there was nothing wrong with Amanda Brody.

They spoke for almost an hour. In fact, Amanda enjoyed the experience. She spoke about the stresses of her job, because she knew it was a common topic for them both to agree on. She even coaxed the clinical psychologist to talk about himself a little. 'Yes,' he'd agreed, 'job related stress, particularly in our disciplines, is a challenge for all health care professionals.' He seemed to realise he had gone off topic and brought the conversation back onto her. So she spoke about herself truthfully, because she knew he could spot a lie a mile off. She just didn't talk about *that*. She was surprised at how easy it was, to act like everything was alright, like nothing had happened. And it was a relief of sorts to just pretend that it was too. Because as she talked, she began to believe that everything was alright herself. Andrew concluded their conversation with a conspiratorial whisper, 'I can safely say, Amanda, you are in a condition of most robust mental health, with a refreshing lack of reserve in talking truthfully about yourself. I'll tell Edward if I may, he will be greatly reassured.'

Amanda smiled. 'Yes, of course.' Wow, that was easy. 'And while you do, let me go and get changed.'

She left the drawing room, but not to get changed. There was something else much more pressing she had to do instead.

Chapter 18

At the top of the house was a small cluttered room they called the office. Amanda went in there and closed the door, sat at the desk and turned on the computer. Despite being up to date technically on medical matters, she was a novice when it came to social media. Which is the way she liked it, although a couple of friends, including Emily O'Shaughnessy, had urged her to update her Facebook profile. At the very least to add a photograph of herself, and generally become more active, just as they were. But she never had, limiting her activity to merely messaging her children and extended family. It was very effective for that, no more trips to the post office to send letters. But she had no interest in posting pictures of herself, or her latest purchase of shoes, or a half-eaten carrot cake in some city centre café or other, and couldn't understand people who did.

Now, however, she wished she had been more active, wished that she knew more about it. Because now she needed Facebook.

She stared at the computer screen. Where to start?

Jess Roy

She rested her right hand on the mouse and moved the cursor across to the Facebook search box, typed in the name, and pressed return. She went through a list of people, narrowed the search by location – Fiona had been from Limerick – tried again. No luck. Perhaps she wasn't on Facebook? It was a fact, not everybody was. She closed her eyes and folded her arms, thinking. It had been a long time ago, such a long time. They'd met as first year medical students at University College Dublin.

She opened her eyes and stared at the screen. She noticed the cursor was no longer in the search box. Perhaps she had inadvertently struck a key and it had moved. Yes, she decided, that must be what had happened, reaching for the mouse again, but before she could touch it, the cursor started moving of its own accord across the screen in a series of looping motions.

She could scarcely believe what she was witnessing.

She grabbed the mouse, pulling it towards her. The cursor began moving downward across the screen, just as it was supposed to. She sighed. Just a glitch, that's all. But a second later it veered suddenly up again, as if having a mind of its own once more.

As if having a mind of its own.

She considered that.

An icy coldness began to spread through her again, as a thought formulated in her mind. Her eyes drifted upward, settling on the tiny web cam in the centre of the black casing surrounding the screen.

Her dressing gown had fallen open, the top of her nightdress sagging, revealing her cleavage. She pulled it tightly about her.

She stood abruptly, her heart thumping, her panic beginning to rise. Amanda opened her mouth, gulping for air, staring at the web cam. She was certain someone was at the other end staring right back; she could almost feel the malevolent eyes upon her.

She was aware of a sound, two dull thuds, and realised someone was knocking at the door. 'Are you in there?' She looked towards it, saw the handle begin to turn, as an inner voice screamed, *don't let him see you like this.* She snapped her head to the computer again and saw the cursor had jumped back into the search box, letters appearing in it unaided. She felt like she was watching a scene from a horror movie, except this wasn't a movie, this was real, and she was in it.

The letters formed into words. They read: **BITCH. WHORE. DID YOU THINK YOU'D GET AWAY WITH IT? DID YOU REALLY THINK YOU'D GET AWAY WITH IT? WELL, DID YOU? YOU FOOL! YOU STUPID, STUPID FOOL. I KNOW! I KNOW EVERYTHING... HA HA HA.**

Chapter 19

Before...

Had she been sleeping? Her head was heavy, her throat dry. She didn't know what time it was, whether night or day. Nothing. She stared about the room, in darkness now save for beams of anaemic light through mostly unseen windows.

Windows? She remembered the sounds of a shower, so long ago it seemed, and a window high on a wall, a bathroom wall. She looked, and there it was, a small rectangle of light as the images tumbled into her mind, of the swirling mist, the door opening and... Him, standing there, the apparition. But just as quickly the images trailed off and there was nothing left in her memory. She knew that was when she had blacked out.

On reflex she raised her hands and began kneading her tender wrists each in turn, feeling the sharp ache of her arms and shoulders.

It took her a moment to register the reality, that she was no longer tied to the bed, that her arms were free. She turned onto her side, the bed sheet sticking to her back, but

as she continued to turn it fell away, her flesh feeling
puckered and tender. She lay back again, raised one leg,
then the other, scarcely believing it. Nothing was
constraining her. She gave an involuntary shiver, suddenly
aware of the bitter cold carried on the dark air. She took a
breath, held it, a temporary heat rising in her as she
withheld oxygen from her body, straining to hear any
sound, any sound at all. There was none. She knew she was
alone, that he had gone, just knew. She rolled off the bed
and fumbled along the wall for a light switch, her legs weak
and unsteady, found the switch and pressed the light to life.
She felt dizzy, as a pain pressed in against her chest, and her
mind seemed to cloud over, pushing out all thought. She felt
herself growing warm, could feel sweat forming along the
base of her neck, the dizziness increasing. She realised she
was still holding her breath. She exhaled in a loud whoosh,
and began to run.

Chapter 20

She tore her eyes away from the computer and those words on the screen just as the door opened, rushing over to a stack of papers on the floor and rifling through them, like she was looking for something, her back to the door.

'There you are,' she heard her husband say from behind, his voice surprisingly affable and relaxed.

She stiffened, picked up an old bank statement, turning it over, pretending to read it.

'Wh-what? Oh yes,' she stuttered. 'I was looking for this.' She turned to him now, and beamed a smile. 'Did you want me?'

He seemed to appraise her for a moment, then he smiled too and crossed to her. He rested a hand gently on an elbow and kissed her cheek, the nice, caring Edward. She glanced to the computer. With a sickening feeling she realised she had not turned it off, the words were still there, goading her: **BITCH. WHORE. DID YOU THINK YOU'D GET AWAY WITH IT? DID YOU REALLY THINK YOU'D GET AWAY WITH IT? WELL, DID YOU? YOU**

FOOL! YOU STUPID, STUPID FOOL. I KNOW! I KNOW EVERYTHING... HA HA HA.

'You had me worried for a while,' he said.

'I was only looking for this, that's all,' a tremor in her voice.

He shook his head. 'No. Not that. The way you're... well, behaviour, the way you haven't been yourself lately, let me put it like that. I was worried sick. We all were. Andrew has greatly reassured me.'

Amanda was a little unsettled by her husband's soothing concern. She had expected the opposite, had been prepared for it. But not this. She went quickly to the computer, standing in front of it to block his view, and clicked out of the page. She turned to face him again, saw the questioning expression.

'I'm sorry,' and she genuinely was. 'I really must have caught a virus, I'm certain I had a high temperature. It made me act all weird.'

He stared off into the distance. Did he believe her?

'Well, we can deal with that.'

'Yes,' she answered, glad for the change of subject, 'we certainly can.'

He nodded and came to her again, embraced her tightly, then quickly dropped his hands, took a step back, his nose crinkling.

'Yes, I know, I need a shower,' she said.

'Phew. You certainly do.'

Her eyes wandered to the computer, a glint of light reflecting on the small black circle that was the web cam. They were being watched, she felt certain of it, by an enemy, an intruder, one she did not know but yet was mere inches away. She forced herself to pull her eyes from it, before Edward became suspicious.

He began to walk towards the door.

'Have a shower,' he said, 'I really can't stand that smell any longer.'

'Of course,' she said meekly, 'of course. Sorry.'

Later that evening, after a lovely dinner cooked by Lauren, she took her chance and left daughter and dad chatting in the living room while she went into the conservatory. She did not trust the desktop computer in the office any longer and would have to think of an excuse to get rid of it, even if it was less than a year old. She sat in a chair and instead used her tablet to search the Web. As she typed the name Dr Fiona McBride into the Google search box she wondered if her phone was safe. She imagined it would be much more difficult to hack into a networked mobile phone than a computer. But she might be wrong about that. In any case, she had little choice. She scanned the first page of returns on the small screen. None was what she was looking for. Her one time colleague and friend had probably married, so her surname had likely changed. She didn't know anything about Fiona now. Nothing. After that night they'd drifted apart, a few months later had gone their separate ways, never to see each other again, never to hear from one another again either. Amanda closed her eyes, the coldness again spreading through her, trying not to think back to those times, but knowing she had to. She opened her eyes and typed, "Dr Fiona, Limerick". There was a photograph among the returns, of a group of people, a formal occasion, black ties and elegant dresses. She clicked on it and a sidebar popped up, an enlarged copy of the photo with the heading: *Munster Sports Psychiatry Association Annual Dinner Dance.*

Which would make sense, because Fiona McBride had been studying to be a psychiatrist. Her eyes scanned the faces, and returned to one in particular, a woman third from the end on the left, dressed in sombre black dress, long sleeves, high neck. She scanned the names in the caption beneath, felt something fizz through her as she read the name, *Doctor Fiona Crowley.* This was her... Or was it? She raised the Smart phone to within inches of her face, peering at it intently. She couldn't be certain. Just like a question in a pub quiz, where the initial certainty of the answer fades to doubt. Fiona, she remembered, conjuring up her image, was of medium build, with black cropped hair, wide brown eyes holding a hint of something - pain perhaps? The woman in the photo looked similar, a little heavier certainly, but the hairstyle was the same. As for anything else, the photo was too indistinct and her memory too vague to be completely sure. She noted the date, December 12, 2018.

Amanda closed out and returned to the search results page, noted now above the photograph a line of text, which she had initially missed, because her attention had been taken by the photograph. She read it now, scarcely believing what it said: **Psychiatrist struck off for failings in care of vulnerable patient, repeatedly ignored threats of suicide, eighteen year old youth subsequently drowning in river.** She clicked on the link and the story appeared, from a national newspaper dated March 2019: **Limerick Doctor Fiona McBride Crowley** –so it was her, had to be – **was struck off by the General Medical Council following a hearing in Dublin today (Tuesday) for failings in the care of a vulnerable patient, who died by drowning after repeated threats to end his own life. No further details were given, but the council President, Professor Anthony Brady, said such behaviour was inexcusable and broke every bond of trust between patient and**

doctor. Fiona McBride Crowley apologised for her failings and said her actions were unacceptable. She remarked that she will have to live with the consequences of what she had done for the rest of her life.

Amanda considered what she'd read, staring at her phone. She closed out of it and dialled Pri. The phone was answered on the second ring.

'Amanda, I've been waiting to hear from you,' urgency in Pri's tone. In the background was the sound of a door sliding open and closing again.

'I'm sorry it's taken so long,' Amanda said, her voice low. The light outside was dim, casting reflections on the panes of glass. She looked ahead to the house at the top of the garden, watching for anyone's approach. There was the sound of footsteps on gravel in the background on the phone now, and another door opening.

'Something must have happened,' Pri said, the door closing with a metallic clunking sound. Amanda knew she was sitting in her car, where she often went for a quiet moment on the phone. 'I mean, to have you go to Dublin like that–Lauren told me about it by the way, she said you had a... well, a...'

'Meltdown?'

'Crisis, was the word she used. But what I want to know is, how are you now?'

'I'm fine. I panicked, I know that now. Everything just overwhelmed me. I couldn't cope, and I needed to get away. That's what happened. I feel better now, stronger, you know.'

'Good.'

'Look, I have to deal with this, Pri. Just have to. Because it's not going to go away.' She quickly recounted the messages she'd received on her phone and computer.

'Jesus Christ,' Pri spluttered. She only ever said those words when completely taken aback. Amanda imagined her quickly blessing herself, as she always did immediately after she'd said them. Not that she was religious, she wasn't, rather it was an inherent sense of Catholic guilt shared by most Irish people that made her do it. 'You know you have to go to the police with this, don't you? You just have to.'

Amanda was silent for a moment, then: 'I can't, that's out of the question.'

'Why is it out of the question? This is getting serious, Amanda. Come on.'

'Because. I told you...'

'This bloody secret. Come on, Amanda, get things into perspective here. Nothing is worth...'

'Pri. Don't tell me what to get into perspective. This is serious, and I don't want anyone to know about it. Can't you just accept that?'

Like you did when it was your secret. It was on the tip of her tongue to say it, but she didn't.

'I shouldn't have told you about it,' Amanda said instead, 'it wasn't fair. I should have kept it to myself.'

'I apologise. I just want to help, that's all. Amanda, I'd be hurt if you'd kept this to yourself, what you're going through. This's what friends are for, Amanda...so won't you tell me, please, of how I can help? If you at least told me what this was all about, I might be able to.'

'Answer me a question,' Amanda said. 'That will help.'

'Of course.'

'And I will tell you, I promise, I'll tell you everything, but not just yet. Okay?'

'Okay.'

'This is the question. Suppose you were me. And something came back, from your past, out of the blue, like it has. And there was one person, from way back then, whom you were friendly with. Who knows a little about what went on, but they don't know everything. My question: what would you do? Would you contact them? Even though you haven't seen or spoken with them since that time, which is almost twenty five years ago now. You didn't stay in touch because you're ashamed, and you want to forget, although you never can, that's impossible. What would you do?'

Amanda could hear Pri take a breath, hold it, release it again slowly.

'I have to say, Amy, this would be intriguing, if it weren't so bloody scary. I wish you would tell me... yes, I know, I know, you will, but not just yet. Anyway. A thought. You say you're ashamed of what they, this person, might know, indeed, of the little they actually do know. But what do they know? I'd like to ask. Maybe they know nothing at all. Have you ever thought of that?'

Again, Amanda fell silent. 'In a way, you've just answered my question,' she said.

'I have?'

'Yes. I realise now, I do need to contact them. I should have done it a long time ago, should never have carried this for as long as I have, like a festering sore. Now it's forcing me to face up to it...Still, on the bright side, maybe something good will come out of this in the end, every cloud has a silver lining and all that. But it's hard to imagine that at this particular moment. I don't know how to find them. In fact, I've already been trying; I've been trying Facebook, Google, no luck.'

The only sound on the line was that of static, and it stayed like that for a long time.

Finally, Pri spoke, an excitement in her tone.

'I just thought of something.'

Amanda waited for her to continue.

'I'm looking at it right now. Here. In front of me. You'd never think of it.'

She fell silent.

'For God's sake,' Amanda said, 'will you just tell me? What is it?'

'A phone book. That's what. Remember those? This one is big, says   "National" along the side, the year nineteen ninety eight. Bit old. Still, worth a look. What'd think? She might be in it.'

'Of course. Go on, have a look.'

'Give me a name, and the details? I'll do it. Right now.'

It was that simple. There it was. In a good old fashioned phone book. The entry read, "Dr Fiona McBride Crowley, Castle House, Raheen, Limerick". The actual telephone number didn't seem correct, though, it didn't look like it had enough digits. A quick Google search by Amanda revealed an extra prefix, zero, had been added some years before. That's all that was missing. As they said their goodbyes, Pri added: 'This could be the person who's doing this to you. Be careful. Talk to me before you do anything about it, okay?'

Amanda assured her that she would, and hung up.

She sat silently staring at her phone, thinking things over. It was dark outside, the lights were on in the house, and because of this she kept the lights off in the conservatory. This way, the house remained clearly visible and allowed her to continue being able to see if anyone approached but without being seen herself. She checked the time on her phone: 9:15. It was a little late, so would be best to leave until morning. In any case, Lauren or Edward, she felt sure, would be coming to look for her soon.

Still... she found herself bringing up the keypad on her phone, dialling the number, hovering her index finger over the call button, forcing any internal objections from her mind and, pressing...

Her heart jumped as it began to ring. She wasn't certain, of course, that this number was still Fiona's, and she imagined someone answering, telling her it wasn't, apologising and having to hang up.

This tempered her excited anxiety. But instead of someone answering, there came a high pitched piping noise, and she knew she was being connected to an answering machine. No message was on it telling her when to speak, just a click followed by a low static sound. 'Um,' she spluttered. 'Hello, my name is Amanda Brody, Doctor Amanda Brody... Is this?... Look, I don't like talking into an answering machine. I'll ring back another time. Goodbye.'

She dropped the phone onto her lap, annoyed, frustrated, and feeling a little sorry for herself. Why couldn't she just be left in peace? Was that too much to ask for? Hadn't she been through enough already? Why had she now to deal with this?

Then her heart jumped again as the telephone screen illuminated the way it always did just before it rang. She snatched it up, cutting off the first ring tone.

'Hello.'

'Doctor Amanda Brody?'

'Yes.'

'You just rang my number.'

The voice was deep, a smoker's perhaps, or this person had just woken up and was groggy, but it was female, with the sing along accent of the southern counties. The same accent, she remembered, as Fiona McBride.

'It's you, isn't it?' she said.

'Who?'

'Fiona... Fiona McBride?'

'That Dr Amanda Brody. I was wondering. What do you want? You do want something, don't you? Otherwise you wouldn't be ringing me after all these years?'

Amanda was taken aback by the confrontational tone.

'Well yes, you're right. I do want something. I want to talk to you, that's what.'

'You took your time.'

'W-what does that mean?'

'You know what it means. That night. It's that night, isn't it? You took your time.'

'That night,' she repeated, the now familiar icy chill coursing through her.

'Yes. That night. How many times must you say it? And you want to talk to me?'

'I do.'

'Not on the phone. I don't trust phones. If you want to talk to me, you'll have to come and meet me.'

That icy chill ran colder.

'Why?' she asked, 'why must I come meet you? Can't we just talk... now?'

There was a chuckling sound, and Amanda realised that Fiona was laughing.

'What's so funny?' she asked, her voice rising slightly.

'Well, you wanted to meet people that night, didn't you? It's why we went out, remember?'

Amanda spoke before she realised what she'd said. 'Did I?' Because much of that night was a blur, much of it she could not remember, but all of it she would never forget.

'I've been getting notes,' she said, 'messages on my computer, and phone, about what happened. Someone...'

'Someone what?' when Amanda didn't finish. 'You mean someone... you mean me, don't you?'

'I didn't say that.'

'No, but you meant it, didn't you. I can tell, by your voice, I can tell a lot, just by that, I spent my life, you know, scraping through the layers, down and down, to find out what lies beneath in people, to release the bile and puss, the rot, to help people heal, to set them free... and what thanks did I get?'

You still haven't said if it was you, Amanda thought, who left that note on my car? And all the rest of it?

'I don't want to talk anymore,' Fiona snapped. 'I told you, I don't trust phones. Someone could be listening. They do that you know?'

Oh, I know, Amanda thought, I know.

'The King John Hotel, you familiar with it?'

Amanda was. On the outskirts of Limerick City, she'd been there once.

'Yes, but...'

'No buts. Tomorrow morning at eleven. I'll be there, sitting in the foyer, watching the door. If you want to talk, be there. If not, don't bother me again.' And with that she hung up.

The Fiona Amanda remembered had been soft spoken, kind and reserved. Not any longer, that much was apparent. She noticed the back door to the house open, the familiar silhouette of Lauren appear and step out into the night, walking through the hollow of light towards her. She suddenly felt an overpowering sense of love for her children. She had to protect them. She had to protect herself. She knew what she had to do.

Go to Limerick, and meet Fiona. That's what.

Chapter 21

Tuesday, 10 September, 2019

L auren went back to Dublin on the early train, having reached her decision after talking with her dad the night before. It was just gone nine o'clock now and Edward – who was still being unnervingly kind to her – had left for work, while Amanda was about to leave on the forty-or-so minute drive to Limerick to meet Fiona. More lies, because she had assured Edward she would not leave the house. She felt she had no other choice.

Earlier, as Edward had showered, she had checked her car. There was no note. Maybe whoever had placed it there did not know her address, but she doubted that was the case. As she drove through the automatic gates and swung onto the road, she felt at least now she was taking action, perhaps embarking on the first leg of a journey that would take her to the heart of all this – this nightmare. And if that were the case, what would she find? The thought of it petrified her as much as anything else. But she drove on.

She had just turned onto the dual carriageway for Limerick when her telephone rang, it seemed shriller, louder than normal, Edward's name flashing across the Bluetooth-

connected dash consol. She clicked the button on the
steering wheel and answered it. Edward's voice boomed
through the speakers so loud it caused her to wince:
'Amanda, where are you?' What he said next hit her like a
gut punch. 'I'm here, at home, and you're not. You're not
allowed to leave this house. Where the hell are you? Come
on, tell me.'

'You're at the house?' scarcely believing it.

'Surprised, aren't you?' he bellowed. 'Yes, I came back
for something, and you're not here. Where the hell are
you?'

'Please, Edward, can we talk about this when I get back?
I'll be home later. I had to go out. We'll talk then, I can't
talk now.'

'No. We won't talk then. We'll talk about this bloody
well now. Where are you? I demand to know. How dare you
not tell me.'

'I can't talk, Edward, I just can't. We'll talk when I get
home. I'm sorry. I have to go.'

'Don't you bloody well hang up on me. Don't you
dare...'

Amanda ended the call, and immediately switched the
phone off.

'Oh God,' she said aloud, 'that's all I need.'

As she thought about it she wondered when she returned
home if he would be livid enough to... no, no, he wouldn't,
he couldn't, that was years ago, it had happened just once.
But it had happened, she reminded herself. Yes, it had, one
time or not, it *had* happened. When Edward had hit her.
God knows she'd had enough warning beforehand, when
he'd thrown cushions, punched the settee... she really
should have known better, shouldn't have antagonised him
like she had, should have realised he was in a foul mood,
should have just left him alone, walked out of the room, left
him to himself. She couldn't even remember what the row

was about now. But after he'd thrown the cushions, after he'd punched the settee, well then, he'd punched her. She remembered it clearly, that blow to her stomach, powerful, solid, the pain excruciating, leaving her gasping for breath.

He'd regretted it immediately of course, his mood instantly switching, contrite, promising he'd never do it again, saying how sorry he was, how much he loved her… but adding, at the end, his voice so low she could hardly hear, and so was never completely certain of what he'd said, but thought it was, 'you bloody well drove me to it, you know, you pushed me too far. This is your fault.'

And he had never done it again. So she forgot about those words. But he had done it.

He had done it.

The question was: would he do it again? She felt that he might.

Oh Christ, my life is disintegrating around me.

She contemplated turning round and going home, fearful now not of what might lie ahead later this morning, but of what her husband might do when she returned later that evening. She couldn't help but begin to sob, feeling miserable, yet kept on driving ahead all the same. Might as well, she decided, because this day can't get much worse.

She was wrong about that.

It could.

And it soon would.

Chapter 22

S he turned from the dual carriageway onto a road with a sign next to it that announced, *This way to Raheen.* A little later the King John Hotel appeared at the end of a tree-lined avenue. She was looking ahead so intently that she failed to check her rear-view mirror, didn't see the flashing blue lights on this occasion, even though she was aware of the wailing of sirens, loud and piercing, like something from another world, unconnected to hers. Because unlike on the motorway to Dublin the other day, it never entered her mind that those sirens and lights might be coming for her. Even when she eventually noticed the row of flashing blue lights behind her, she still thought this.

But she was wrong.

Because they were.

They were coming for her.

They appeared all around her as she reached the hotel entrance, like an angry swarm, a police car swooping in front, another behind, and yet another alongside. She realised she was being boxed in, which she thought absurd. Whatever this mix-up was, all they had to do was ask, she thought with incredulity. She jammed on the brakes and came to an abrupt stop, stared ahead, completely frozen, as the door was yanked open, and voices sounded, aggressive and loud, and a hand, a big hairy hand, clamped onto her wrist and began to pull her from the car, with something unseen tugging her backward, sharp and painful, tearing into her shoulder.

'The seatbelt,' a female voice shouted, 'the bloody seatbelt's holding her in.' A body leaned across her, gone again just as quickly, the seatbelt was released and she was being dragged out through the open door, *oomph,* landing on her arse on the road, pain juddering up her back, staring at the bodies gathered round. She felt hands on her, searching, a female voice, stressed, a little fearful, 'Any sharp objects? Tell me!'

'No,' Amanda spluttered, 'of course not. What is this?'

Another voice, male. 'You and your vehicle are being searched under Section 23 of the Misuse of Drugs Act. Information has been received that you are in possession of Class A drugs for sale and supply. Now, where are the fucking drugs?'

Amanda couldn't believe this, and froze, unable to move. As she was being pulled to her feet and led away, she could see that someone was standing on the pavement, staring at her, a woman, the woman in the newspaper: Fiona McBride Crowley.

Drip, drip,drip. The tap in the steel sink in a corner of the cell at the police station was faulty. The sound of the dripping water seemed to drown out all else – the voices outside, the banging of doors, the ringing of telephones – echoing around her head, becoming louder, louder... LOUDER. She was sitting on the side of the hard, thin mattress on top of the fold-out steel bed, bent double, hands pressed against her ears. The horror movie continued, becoming scarier and more desperate at every turn, with no end in sight. She had been brought here in the back of a police-car between two burly officers. They would not speak with her, even when she had tried to tell them that they had made a terrible mistake, that she was the victim of malicious false information, a hoax. She had been further humiliated at the station, forced to undergo a strip search – *a strip search* – so a stranger could inspect her most intimate places. She had never been so degraded, so humiliated, in her entire life. They were treating her like a criminal, an animal. She was neither, she was a respected medical doctor.

Drip, drip, drip.

'Amanda.'

She looked up. She hadn't heard the cell door open. The officer was looking at her without expression, her eyes cold.

'Come with me,' the officer said.

'Where?'

'Detectives want to talk to you. Come on, they're waiting.'

'No. You can't treat me like this. I have rights. I want a solicitor.'

'Fine,' the officer began closing the door again. 'I'll tell them you said that.'

'Wait. What about..? Why do they want to talk to me?'

The officer had almost closed the door. She pushed it open again. 'Why do you think?'

'Me? What do I think?'

The officer threw her eyes to heaven. 'Yes. There's no one else here, in this cell. Why would they want to speak with you? Tell me.'

103

'Do you speak to everyone in this way?' Amanda asked softly. 'No, I don't think so. Because I've done nothing wrong. I'm a completely innocent person. How would you like it if someone spoke to your mother, or your sister, the way you're speaking to me?'

The officer blinked, apparently stung by the comment.

'You don't sound very convinced of that,' the officer shot back, 'if I'm honest.'

'I want a solicitor.'

'I know. You just said. I'll go and tell them. Look, they only wanted a friendly chat, you haven't been charged with anything, not yet, you're simply being held while we search your car, that's all… 'course, if you want to make it into something a lot bigger than it is, then that's up to you.'

Amanda dropped her head. She didn't want to stay here a moment longer than was necessary.

She got to her feet.

'I'm coming.'

There was a smell of sweat and bleach in the small, windowless, clammy interview room. She sat down on a metal chair, realised it was lower at the front than the back, which meant she had to constantly push herself into it to stop herself from sliding off. Two detectives sat behind an unusually high desk, high enough that she had to look up at them. A male and a female, neither looked older than her own kids. They peered down at her, and she felt utterly alone, desperate, and scared.

The male detective, he had gelled back black hair and bad skin, turned on a recording machine having told her she was being questioned in connection with the sale and supply of Class A drugs. He gave his name as Broderick, his partner as Kinsella. Kinsella was attractive with big blue eyes that Amanda imagined were normally friendly, but not now.

'Where were you travelling to when you were stopped?' Broderick asked.

Amanda said nothing.

'All the way from Galway,' Kinsella added. 'Where were you going?'

Now Amanda did speak.

'I was visiting someone, that's all. As for anything else, drugs, I've no idea what you're talking about.'

'Who're you visiting?' it was Broderick.

'Does it matter?'

'Actually,' Kinsella said, 'it does.'

'Fiona McBride, if you must know,' Amanda said. 'Fiona McBride Crowley. I went to college with her. She... well, she was a doctor.'

Broderick sat back in his chair, raised an eyebrow.

'Until she was struck off the medical register, you mean,' he said. 'I've heard all about her, worked with a colleague involved in that case, as it happens. Why would you be seeing her? Can you tell me that? Do you two often get together for a chin wag?'

Amanda shook her head. 'No.'

'Then why now? Why *were* you going to see her?'

'I can't say, it's a private matter.'

'Hmm,' Broderick said, leaning forward again, placing both hands palm down onto the table. 'We don't receive information about people like yourself, a respectable doctor, every day of the week, carrying thousands of euros' worth of drugs. You're not our usual type of client, I'll grant you that. And I can tell you this, Fiona Crowley, despite everything, isn't either.'

'I'm glad you're beginning to see it,' Amanda said, 'because, do you seriously think I would do such a thing? I mean, why would I? I'm a physician, as is my husband. I don't like to have to say this, but we're well off, very well off. I mean, why would I even dream of doing such a thing? Tell me that, please? And by the way, I abhor the use of illegal drugs, I've seen the terrible consequences they can have. I'm totally against it. '

Both young detectives exchanged glances. They didn't seem so certain of anything anymore.

'I dealt with a barrister once,' Broderick countered, puffing out his chest, 'who liked to shoplift clothes. We gave her the benefit of the doubt the first time. But she kept doing it. I wouldn't mind, but the clothes weren't anything special, general department store stuff, often out of the bargain bin. She could offer no explanation for her actions. It destroyed her career. People can be peculiar, wouldn't you say?'

He smiled, self-satisfied, but still, he looked uncertain. Then he appeared to think of something. 'If this is a hoax, as you say, I suppose you'll be making a complaint to that effect. It'd come under malicious intent, or something similar, I'd imagine, I'm not quite certain. Anyway, I'll have to check, when you make your complaint that is, yes?'

His eyes narrowed as he looked at her. Amanda looked away, said nothing.

'I thought so,' Broderick said.

There was a knock on the interview room door.

Broderick got up, crossed and opened it, mumbled something to the person standing there, then stepped out, closing the door behind him. Kinsella said nothing, her eyes boring into Amanda, the silence becoming insufferable, suffocating, the warm thick air becoming even warmer and thicker. Amanda started to sweat, her hands moist, her blouse sticking to her flesh. If this went on much longer, she'd faint.

After what seemed like forever, the interview room door opened again and Broderick came in. A cool breeze momentarily followed, floating around Amanda like a welcome, gentle embrace. Broderick stood inside the door and glared at her, his face like thunder, before using the back of his foot to kick the door closed. And the cool embrace was gone, in its place the clawed hands of fear pulled at her again.

'Well, well,' he said, the tone smug, resuming his seat behind the desk.

Amanda grabbed the legs of her chair with both hands, pressing her body back into it, realising almost too late that she'd been sliding off it again. She felt weak, so weak, using all her strength to do it.

Broderick leaned towards his colleague and whispered in her ear. Then they both looked at her. A smile crossed Broderick's face.

'Now, Doctor Brody, is there anything you'd like to tell us?'

She looked at Kinsella, whose big blue eyes gave nothing away. The same, cold, hard expression on her face. Broderick's smile had broadened, delighted with himself.

'I can't take much more of this,' she said, almost in a whisper.

'What?' Broderick demanded. 'I didn't quite catch that. Can you speak up?'

'I said,' louder this time, 'I can't take much more of this.'

'No…' Kinsella said, her voice low and husky, 'I suppose you can't. Then why not just tell us? Get it over with.'

'What? What did you say?' Amanda asked. 'Tell you? Tell you what?'

'Suddenly hard of hearing, are you, Doctor Brody?' it was Broderick.

'I want to go home,' Amanda said. 'Why this? This change of attitude? What is it? What's happened?'

'One last chance,' Broderick said, 'is there anything you'd like to tell us?'

Amanda paused, staring at them both. What was this about?

'You've gone very quiet,' Kinsella said, and in that moment Amanda knew how it must look, how guilty she must appear.

She dropped her head into her hands.

'There's nothing in my car,' she said, 'there's nothing on me either.'

Because of both she was certain.

Or so she had thought.

When Broderick spoke, her hands fell away and her head snapped up to look at him.

'That's where you're wrong,' he said. 'We found plenty in your car.'

He tossed something onto the desk. He must have concealed it when he'd re-entered the room, keeping it for the right moment. It was an A4 plastic bag, written across the front: 'Evidence', inside it another, smaller zip bag, and inside that a white, fine powdery substance.

Amanda's stared at it.

'W-what is it?' she stuttered, her voice child-like.

'We thought you could tell us,' Broderick said.

'What? Are you saying that was in my car? That that's where you found it?'

Again, that half smile from Broderick.

'Nice one, Doctor Brody. You could convince me if I didn't know the

truth. Yes. Of course. We found that in your car. Look, you're not helping yourself. So I'll ask again, what is that substance?'

'I don't know. I have no recollection. Maybe it dropped from someone's...' She fell silent. Maybe it had dropped from Danny's pocket. Her mind swirled. When was the last time he'd been in the car? She couldn't remember. Maybe it happened when she'd been in Dublin? Who had driven the Mercedes home? She'd never enquired. Was it Lauren? Had to be, because she was the one at home; Danny had remained in Dublin, and Edward had driven his own car. So Lauren had to have been driving hers. But she couldn't implicate either of her children. No way.

'Pocket? Is that what you're trying to say,' Kinsella asked.

'Maybe,' Amanda replied, 'because I have no idea. Honestly.' She looked from one detective to the other, slowly. 'You've got to believe me. I know nothing about this. Please, you've got to believe me.'

'Hmm,' Broderick said, like he was contemplating, 'we're going round in circles here. You're not going to tell us, are you, Doctor Brody?'

'There's nothing to tell. I know nothing about it.'

'Fine. It's going for analysis, then we'll know for definite. But what I failed to say is that if it dropped from someone's pocket, how did it end up taped to the underside of the car-jack in your boot? You don't even look surprised, Doctor Brody, I have to say.'

'I'm overwhelmed with it all, that's why. I have no answers. None.'

'Oh,' Kinsella said, 'I think you do – rephrase, I'm certain you do.'

No one spoke, the thick air suddenly thicker and the silence heavier.

'There is nothing else we can do today,' Broderick said, his tone one of resignation. 'When the results of the analysis come back, I have no doubt we'll be talking to you again, Doctor Brody.'

He then whispered into Kinsella's ear. She nodded and stood, left the room. He turned off the tape recorder.

'Right, come with me,' he said, standing and walking to the door without waiting for reply. She followed him quickly out of the room, along the corridor, up a short flight of stairs at the end, along another corridor to a door. He stopped, punched in a number on a security pad and pushed it open. He indicated for her to go through. She passed into the foyer of the station, a counter running along the length of one wall, a glass hatch open in the centre. He went to the hatch, took something from the officer standing behind it. As he returned she saw it was her handbag.

'Your car's out front,' he said, giving it to her, 'we'll be in touch.' She inspected her bag, and when she looked up again, Broderick had gone. She was standing in the foyer of the police station, feeling utterly alone and abandoned.

She walked across to the main door and out into the bright, cold sunshine, stood on top of the station steps. A man in a bright, fluorescent tracksuit bounded up and gave her a toothless smile as he passed through. 'Alright, love?' he said. She went down the steps quickly and squinted, looking up and down the street. She spotted the Mercedes a short distance away, parked front end against the kerb. She hurried to it and tried the door. It was not locked. The key was in the ignition too. She sat in, noticed the floor rugs had been haphazardly replaced, the glove compartment door was open, the contents topsy-turvy, and the front passenger door panel had not been properly screwed back in. She used to love this car, but now she felt she hated it, because it, like her, had been violated.

Amanda became aware of a person sitting on a wooden bench further along the street, in the shade of a tree. The person stood. It was a woman. She began to walk towards the car, her gait angled slightly forward, like she was walking on her toes. It was the same woman who had watched while she was being dragged from her car earlier. It was Fiona McBride. Amanda stared through the windscreen at her, undecided what to do. But as the woman drew closer she could not help but shudder. Now she could see those eyes, those wide eyes that had once held something – pain perhaps? But now held a craziness, mixed in there too with a malevolent anger, and it scared her. She turned the key and the engine came to life. Fiona McBride broke into a run, and Amanda could see she was holding something in her hand. She didn't know what it was, but it glinted in the sunlight. She turned the steering wheel, stomped on the accelerator and reversed from the kerb, crossing into the path of an oncoming articulated truck, the driver blasting his air-horns in response. She rammed the car into forward gear and darted away with a screech of tyres, glancing in her door mirror to see Fiona standing in the middle of the road, staring after her.

Chapter 23

Before...

S he ran along a narrow hall, the light from the
bedroom behind her showing the way. At the end was
a door, slightly ajar, enough for her to see the street
outside. She stopped, pulled it open tentatively, wide
enough to poke her head out, peered up and down the street,
at the rows of narrow houses on either side. It was a housing
estate, one she was not familiar with. She stepped out, the
pavement cold and wet against her bare feet, the air sharp
and icy on her flesh, and realised–that she was still naked.
She darted back inside, and stood, rooted to the spot.

What now? She would have to leave naked, she had no
other choice. As she turned towards the door again, her eyes
fell on the staircase next to it, and the pile of clothes on the
first riser, as if waiting for her. She recognised a small
brooch on the tunic of a jacket as it glinted in the glow of a
street light from outside. These were her clothes. Quickly,
with her hands shaking, listening out for the approach of
anyone, she began pulling them on. Beneath the pile was
her handbag. She grabbed it and opened the door, ran from
the house, this time never once looking back, and never

once stopping, through a labyrinth of streets, until she eventually emerged onto a main road, breathless, her lungs on fire, as she leant against a wall, holding on desperately to stop herself from collapsing. After a moment she heard the sound of an engine and looked to see a car pull in against the kerb, a light shining on its roof.

'Oh God,' she muttered, pushing away from the wall, about to try and stumble on, but unable to, it was all she could do to merely stand.

The window of the car wound down and a man's small head poked out, a tuft of white hair above each ear.

'Alright, love? Need a taxi? You look like you do.'

Amanda saw now the roof light was actually a taxi sign. She staggered towards the car as the rear door opened, flopped in onto the seat.

'Where to?' the driver asked.

'Drive. For God's sake. Just drive.'

Chapter 24

A pain pressed in behind Amanda's eyes as she drove back to Galway. She could smell the stale sweat from her body. Her hands were shaking. She'd had nothing to eat or drink. No one at the station had offered her so much as a cup of tea. Her mouth was dry and acrid. They – the Gardaí – had been through her car with a fine-tooth comb, there were dog hairs everywhere. They had pulled the Mercedes apart, and it didn't feel the same, nothing felt the same any longer. On top of everything she had a new fear now: Fiona. And she had not turned on her phone since Edward had last rung. He would be livid. She would not, could not face him, but she knew she soon would have to. She drove on, trying to block everything from her mind, but everything churned none-the-less, threatening to overwhelm her, as the pain pressed in behind her eyes.

She turned from the main road onto Ocean Drive and immediately began sweating again. She slowed down, right down, her hands becoming clammy once more, her crumpled blouse losing its prickliness and becoming sticky as the moisture from her skin seeped in. A sound began to push through above the noise of the car engine. It was that familiar sound she'd been hearing a lot of lately, it was her heart, pounding as loud as a drum in a deserted auditorium.

She swung the Mercedes in front of the closed driveway gates and stopped, pressed the in-car remote control button and the gates began to slide open. She did not drive in immediately, but remained, wary, sitting so far forward in her seat her face was almost pressed against the windscreen, as she looked ahead, trying to spot Edward's car. She'd never felt so tense, her body rigid, limbs like wood, stiff and awkward. She couldn't see his car, and exhaled loudly, collapsed back into her seat, arms flopping by her sides. Amanda felt dizzy with relief. Yet it shouldn't come as a surprise, because Edward wasn't due home for at least an hour yet.

She drove through, slowly advancing along the driveway, her eyes still scanning ahead, sweeping across the house in the near distance, to either side of it, and over the gardens. Watching, noting everything. It no longer felt the same. Suddenly her comfortable, safe, cosy refuge had changed. Ocean View House had taken on a malevolence, a prop in that scary movie she was living through, and it broke her heart. She could not see Edward's car anywhere. She glanced at the clock in the centre of the console: 4:25. Of course, he was still at the hospital. He very rarely got home before six. But he must have been home at some stage during the day because he'd known she wasn't there, that time he had rung, fuming. He said he was at home, but had he? And then she remembered the computer, its webcam, the feeling she'd had of being watched the other day.

Was it possible? Could Edward have been observing her? Is that how he had really known she wasn't there? And if so, were there other cameras in the house too? No, no, no, she thought, I'm losing it. That's not possible. Edward would never do such a thing. If he was to, he would have done it well before now. Why wait?

She was almost at the house now. Her dark, heavy mind churned again, throwing out that memory…of that time. That one time. When he had hit her.

No, you fool, he's not going to do that again, of course not, he wouldn't dare. It was a once off, a once off, that's all.

But she could not remember a time when her husband had been as angry as he had on the telephone earlier. He had scared her, really scared her. And if he had punched her that last time, then what about now? He could do it again.

But he'll have calmed down, won't he? Yes, he will. Oh God, he will, please, please, let him have calmed down.

She parked the car right next to the front door and got out, pausing again as she listened, before striding over, placing the key into the lock, turning it, pushing the door open, standing there once more, listening intently.

What was that? Had she just heard something? A breeze rustled the trees again and she realised it was just the groaning of the branches she had heard.

She stepped into the foyer. The house was still, quiet, empty… eerie. She didn't like this, being nervous and scared. This was her home. And Edward was her husband. She must not be scared of him, because essentially, he was a good man. Then she thought, sadly, of all that had been happening lately, it had not brought them closer together – instead, it was pulling them apart. She thought she was not being fair to her husband, because Edward had no idea what any of this was about.

She reached the staircase and started up it, heading for the office. At the top she crossed the landing and went to the office door, pushed it open, spotted a thick, heavy dictionary on the floor and dragged it with her foot up against the door to hold it open. Then she walked across the room and...

Froze.

There was a sound, unmistakable, definitely not the trees swaying outside the window, or anything else. The sound was inside the house. Inside the room. Inside *this* room. It was the sound of the dictionary being pushed across the floor, and then of the door closing. Still standing, frozen, unable to move, she attempted to rationalise it. Perhaps the dictionary hadn't been strong enough to hold the door open after all? But she knew it was, it weighed the same as a small bag of potatoes.

There was someone standing there. *Behind her.* She detected a scent, and knew who it was. As she turned, she said his name, softly, soothingly, like she would to a child.

'Edward?'

He was dressed in a red polo shirt and beige cargo pants, white sneakers, leaning against the door. He caught her looking at his clothes and read her mind.

'Tuesday afternoon. Remember? I told you. Hospital Director's talk on transparency in the delivery of primary care, or some bullshite like that. I had a great excuse. I was worried about you. So I came home. As any good husband would do. But I chose to park my car behind the house, I just knew that would be a good idea, and it was. I saw you looking for it.'

He smiled, and she smiled in return. He didn't appear to be angry with her. She had been correct, his anger had dissipated, had exhausted itself. He came to her, opening his arms, about to embrace her. It was what she needed right now, more than anything else, reassurance, from her husband, that all would be alright, that they would be alright. She stepped towards him but noticed his arms had stopped expanding, there was not enough space between them for her to fit. And then she noticed his hands turn upward, palms out, like the buffers of a train, and draw back, before springing forward again, each catching her square on a shoulder, sending her sprawling backwards. She hit against something, sharp and angular, and knew it was the edge of the desk. Her body was at such an angle that for a moment she couldn't move, a ship floundering on rocks, as the tempest that was Edward approached.

'You've been treating me like a fool, haven't you?' his voice like escaping steam.

'What?... Edward. Stop this. Edward! Please!'

He mimicked her. *'Stop this, Edward, please...* Yes, you have been treating me like a fool, haven't you? The way you've been acting. A fever you said. I even had Andrew O'Shaughnessy take a look at you, as if asking him wasn't embarrassing enough. But you didn't care. You lied. I'll stay home, you said. I won't go anywhere, you said. And then what do you do?'

Amanda pushed herself from the table and stood.

'For God's sake, what's gotten into you, Edward? What? You're scaring me.'

'Good,' he said, taking a step closer so he was right in front of her. He grabbed her wrist and squeezed. 'Good,' he repeated. With his other hand he pressed the computer to life, brought up Google, typed awkwardly with an index finger, stabbed the return key. 'There. Take a look at this,' he said, 'you just have a look at this.'

He yanked on her hand, hard and sharp, spinning her around, so she was looking at the computer, her confusion growing, seeing on the screen a frozen image, at the top the

sky visible through overhanging tree branches, at the
bottom glimpses of a stone wall running by a pavement next
to a road, to the forefront a collection of cars – police cars –
haphazardly abandoned. It was then she recognised the
road, it was the one outside the King John Hotel, where
she'd been stopped. And in the middle of the police vehicles
was a lime green Mercedes car. She recognised that too, it
was her Mercedes.

He scrolled back the video bar to the beginning and
pressed play, the screen coming to life. For a moment all
appeared tranquil, the trees gently swaying, the rustling
sound of the branches, birds singing. Then the sound of
sirens – approaching fast. Her Mercedes entered right of
screen, moving at a moderate pace, as a police car overtook
her, travelling very fast, and then she saw two other police
cars behind her. One swooped out to the side of her, while
the other came up close behind, almost bumper to bumper.
All the cars came to a stop at the opposite side of the screen,
and there were the sounds of opening doors, running feet,
and finally agitated voices yelling at her to get out of the
vehicle, and, above it all, a female voice, shrill and piercing,
'The seatbelt. The bloody seatbelt's holding her in… any
sharp objects? Tell me!'

Someone had videoed the entire scene, the whole lot,
everything, it was all there, her being stopped and dragged
from the car, and had uploaded it to YouTube. She felt sick.
She stared at the screen, scarcely believing it, as she
watched herself being dragged from the car and plonked
onto her arse on the roadway. She noticed a collection of
numbers next to a variety of emojis, mostly of smiling faces
with thumbs up icons among them. The numbers meant the
amount of people who had already viewed the clip. It
was12,456. Really? And they had liked it? What? She

couldn't help it, as her eyes wandered to the comments box beneath. The first was enough: **Rich bitch drug dealer getting what she deserves. And she's a doctor I hear! Unbelievable. No sympathy! Lock her up! Throw away the key!**

'My God,' she muttered.

Edward spoke, his voice low, compressed. 'You know how hard I work? You know how much it took to get where I am? You know how much it takes every single day to hold onto the respect I've built up over the years, that I deserve. And you… you, just go along and blow it all away. A drug dealer! A drug dealer! Now that, I'd never have expected. How dare you treat me like a fool. What have you been up to? What?'

He released his grip but swung his open palm through the air, about to strike her. Amanda turned away, cowering, waiting for what was to come.

'Don't even think of it,' the voice said.

She turned her head, just as Edward snapped his towards the door too. Pri was standing in the doorway.

'Good job I decided to come over. I was worried about you, and rightly so.'

Edward's demeanour immediately changed, his arm fell to his side and his head dropped, shoulders folding. He said nothing for a moment, and the only sound was that of Amanda's frantic breathing, like a bellows on damp kindling.

He smiled, his professional smile, his mask. 'Pri. Ah, look, Pri, this is not what it looks like, not at all, a domestic issue, that's all, everything's fine. Now, will you please leave us to deal with it. Tell her everything is alright, Amanda. Go on, darling.'

'Amy?' Pri said, the word a question mark.

Both women stared at one another. The seconds dripped by in a loud, screeching silence, so loud Amanda wanted to clamp her ears shut against it. She turned to her husband, her eyes lingering on him, giving nothing away.

'No, Edward,' she said finally. 'Everything is not fine. It hasn't been fine for a long time, if ever. I can't stay here any longer. I've leaving.'

Edward attempted to pull back his shoulders and straighten himself, hoisting up his head a couple of inches.

'What nonsense are you talking now?'

'I can't put up with it any longer, that's what I'm talking about. And don't tell me you don't know what I mean. I've had enough.'

'I-I don't know what you mean. I don't. And look around you. What could be wrong? You have everything here. This house. Look at it. Everything is here. Tell me what's wrong. What?'

Amanda dropped her gaze to the floor. 'It's not about that, for God's sake. You just tried to hit me.' And looking up again. 'Think of that. And you ask me what could be wrong?'

His eyes flared. 'I didn't. You're mistaken. I don't hit women, I've never hit a woman in my life.' He threw his hands into the air. 'I'm not a, a... wife beater.' He glared at her. 'In any case, well, if that's what you want, then go ahead,' his arm shot up as he pointed, 'there's the door... leave, go on, get out.'

'Wait,' Pri came and stood next to Amanda. 'Why should she leave? You leave. Go on. You get out. I witnessed what you just did. And I'll make a statement to that effect. If the police were to come here, that's what they would do. They'd request you to leave, and if that didn't work, they'd make you leave.' She stabbed a finger at him. 'You. Are. The. Aggressor. You get out.'

Edward laughed aloud, and his expression became a sneer. The real Edward, lurking beneath the thin veneer of respectability that he'd been hiding behind all these years. 'Good God woman, if they were to remove me, I'd be back in the morning. Don't you know that? Are you that stupid? They have no powers to remove me from this house permanently. This is my home.' He snapped his fingers. 'What? You thought they could? Just like that? Honestly!''

He turned and looked at Amanda.

'Come on. Enough of this nonsense. I'm sorry, okay, I don't want you to leave. Tell Pri everything is fine. We'll sort this out ourselves, like we always do.'

Amanda was silent for a moment, then shook her head.

'No,' she said softly. 'I'll leave. For now. But this is only for now, Edward. And I'll be back, yes I will, after you've gone. God, how did I put up with you for so long? How? I ask myself.' She clicked her fingers. 'But no longer.'

Edward went instantly pale.

'You can't leave, you can't, not really.'

'Can't I, just watch me.'

'But you can't,' he spluttered, 'you can't, because I forbid it, I don't give you permission. I am your husband. Listen to me. You do as I say. *Me.* You can't.'

Then Amanda did something which took even her by surprise. She burst out laughing, releasing some of the tension of the recent days. Edward squirmed. She had recognised something in his voice that she had never heard before, a pleading.

'You're pathetic,' she said, 'all this time, the snide remarks, the put-downs, the gentle asides, oh, nothing like what you did that one time, when you punched me and would have done so again just now if...'

Edward looked at Pri.

'I never hit her,' he said, his voice a whine, 'I never...'

'Don't,' Amanda cut him off, 'don't you dare deny it. You did. You know you did. We both know you did. But fool me once, shame on you, fool me twice, shame on me. You've been punching me for years, verbally that is, nothing I could ring up about and complain, there were no bruises after all, physical that is, never enough to make me realise for certain what you were doing, but just enough to have me doubt myself, blame myself, have me always think it was my fault. You absolute manipu...'

'And that's my fault too, is it,' he snapped suddenly, like he had to get the last word in, 'getting stopped by the police was my fault too? Getting dragged from your car and searched like that? That was me too, was it?'

'How do I know? Maybe it was? I would never have thought you were nasty enough to do it before, but I do now.'

'Who the hell are you?' he yelled. 'I don't know you. I don't think I ever knew you. Like I say, if you want to leave, then go,' he pointed once more, 'there's the door. Go on. You... you... bitch. Go!'

'That make you feel better, does it?' she shouted back, 'telling me to leave, insulting me, give you some control, does it? Ordering me out of my own house? I'm leaving, but of my own accord, don't make any mistake about that, and like I said, I'll be back, that's a guarantee.' She turned to Pri. 'I'm sorry, Pri, you had to hear and see all this. Will you come with me while I gather a few things?'

'Of course I will. What? Did you think I was going to leave you alone?' She nodded. 'All alone, with him? I don't think so.'

Edward's eyes narrowed, he opened his mouth, like he was about to say something, but then closed it again. Amanda looked at him, at the silent pleading in his eyes, the boyish, lost expression, and felt her determination wilt. Had she been too hasty? Edward seemed to sense her crumbling resolve, but then something passed behind his eyes, something she couldn't be certain of, a smugness maybe, but something she didn't like.

'Come on,' she said to Pri, 'let's go.'

Chapter 25

P ri had insisted that she come stay with her for a while, and she followed her old Jag now in the Mercedes. Pri's home was an ultra-modern glass and steel, flat roofed structure overlooking the river Corrib on the western edge of Galway city. Pri and her husband, Liam, had one child, Marie, currently on a year long working visa in Australia. Liam was an ecologist and obsessed with all things environmental. He had built the house himself, and his attention to detail was such that not a single weed *or* a blade of grass dared venture up between the cream coloured gravel of the driveway. Amanda drove behind Pri along the driveway to the parking area at the back of the house. Behind that was a small wind turbine – still twice as tall as the house – which, coupled with solar roof panels, provided much of their electricity needs. The property was straight out of the pages of a Nordic sustainable living magazine, except it was in the west of Ireland. A small orange car was plugged into an electric charging point just down from Amanda by a log wood shed. Despite everything, Amanda allowed herself a small smile.

Jess Roy

The differences between Pri and her husband could not have been wider and were not hard to spot.

'I rang and told him to get the spare room ready,' Pri said as Amanda got out of her car.

Amanda noted Pri had not even bothered to use her husband's name. A guilty thought struck her: why can't I have a man like Liam? Pri doesn't deserve him. She felt herself blush, and hoped Pri didn't notice.

She walked quickly to the rear of the Mercedes and opened the boot.

'What I've packed won't last long,' she said, hoisting out a black roller bag and dropping it onto the ground.

'An excuse to go shopping then,' Pri said with a laugh, 'out with the old and in with the new.'

But Amanda didn't laugh.

'Sorry,' Pri said. 'I know it's not easy, just trying to lighten the load, that's all.'

Amanda looked ahead to the cube style house. For the first time in her life she had no home to go to. She felt tears well in her eyes, as Pri stepped over and wrapped an arm around her.

'Come on inside, you'll feel better,' she said.

'I need to speak with the kids. Before Edward does. To explain, being stopped by the guards, everything.'

'Can't it wait?'

Amanda shook her head. 'No, Pri, it can't.'

'Come on then, let's go inside.' She led her towards the house.

The spare bedroom was large and airy, with a bay window that looked out over the river. She was surprised to see Liam out there. He was chopping wood on the other side of the shed, tall and gangly with a mop of receding dirty-blonde hair tied back in a ponytail. She sat on the cushioned stool at the dresser by the window and switched on her phone. Her belly tightened as she looked at it, at the

126

multiple missed calls from Edward, fifteen voice messages, as well as calls from Lauren and Danny. But mercifully, nothing else. She looked again, to make sure she had seen correctly. Yes, fifteen voice messages from Edward. She didn't listen to any, instead deleted them all. She took a deep breath, brought up Danny's number and pressed call. She spent the next half hour talking to each of her children in turn. She was pleasantly surprised they both accepted her explanation, because their mother being dragged from her car and searched for drugs was so alien, so out there, it could only be the result of a terrible mix-up. Either that or they were too much in shock to express themselves properly. Or perhaps it was a mixture of both. It was when she explained that she was no-longer at home, and would not be for the foreseeable future either, that everything changed. Not for Danny, who sounded relieved. 'Best news I've heard in ages,' he said, 'should have done that years ago, Mum, like I told you. You were never happy, not really. I love Dad, y'know, but still, I think you two are better off apart.'

How prescient she had thought. She really had under-estimated her son.

'As for the YouTube video,' he added, 'hard core, Mum. You rock, girl.'

'Danny, that's not funny.'

'I know, I know. But don't you worry about it, Mum. And I'll see if I can't have it taken down.'

'Really?'

'Ya, I know a fella had something taken down, I'll talk to him.'

Amanda didn't ask any further questions, because she didn't want to know.

She finished with Danny and rang her daughter. But with Lauren it was a different story. She was the apple of her dad's eye and they'd always been close. The silence when she told her lingered.

'Lauren,' Amanda said, 'please talk to me.'

'I love you Mum,' she said. 'But I also love Dad. I hate this. Is it temporary? Please tell me it is.'

Now it was Amanda who was silent, and when she told her the truth, that it probably wasn't, Lauren began to cry, which broke her heart, and as she began to try and reassure her, her daughter spoke. 'Not now, Mother,' she said, 'I don't want to talk anymore,' and the line went dead.

Amanda stared ahead, but could see nothing, too worried about her daughter, thinking, *what have I done?*

She had slumped low on the stool, and she hurriedly pushed herself upright and fixed her skirt, ran a hand through her hair, thinking of all the reasons why she was here: the note, the message on her computer, being stopped by the police and dragged from her car, the YouTube posting, the confrontation with Edward... and further back, way back, believing that this was all connected... to that one night.

Chapter 26

Before...

It was a Friday, and for the first time since that night, they both had the weekend off. But it didn't matter. Because it was gone. The laughter they had shared, the laughter that had signalled something else, their friendship. Gone. Amanda and Fiona hardly spoke now, indeed, Amanda could scarcely bring herself to even look at her.

Their apartment was quite large, in a wing of the hospital reserved for student doctors, but with the elephant in the room now living there as well, there was hardly any room left for them to move about, let alone to breathe. They both knew it. But they both didn't speak about it. And the elephant continued to grow, getting bigger and bigger, and still they pretended that everything was as it should be, when it would never be the same ever again.

Amanda carried her small bag of groceries and put them on the kitchen counter. The apartment felt different somehow too. There was a silence about the place, an empty silence. She stood still, listening for any sound. She had dreaded this weekend, a part of her feeling that, alone together, Fiona would bring up the subject. Fiona was always the more open, studying psychiatry as she was, and Amanda thought she was just biding her time, waiting for the right moment to say it.

She noticed the telephone answering machine blinking. She went over and pressed 'play'. The tinny sound of Fiona's voice came from the speaker.

'Amanda, I've left Dublin, and I won't be back. I know this will come as somewhat of a shock, okay, it's quite a big shock, but I had to get away. I've been transferred to Limerick. I would have talked to you about it, about everything, you know what I mean, but I know you don't want to; you don't want to even mention it. It's painful for me too, Amanda, just so you know. Hope it'll get easier, for both of us. Goodbye, Amanda.'

The call finished and Amanda stood staring at the phone. "For both of us" Fiona had said.

It was the first time that she knew, too caught up in her own turmoil to have considered it. But she did now. Because now she knew it wasn't just her. On that night, something had happened to Fiona too.

Chapter 27

She stared ahead, unable to believe that her past had come back to haunt her like this, unable to move, sitting at the dresser in the spare bedroom of Pri's house.

How was that possible? How?

That everything – her life – had turned to this so quickly? Did she deserve it all? Was it all her fault? But she knew too, this was not the time for self-pity.   This was the time when she needed to be strong.

She ran her tongue over her dry lips as the door opened.

Pri was standing there, clutching an enormous mug. She smiled, 'Tea, with a drop of something in it.' She crossed to Amanda and placed the mug onto the dresser. 'And,' she added, 'whenever you want to talk. I'm here.'

Amanda nodded, 'I know.'

'Right. I'll leave you to settle in.' She turned to leave again. 'You come down when you're ready.'

'Pri?'

'Yes, honey?'

'Thank you. I mean it.'

'I know you do. But you don't need to thank me. I know you'd do the same for me if the shoe was on the other foot.' She smiled, and left the room, closing the door gently behind her.

Liam's sandals made a flopping noise as he moved about the large kitchen, washing his home grown vegetables at the sink, moving to the granite worktop, chopping them finely, then to the cooker, piling them into a huge frying pan. He presented his offering a little later, still in the pan, which he set down on the table onto a thick wicker mat.

'It's called Liam's Special,' and with a smile. 'Just made that up, by the way. Hope you like it.'

Pri threw her eyes heavenward. 'Cringe time,' she said. 'Vegetarian, I suppose?'

He picked up a bottle of wine and began to peel away the foil seal. 'Well, yes, that's okay, isn't it?'

'It'll have to be,' and looking at Amanda, 'this is the latest fad, vegetarian.'

'Excuse me,' Liam said, positioning the corkscrew into the top of the bottle, 'I've been vegetarian a couple of years now, at least,' and began to turn it.

'Oh how time flies when you're having fun,' Pri said. Liam began to fill her glass. She lifted it and took a long sip. 'Not.'

He said nothing, pouring two more glasses, scooping food onto a plate and passing it to Amanda.

'What do you think?' he said a little later as she ate, looking at her.

'Lovely, really nice,' she replied, swallowing. In fact, it was delicious, but she couldn't bring herself to say it, not with Pri sitting there silent, picking at her plate.

'And there's loads more,' he added, 'so don't be shy, help yourself.'

Pri refilled her glass, leaving the bottle empty. She got up and brought over another, held it out to Liam.

'Open Sesame,' she said.

Liam hesitated before taking it, long enough to stir something in Pri.

'What? You have a problem with me having another glass of wine now, do you?' She glanced at Amanda. 'What goes on behind closed doors, eh, Amy, you'd never guess. Hope we're not embarrassing you, sweetie?'

'No, of course not.' But actually, it was making her feel a little uneasy.

'I don't think it's me who's embarrassing anybody,' Liam said, twisting his hand around the neck of the bottle. 'Here, it's a twist off, didn't you notice?'

Pri glared at him, before snatching the bottle and refilling her glass, and, like it was an after-thought, held up the bottle. 'Anyone else?'

Amanda shook her head, while Liam just stared at his plate. They finished eating in an awkward silence, then Liam got up and began to clear the table.   Amanda started to push back her chair, about to help him, but he shook his head.

'I got it, Amy, it's fine, really.' He smiled, and again Amanda wondered what the problem was with this marriage?

It was getting dark outside and she felt suddenly very tired. Tomorrow was a busy day. Somehow she needed to get her head in order.

'You look tired, sweetie,' Pri said. Amanda noticed her friend's eyes were beginning to drift, like little buoys breaking free from their anchors.

'I'm working tomorrow,' she said. 'I'm scared about it. I don't know what to expect.'

Pri waved a hand through the air. 'It'll be fine, sweetie, you'll see.'

Amanda lowered her voice. 'I told you my car was searched, but I never said if they found anything. They did. And if it turns out to be drugs, I could be struck off the medical register.'

'No. They have to prove it's yours first.' Pri said, and added cheekily. 'It's not, is it?'

'Of course it's not. This is serious, Pri…'

'I know it's serious. Very serious. That woman, Fiona…'

'Yes.'

'Well, she sounds like a right loo-la, doesn't she? You said she was there, watching, when you were stopped. Really?'

Amanda nodded. 'Yes. Really. And later, outside the station. She ran after me, there was something in her hand.'

'Like a knife?' Pri's wine glass was almost empty again, her voice rising.

'Maybe.'

'Jesus Christ.' Pri quickly blessed herself. 'You could still report it you know.'

Amanda shook her head emphatically. 'No. I just won't contact her again. That was a mistake. And I won't do it again.'

'And what,' Pri said, a shrillness to her tone, 'you think that'll do it, that'll be enough? She'll just go away and leave you in peace? I have a bad feeling about this, Amy, I have to tell you, I really do. I don't think she's just going to go away that easily. Sorry.'

'I have to be able to hope, I have to have that, don't I?'

'I still think you should report it,' Pri said, draining her glass.

134

'No. I can't.'

'Because of this bloody secret. You said you'd tell me, when you were ready. It must be some bloody secret, Amy, sorry. You didn't kill anyone, did you?'

'Of course not,' getting to her feet. 'I need to get to bed. You're very good to let me stay, but I'll sort something out a little more permanent in the next couple of days.'

'No you won't. You have enough on your plate as it is. You stay here as long as you want. End of.'

I don't think so, Pri, I can't listen to you and Liam endlessly sniping at one another, and something else is making me uncomfortable – your drinking.

'Thanks again for everything, Pri,' she said. 'I'll see you in the morning.'

She leant down and kissed her friend on the cheek, the smell of red wine pungent and sour. When this was over, they needed to have a talk.

Chapter 28

The next morning, Amanda was already awake when the dawn light finally crept into the room, dissolving the black into a drab translucent grey. She'd been awake for hours, tossing and turning. Her eyes were sore and tender, her head heavy, and she felt utterly exhausted. What if I were to just lie here and not get up, she thought? Like, ever again. What would happen then? After a few days, she guessed, an ambulance would be summoned and she'd be taken to a hospital, and then, later still, she'd likely be transferred somewhere else, to a nursing home perhaps. She liked the idea of a nursing home, because she'd be safe in a nursing home, she'd be looked after, everything would be provided for her, she wouldn't have to worry, about anything. If I just stay in this bed, just stay right here, I'll be safe, everything will be looked after.

She pulled back the duvet, dismissing the absurd thought, turned and plonked her feet onto the floor, standing awkwardly, shuffling to the en-suite. Standing over the sink she turned on the cold water tap, dipped a finger into the flow and ran it over her eyes. They stung, and when she opened them again the water clung to her eyelids like a viscous invisible cobweb.

Amanda returned to the room and squinted at her watch on the dresser, it was just gone six o'clock. Lack of sleep accentuated her already fraught emotions and stirred up the darkest of thoughts, telling her everything was useless, her marriage was over, and this was all her fault, and the past had come back to haunt her, seeking revenge, and overall, that her life was a battle she could no longer wage. But she knew this was merely her tiredness and fatigue talking, and pushed the thoughts away, instead concentrating on her breathing, on the silence of the room, on the beating of her heart, gradually resettling her emotional core. Because, she told herself, it was more than enough to have to deal with the here and the now, just this very moment. That was enough to deal with, more than enough.

It was too early to stay up, she considered. If she ran the shower, the sound might wake Pri and Liam. Likewise if she went downstairs to make a cup of coffee. These were what one had to consider when in someone else's house. She lay down on the bed again, and closed her eyes, not imagining for one moment that she might actually sleep. And because she was no-longer chasing it, that's exactly what happened.

She dreamed. In it she could hear a knocking sound, it was not very loud, but still, there was no doubting its insistence. With it a voice, one she recognised as Pri's, that said, 'Amy, is everything alright in there? Are you getting up today?'

Amanda's eyes snapped open. It wasn't a dream. It was real. It was the sound of Pri knocking on the bedroom door.

'W-what? Pri? What time is it? Come in. Come in.'

The door opened.

'It's half past eight, Amy,' she said, entering the room. 'Aren't you supposed to be working this morning?'

'Half past eight,' Amanda practically shouted. 'I have to be at the clinic in half an hour. My God.'

She jumped from the bed, heading for the shower.

'Anything I can do to help?' Pri asked.

'No,' Amanda called over her shoulder, 'this'll take me five minutes. I'll see you downstairs.'

When Amanda got to the kitchen, Pri was sitting at the table, a steaming mug in front of her.

'Aren't you having any breakfast?' Pri asked. 'I can get you something.' But she made no attempt to move. Amanda noticed that her eyes were bloodshot and her complexion pale.

'No time. I'll grab something later.'

She wasn't hungry anyway. She wasn't anything. The frantic rush to get ready had pushed everything to the side and, although it was no doubt temporary, Amanda was glad for the diversion. Workaholics would understand that logic, she assumed: too busy to feel the pain.

She smoothed down her tweed knee length skirt and adjusted the matching jacket, complimented with a cream blouse and brown, patent leather pumps. She was about to ask Pri if she looked okay, but Pri was staring blankly into her mug. Instead, Amanda grabbed her handbag and headed for the door.

'See you later,' she called as she opened it.

Pri raised a hand and twiddled her fingers, looking up. 'Go get 'em tiger. See ya later,' but her voice was a flat monotone.

As Amanda closed the door, she wondered just what her friend did all day?

When she met her first set of red traffic lights a little
later, all she could think about was how late she was
running. Her eyes kept straying to the dashboard clock, as if
this was going to speed things along. It didn't, instead
merely seemed to slow everything down. Her anxiety was
like a fizzing, damp firework inside her. She asked herself:
am I crazy going back to work? I haven't fully thought this
through, have I? Understandable though, isn't it? What with
everything that's been happening. But I should have at least
rung Layla, got a heads up on my schedule for the day. I
didn't even do that. I thought I'd be in time, thought I'd be
able to go through it all just before I started. Now look at
me. I'm running late, nothing done. How unprofessional is
this going to look?

The light changed to green but she didn't notice. A car
behind honked its horn, snapping her from her thoughts, as
she revved the engine and darted forward. She fumbled with
her phone, dialled the White Rock Clinic and switched to
speakerphone, listened to the hollow echo as it rang. Layla
should be there by now, her starting time was 8:30, and it
was now 9:20. Still, her call went unanswered.

Fifteen minutes later, at 9:35, she rushed through the
revolving door of the White Rock. She passed the main
security desk and walked quickly along a corridor to her
clinic suite. All medical suites were on the ground floor for
ease of access. As she pushed open the door she could see
Layla's head bowed behind the desk, her long blonde hair
like golden brush strokes. She went to the desk and stood
before it, feeling awkward and nervous. She told herself she
didn't need to feel this way. Layla was her secretary, not the
other way round.

She coughed, feeling a little pathetic.

Jess Roy

Layla looked up lazily, her eyes settling on Amanda, unable to hide her surprise, her expression like she'd just spotted an overcharge on her Tesco receipt. But still, her cherry-red-lipsticked lips – which Amanda had always thought too garish for daytime wear but never said anything about – stretched and raised themselves at the corners to give a half smile. But nothing else smiled, the eyes remained the same. Still, Amanda thought, she's smiling, that's something.

Just then, she heard the door of her surgery open behind her. She turned. A man emerged, mid-thirties she guessed, dressed in grey slacks and open neck white shirt. He smiled as he approached the desk, leaned over it to speak with Layla. Amanda couldn't help but stare at what he wore around his neck: a stethoscope. She realised her mouth had dropped open, and quickly closed it again.

'I've a little time,' he said to Layla, 'I'm going to the canteen, be back in a couple of minutes, you want anything?'

'No thank you, Doctor Farrell,' Layla replied, folding her lips into a smile so wide Amanda thought a little guiltily that she looked like a horse. As Doctor Farrell walked away, her smile receded as she turned to Amanda. 'I'm sorry, Doctor Brody. I was told you weren't coming back until next week. Doctor Farrell is the locum sent to replace you.'

Amanda tried not to show her hurt and anger as she took in this news. 'I gathered as much, Layla,' she said with false calm. 'Who told you I was back next week, by the way?'

'Oh, Mr O'Dowd of course.'

The clinic's director. Amanda could not betray her surprise this time however.

'Layla,' she said, 'you've seen the YouTube video I take it. Haven't you?'

Layla looked away, dropping her head, and Amanda was staring at the golden brush strokes again.

'Yes,' she said without looking up, 'everyone has, Doctor Brody.'

'Just so's you know. It's not true. I would never have anything to do with drugs. Anyone who asks, you can tell them that from me.'

Layla looked up now. But her expression had not changed. She was still looking at her Tesco receipt.

'Yes, Doctor Brody, of course,' her tone uncertain. She seemed to realise it and quickly added, with a flicker of a smile. 'I mean, of course it's not true.'

'Thank you, Layla,' Amanda said, turning. She strode out of the surgery, feeling Layla's eyes burning into her back.

The management and operational offices were on the third, and top floor, of the White Rock, with wall to wall glass offering panoramic views across the city. Amanda reported at the reception desk and asked to see Mark O'Dowd. She was asked to take a seat and wait. She sat on a bright red fabric chair at a coffee table loaded with glossy magazines, focusing on her breathing, pushing back against her anxiety. She had been to the director's office a mere handful of times in her ten years at the clinic, once when offered the job after having been headhunted from general practice, and a few times afterwards for a variety of mundane, work related reasons. But nothing like this. Fifteen minutes went by before Mrs Winters, Mark O'Dowd's secretary, emerged from a corridor to the side of reception, heading her way.

'Hello, Doctor Brody,' she said with a beaming smile, stopping before her. Unlike Layla, Amanda could not detect any sign of reserve or suspicion. But then, Mrs

Jess Roy

Winters had enough experience to be adept at hiding it, unlike the much younger Layla. 'Mr O'Dowd will see you now.'

Amanda stood, but forgetting that she'd been cradling her handbag in her lap, it fell, tumbling to the floor. She'd also forgotten to close the zipper, so the contents spilled out onto the mauve coloured carpet patterned in the White Rock Clinic logo of a two tone blue and white medical cross inside a black circle.

'Oh, my God,' she said, bending, 'sorry, sorry.' She righted the bag, began scooping the contents up and placing them back inside, and stood. The effort made her dizzy, which she knew was a combination of having not eaten that morning coupled with her general tiredness. The room momentarily lurched. She felt something on her arm, realised it was Mrs Winters's hand, steadying her. Amanda took a breath, closing her eyes, waited a moment, then opened them again, the dizzy spell having passed.

Confusion pushed through the secretary's mask now, and Amanda could see mixed in there too a certain wariness.

'Are you alright?' she asked.

No, I'm not alright, isn't it obvious?

'Yes thank you, yes, just, whooo, low blood sugar I suppose, I haven't eaten you see.'

'Oh… well, if you're sure.

'I'm sure.'

'This way then, Dr Brody.'

Mark O'Dowd was standing by the window of his office when she went in. The office was huge, taking up a corner of the building. It was an in-house joke that most of the photographs on the wall were of himself. Which was true. He turned, looking at her, dressed in a shirt so white it

142

seemed to reflect the light from the fluorescent bulbs overhead, accentuating his year roundpermatan, which probably was the whole idea. He indicated a chair on the other side of his desk and she crossed the room and sat in it. He remained standing for a moment, then stepped behind the desk and leaned forward onto it, peering down at her, like she was an exhibit of some sort, she considered. She took a slow, deep breath, ignoring it.

'Doctor Brody,' he said, like an announcement. 'Amanda, what brings you in here today, if I may ask?'

He'd spent some years in America, and his vowels in places were slow and stretched.

'To work. It's Wednesday, Mark. I'm due back today… well, am I not?'

He pushed himself upright and slid into his seat.

'No, actually, you're not.' He ran a hand through his thick grey hair. He was mid-fifties, but that grey hair still ringed his head like a miniature forest. 'I…' he stabbed a button on his desktop computer keyboard, stabbed it again three or four more times, 'have it right here. Doctor Amanda Brody will not be returning until further notice. HR will speak to her later and further details to follow.' His gaze shifted from the monitor to her. 'Right there, from HR. I mean… I've had to arrange a locum, which is costing over two and a half thousand a week, by the way, but no matter.' He paused, his eyebrows knitting together. 'I have to tell you, Amanda, this is highly unorthodox. Why would you think you'd work today? And the, um, I have to mention it, that YouTube video. I know about it. We all do. In light of it, I think it's best, anyway, that you not return to work at the moment, for the foreseeable future at least, until things settle down.'

143

'Really,' she'd actually forgotten about the video, just for a brief moment, 'what do you mean?'

'Exactly what I just said. That it's best you're not here at the moment. People want to have complete faith in our medical staff, you can understand that surely, can't you?'

His words stung. 'And you mean they won't, not if I'm around, is that it? But I'm innocent, doesn't that count for anything, anything at all? I've done nothing wrong. My patients can have complete faith in me.'

'We'll see,' he said.

Amanda couldn't believe it. Is that what it boiled down to? *We'll see.* Her ten years of unblemished record at the White Rock could be summed up with nothing more than that: *We'll see.*

'By the way,' he added, 'I've ordered an audit of all your prescriptions issued over the past twelve months... Just a precaution, you understand.'

For the first time, she felt it stirring inside her: Anger.

'No, I don't understand. What, you think I've been writing out prescriptions, is that it? And for what, and for whom exactly? For myself you mean?'

He said it again. 'We'll see.'

'Yes,' she said, getting to her feet, 'we will. We will see. When you're proven wrong, as you will be. I have options, just so's you know.'

His forehead creased. 'Meaning?'

'You know what I mean. You're questioning my reputation. That to me is everything, it's sacrosanct. I will defend myself. You don't need me to tell you how.'

He forced a smile. 'Come on, there's no need for that, Amanda. Amanda. Amanda. How's Edward, by the way?'

'Edward, what's he got to do with anything?'

144

'Have you spoken to him about any of it at all?' He leaned forward. 'Look,' his voice almost a whisper, 'there's no easy way to say this, you're ill, Amanda. Lauren, your daughter said so when she made the initial phone call... and now, it's very obvious, your mem...' But his voice trailed off.

'Sorry, Mark, my what? You didn't finish.'

'Okay, Amanda. Your memory, that's what I was going to say.'

'What?' she said, her voice rising sharply.

'Can't you remember?'

'Remember?'

'The telephone call?'

'Please,' a pleading in her voice that she hated, 'what are you talking about?'

'Ask yourself, why would I say you weren't returning to work until further notice? Where would I have gotten that from? Would I have just made it up?'

'This isn't a quiz, Mark, just tell me.'

'Right, I will, because you clearly won't, because you don't know. Which, I have to say, proves my point. It was you who rang HR. It was you who said you wouldn't be returning until further notice. It was you, Amanda. *You.'*

She opened her mouth, but nothing came out of it. She was speechless.

Amanda could not remember a time in her professional life when she'd felt as humiliated. Even as a junior doctor, subject to the whims and moods of bad tempered consultants and patients, she'd never felt the way she did now.

'Me,' she repeated, 'but that's impossible. I didn't make any telephone call.'

'You can listen back if you want?'

But she didn't want to do that. It would prove nothing. Someone had rung posing as her. That much was apparent. What she wanted was to get away from here as quickly as possible. She stood.

'I can't stand this any longer,' she said. 'I've got to get out of here.'

She left the office without another word, walked out of the clinic in a daze, feeling nothing but the searing heat of that humiliation, which clung to her, burning deep into her soul like napalm.

There was a heavy downpour, shimmering sheets of rain. But she was immune to it, to everything, nothing could penetrate that searing heat of humiliation. As she reached the car and raised the key-fob to open it, her eyes fell on what looked like a small grey rag beneath a wiper, the rain sticking it to the windscreen. A sudden, powerful, invisible jolt pushed her, snapping her mind back into the present. The rain cascaded down her face, dripping into her eyes, making her blink. She stepped closer and raised the wiper, realised it wasn't a rag beneath it at all, but a rectangle of saturated cardboard. She peeled it away from the glass, held it by the corners gingerly. Part of her wanted to cast it aside, for it to disintegrate and the rain wash it away, but she found her hands switching the edges, turning the piece of paper until it was facing her, and she could read the words, the letters resting within cobwebs of smudged ink lines, each one cutting into her as surely as a sharpened blade. Three words:

Ha Ha Ha

Chapter 29

Before...

Amanda sat outside on one of the hard wooden benches just down from the staff entrance to the hospital. It was an unusually hot and muggy August afternoon, but the benches had been placed beneath an overhang that offered shade. The aroma of cigarette smoke drifted up to her from a bunch of nurses sitting a couple of benches away. Work had become her refuge from the madness of that night sometimes. Even at the end of a crushing twelve hour shift, she didn't want to leave the hospital, didn't want to go home.

'There you are.'

She looked up. Doctor Rae Brennan was standing there. The small, petite gynaecologist with the abundance of perfectly coiffured blonde hair sat down beside her and turned.

'It's positive, I must tell you that immediately. I just got the result.'

Amanda released a long sigh and sat back, resting her head against the concrete wall behind. She stared ahead, but saw nothing. The whoop of a particularly loud siren yanked her back into the present.

'I thought so,' she said, 'I didn't want to believe the home pregnancy test, I prayed it was wrong,' and, lowering her voice, 'Please, I don't want anyone to know about this. This is strictly between the two of us.'

Doctor Brennan raised an eyebrow. 'Come on, you think I'd mention it? I'm a doctor, you're a doctor and you know I can't mention this to anybody, not a living soul.'

Amanda gave a weak smile. Doctor Brennan wrapped her arms around her.

'You poor baby. This should be the happiest time of your life. Is it?'

'No,' Amanda said, beginning to sob, 'it's not, it's the worst time of my life.'

She felt Doctor Brennan's hands on her shoulders, gently nudging her back so that she could look into her eyes.

'This can be the best time of your life if you want it to be. You have a life inside you, and that's more precious than anything. The amount of couples I see everyday heartbroken because it just doesn't happen for them. Sometimes for no reason whatsoever. It's just the way it is, okay? You've got a life inside you… by the way, you want to keep the baby, don't you?'

Amanda hadn't time to consider that question. She hadn't time to consider anything. Her expression told it all.

'I hope you do,' Doctor Brennan said, 'I really do…'

Amanda held out her hand and Doctor Brennan took it. The gynaecologist had been nothing more than a work colleague until now. But one she felt she could trust. Now she had become a friend.

'Thank you,' Amanda said, 'from the bottom of my heart.'

Doctor Brennan smiled. 'You tell him yet?'

'Who?'

'Your boyfriend, of course.'

Amanda shook her head. 'O-oh, n-no, not yet.'

'Well, maybe you should think about it. Listen, I've got to get back. Remember, if you need anything, anything at all, you just shout.'

Amanda forced a smile. 'Thank you, I will.'

Doctor Brennan got to her feet. 'See you later.'

'Yes, see you later.'

She watched her walk away, as a desperate plan began to form in her mind.

Later that evening she rang Edward.

'Yes.'

She could tell immediately by his tone that he was being cool with her.

'I'm sorry, Edward, I haven't been in touch, it's been mad busy... how are you?'

'It's been a while,' he began, and said nothing more for a moment, no doubt allowing that to sink in, 'since I last heard from you. Two weeks. Do you remember? We spent the night together. Or had you forgotten? Oh yes, you must be really busy.'

'I'm sorry,' she said, 'I really am. And of course I hadn't forgotten. How could I? I won't let it happen again. Did you miss me?'

'Ah-hah,' he said, 'is that what it was? A means to test if I missed you? Well, juvenile as it sounds, that does make sense, I suppose.'

'Yes,' Amanda said immediately, grabbing the life-line, 'I'm sorry, I was being childish, I just wanted to see if you'd miss me. I'm sorry, Edward, I really am, but I wanted to see if you thought about me as much as I think about you, I just needed to be certain.'

There was a soft, dull sound on the line, and she realised he was laughing.

'What?' she said. 'Why are you laughing?'

149

'It's okay, Amanda, I'll indulge you, I'll go along with your little game. Yes, I have missed you. Of course. So there.'

'Oh, Edward.'

'But you're not to do this again, you hear? I forbid it. And all this talk of being casual, come on now.'

'Of course. I'm so sorry to have upset you, please, it won't happen again. But the truth is…'

'Yes, the truth is..?'

'I've been missing you so much.'

There was a short pause.

'And I've been missing you,' a sudden husky eagerness creeping into his voice as he added, 'Meet me then, Amanda, will you, soon?'

'Yes,' she answered.

'The Templeton Hotel? Tell me when you're free?'

'How about right now?'

I Know Your Secret

Chapter 30

She drove from the clinic, taking the route to Salthill, the seaside suburb of Galway City, without any will on her part of actually wanting to do so, as if she were on auto-pilot. When she got there, she sat on a bench in an isolated shelter along the rocky shoreline, staring out at the churning water. A strong wind was blowing, pushing the rain clouds away. For one crazy moment Amanda considered walking out into the ocean, walking in until there was no turning back. That would end it all. She dismissed the thought as quickly as it came.

Ever since she was a girl, it was to here she came when she wanted to be alone, to find peace, solitude, to find *herself.* She could hear her mother's words ringing in her ears, 'where've you been for the last two hours? Staring at the water with your head in the clouds I suppose. Amanda, I worry about you sometimes, I really do.'

In truth, Amanda knew now that what her mother was worried about more than anything was herself, her own mental health, her own fragility. She likened her mother to a pretty flower, and her father to bindweed smothering it. They should never have married in the first place, as Danny had pointed out to her about herself and Edward. Amanda's

151

childhood was one, not of mayhem, but of complete dysfunction, caught between her mother's alcoholism and her father's dour indifference. They pulled against each other, her parents, their relationship always strained and taut, Amanda left to walk the tightrope between the two. One time she'd yelled at them both, 'Why did you have me, why? Why did you bring a child into this world when you can't love her, when you can't even love yourselves?' It was the only time she remembered the tightrope slacken, when they'd seemed lost for words, shocked at the visceral observation of them both by a twelve year old.

She'd spent a summer – a wonderful coming of age summer –before taking up her college place in Dublin, in New York on a J1 working visa. At Shannon airport the day she flew out, lingering in the departures area waiting for her flight to appear on the board. Her father was more irritable than usual, she surmised because he felt inadequate, standing amongst the streams of international travellers while he himself had never left the country in his entire life. Here, he was out of his comfort zone, no longer in control. She knew he would hate that, and he did, snapping at Amanda's mother and saying very little to her. Until it came time for Amanda to say goodbye and pass through into the departure lounge. Then he shook her hand stiffly, and as he released it, suddenly pulled her into a tight, awkward embrace, but an embrace she would never forget, because it was the only time she could remember that he had ever embraced her. Ever. He had whispered in her ear, 'Please, forgive me for everything I've done to you.' When he stood back, he stuck his chest out, told her to watch herself, that there were some bad areas of the Bronx, to keep away from the lower Grand Concourse, and to never, ever, go to Port Morris. She wasn't going to New York, she was going to New Jersey. She said nothing. She knew he wanted to parade his knowledge, all gleaned from books, designed to show that he was still in charge, that he knew things, standing amongst the stream of international travellers, a man who had never left the country in his entire life. She treasured every moment of it, because he had looked directly into her eyes as he had spoken, giving her his undivided attention.

Now, she wondered who she'd been fooling? All these years? Herself, that's who. And who'd she been avoiding all these years too? Well, she couldn't avoid it any longer, she couldn't avoid anything. It had all come full circle, as it always did in the end. Here she was, feeling as low as she'd ever felt back then, her father having been replaced by Edward, her life crumbling around her... because of a secret.

She felt the wind on her face and blowing through her damp clothes. She shivered, and stood. But she knew too, she was strong, and she could deal with this, she would deal with whatever was thrown at her. She began to walk away, the anger she'd felt earlier, at Mark O'Dowd, still present. God, it was good to be angry sometimes, it was better than being cowed and scared, anything was better than that. Her anger deepened as she made her way back to the car, as she thought of that note: *Ha Ha Ha.*

Chapter 31

Amanda stepped into the hallway, was just about to call out a greeting, but stopped. Because Pri might be resting. Which was unlikely, it was only just gone noon, but still. Her Jaguar was outside, so likely she was home. Amanda headed silently towards the stairs and started up them, heading for her bedroom. When she reached the landing she became aware of a smell, like burnt charcoal, with it a noise, of voices in muted laughter coming from behind one of the closed doors across from her. She hadn't seen Liam's orange electric car outside. But he might have put it into the shed. Anyway, she wondered, why am I even thinking about any of this? It's none of my business. She went to her bedroom door and was just about to turn the handle when the door behind her burst open. She looked to see Pri rush out, giggling. Her head was lowered and she was running a hand through her tousled hair. She did not see Amanda. She took a couple of steps and looked up, instantly froze when she saw her, her free hand flying to cover her mouth. Amanda noticed her skin was glistening with sweat, and she had nothing on but a pair of stockings and a suspender belt. Behind her, she glimpsed a male body lying on a bed, looking at the ceiling, smoking a cigarette. Amanda realised this was the source of the smell she had detected moments earlier, cigarette smoke.

Pri took her hand from her mouth. 'Oh, Amanda, you're back early. One minute.' She turned and went back into the room, closed the door. Amanda heard her speaking, feeling increasingly uncomfortable. This was none of her business, she reminded herself again. The door opened and Pri emerged once more, tying the cord of a short satin robe about her.

'Come with me,' she said. She nodded towards Amanda's bedroom. 'In there?' Pri grabbed Amanda's arm and led her into the room.

'You need to change out of those wet clothes,' Pri said when they were inside, pointing, 'or you'll catch your death.'

Amanda thought it ironic, considering what Pri herself was wearing, that she thought she needed to change. Even if she was correct, that indeed she did. Amanda quickly took out a pair of jeans and sweatshirt from her suitcase and changed. Afterward, Pri was standing with one ear pressed against the door.

'He's gone, I just heard the back door closing.'

'Pri,' Amanda began, 'I didn't mean to interrupt anything. If I'd known…'

'You didn't interrupt anything, it was time for him to go anyway.'

They were silent. Pri walked to the bed and sat on the edge, clasped her hands together.

'Look, my affair didn't finish, okay. There, you have it. We still see each other, when we can, but only the odd time,

that's all. I know what I said, that it was over, and it is...
except, well, you know, for the...' her voice trailed off.

'I know,' Amanda said, 'for the odd time.' She couldn't
help but shake her head. She sat down on the stool by the
dresser. 'But what about Liam?'

'What about him?' Pri shot back. 'He's no angel you
know. I'm convinced he's having an affair too, just haven't
caught him yet, that's all.'

'Really?' utter surprise in Amanda's voice, 'are you
sure? Liam?'

Pri nodded. 'Yes, Liam. Good ol' reliable stick-in-the
mud Liam. Trust me, he's not all that he seems to be.'

Amanda felt a hopelessness descend on her all of a
sudden. Could she tell what was real anymore? About
anything? Nothing seemed as it was, as she thought it
should be, even the lives of her friends. She buried her head
in her hands, wanting to cry. But she didn't, and wouldn't.
What was the point? She'd done enough crying.

'Something's happened, hasn't it?' Pri said. Amanda
could feel her hand on her shoulder, 'why are you back so
early? What is it, Amanda? Forget about everything else.
What's happened? Tell me.'

Amanda took her hands from her face and tented them
beneath her chin, staring ahead.

'My life,' she said, 'is literally coming apart at the
seams, that's what's happening.' And she briefly outlined
what had taken place that morning.

'Jesus Christ,' Pri said, but didn't follow with the
customary blessing of herself. 'What're you going to do?
You have to do something, you really do.'

'Yes,' Amanda said, almost in a whisper, 'I know that,
but what?'

'It must be her, the loo-la woman, Fiona. I mean, has to be.'

Amanda nodded. 'It seems the most likely,' yet she could hear the doubt in her voice.

'And she's connected,' Pri added, 'isn't she? To this… secret?'

Amanda nodded again, her secret, her burden, her calamity.

'Pri,' Amanda began.

'Yes?'

'You asked. What happened, that night, my…okay, secret, if you want to call it that.'

'Un-huh?'

'Well…' Amanda began, her gaze drifting, as her mind stretched back, over the years, to that black cauldron of memories, the flame beneath which had never fully extinguished, and was now reignited, the cauldron red hot, the contents bubbling and hissing, spilling out.

Pri was silent, waiting for Amanda to continue.

'When I…' Amanda began, 'was a student, a first year student, in college, studying medicine – it's where I met Fiona, by the way – one night, when we were out, in a pub, The Merchants it was called, my drink was spiked, and when I woke up, I didn't know where I was, I was in a bedroom, and there was someone there, a man, a man who had raped me, raped me multiple times, as a result of which I became pregnant...'

Amanda fell silent.

'What a terrible thing to have happened,' Pri said. 'So, you had an abortion. I understand, Amy.'

'An abortion?' Amanda's eyes widened. 'I didn't have an abortion. It was illegal. I had the baby. The baby is Lauren.'

157

'My God,' Pri's face displaying her shock. She tapped an index finger against her chin. 'Wait, that means Edward's not...'

'Lauren's father,' Amanda finished the sentence for her. 'No, he's not.'

'My God,' Pri said again, 'does he know?'

Amanda shook her head. 'Of course not. Nor Lauren.'

'Oh,' Pri said, 'Now I understand. Yes, that's some secret, Amy. But, but, having a baby, like that, after what happened you, wow, that can't have been easy. I certainly wouldn't do it. Did you ever treat her...'

'Differently? Of course not. In fact, I love her even more because of it, it's not her fault. It would break her heart if she were to know. Really.'

Pri took Amanda in her arms and hugged her tight.

'All these years, you've been carrying this. Oh, Amanda.'

Just then there was a loud, twittering sound. Amanda recognised it as her phone ringing on the dresser top. She went and picked it up, Lauren's name flashing across the screen. 'It's Lauren,' she said, and, answering it, 'Sweetheart, how...'

'Mum, don't talk, just listen.'

As Amanda listened, she felt her blood run cold.

'Edward?' she said, taking the phone from her ear, 'He's been attacked.   He's in the hospital? My God.'

Fifteen minutes later she rushed through the doors of Galway University Hospital.

'Ward B,' the assistant behind the front desk told her, 'that's on the first floor, lifts are right behind you, when you get out you...'

'I know the way,' Amanda said, cutting her off, turning. She knew a quicker route, from her time spent as a junior doctor here. She pushed open the door at the side of the desk. The assistant was about to say something. This led to a staff only stairs, but Amanda had disappeared through it before she could speak and was taking the steps two at a time. She emerged onto the ward through the door at the top, right next to the nurses' station. A couple of nurses were behind it, one filling in details on a form, the other, the older of the two, looking at CT scan results on a computer monitor. The older nurse looked up, recognition crossing her face as she smiled.

'Doctor Brody,' she said, standing. 'Now, don't worry, Ed… I mean Doctor Brody, your husband. Everything is fine with him, relatively speaking.'

'Nurse Connor,' Amanda said, 'what happened? My daughter didn't have all the details, just that he was in the hospital, and to come right away.'

The nurse opened the hatch in the nurses' station and emerged from behind it, stood beside Amanda, resting a hand on her arm.

'He drove himself here, presented at A&E. He was dishevelled and a little disorientated. His clothes were torn and he was bleeding from a head wound. Our first concern was a brain injury. We've discounted that however. We examined him and he has lacerations to his head, hands and legs. Also bruising to his face where we believe he was struck with some kind of weapon.'

'My God,' Amanda said. 'He was mugged?'

The nurse shook her head. 'Doesn't appear to be the case, but we'll leave that for the guards to decide. Nothing was taken, he said he was attacked, somewhere in the city, not quite sure where. But,' the nurse paused, 'his injuries are superficial. He's fine, shook up of course, but he's fine. We're merely keeping him in for observation.'

'Oh,' Amanda said, 'okay, that's good.'

'Now, my dear, let me take you to him.'

Nurse Connor began walking quickly away along the corridor. Amanda hurried to catch up.

'Like I say, Doctor Brody,' the nurse said as Amanda reached her. 'Everything is fine. It could have been much worse, these things can turn out very ugly, as you well know.'

Yes, Amanda thought, they certainly can.

The nurse stopped outside a private room. 'Remember,' she said pushing the door. 'It looks worse than it is. Okay?'

Amanda nodded.

They went in. Edward was lying on his back, his forehead and one hand swathed in bandages, the hair along one side of his head matted to his scalp. The nurse hadn't mentioned that, Amanda thought. His eyes shifted to her, staring. The nurse checked the monitor on the stand, took out the patient chart from its holder at the end of the bed, wrote in it, put it back again.

'Are you comfortable, Dr Brody?'

He nodded.

'Very good. Your wife is here.' She lowered her voice as she spoke to Amanda. 'Not too long. Ten minutes, okay?'

Amanda nodded as the nurse left. Edward had still not spoken, merely staring at her, his eyes full of accusation. She dismissed it.

'You're going to be okay,' she said, 'that's the main thing, Edward. What happened?'

He turned his head away.

'Bit of a coincidence,' he muttered.

She sat in the chair by the bed, crossed her legs, folded her arms tightly across her chest.

'What's that supposed to mean?' her tone sharp. She regretted it immediately. Now was not the time.

He didn't answer. But she knew what he was getting at. Her compassion for her husband in the condition he was in was being eroded by the absurdity that he was blaming her for what had happened.

'I spoke with Lauren,' she said softly, 'our daughter told me. Did you give them her number, as a contact, instead of mine? It would have been better to have given them mine, to spare her the worry, you know what she's like.'

'I know what *you're* like,' he snapped.

'She and Danny will be down later,' Amanda said, ignoring the remark, 'she's getting the evening train.'

'No.' He turned and glared at her. 'I spoke with her. Told her, both of them, not to come here. No. Under no circumstances.'

'Why,' doing her best to keep her voice calm. 'What do you mean?'

He looked at her and she felt herself recoil. Never had she seen such venom in his eyes before.

'You,' he said. 'You know what I mean. It's you. You've brought all this on. Yourself. You.'

She was momentarily transported back, to the way it had been with Edward, the way it had always been, hanging on every syllable, tuned to his every mood, trying to assuage him, calm him, make him happy, trying to please him. She never could, not then, and not now. She touched her throat, her breath catching. She wanted to be kind, to help him, because yes, despite everything, she wanted that. She did not want to see him like this.

He spoke, and his voice was little more than a rumble, coming from somewhere far below, way down deep inside him, dripping with hurt pride and anger.

'Get out.'

For a moment, she was unable to move. She had not expected this, certainly not.

'Go on, get out.'

She blinked, but got to her feet slowly, wanting more than anything, in this moment, despite everything, for him to be kind to her, and for him to allow her to be kind to him. Because he was right. This was all her fault. Somehow, she was responsible. For everything. She knew it.

'Please,' she said, imploring.

'I said get out.'

She fought back tears, went to the door and pulled it open, stood outside in the corridor, people hurrying by in both directions. How much more of this could she take? Not much, she felt certain, not much. She walked away towards the stairs, feeling like she was becoming more and more lost inside a labyrinth, and the more she sought escape, the more lost and hopeless she became, as the light dimmed, the labyrinth becoming darker and darker…

Soon, there would be no light left at all.

I Know Your Secret

Chapter 32

'I don't know,' Amanda said. She was sitting in her car having just come from visiting Edward, on the phone with Lauren: her daughter had just asked what exactly had happened. 'He didn't say,' Amanda added, 'didn't want to discuss it.'

Lauren spoke, her voice beginning to quiver. 'He told me he'd been attacked, that he was walking in town, along one of the streets, a back street, in broad daylight, and he was attacked... oh, Mother. But he said these things happen. You know Dad, doesn't want anyone to worry about him.'

Not true, Amanda thought, he's just achieved the exact opposite, but she said nothing.

'He's not badly injured,' she said instead, 'like I told you. But they'll keep him in for a little while, merely for observation. Try not to worry, sweetheart.'

'And then what?' Lauren asked.

'What do you mean?'

'Well, Mum, who's going to look after him? He can't be left on his own.'

Amanda couldn't help but feel a warm glow for her daughter. She wondered how, as she'd wondered countless times, someone so beautiful could come from something so

163

evil? Her precious Lauren had always put others first. As a child she'd come home fretting about classmates or friends who'd seemed sad or unwell, and once with a puppy she'd found on the street. There was a time when she'd considered her daughter might have been too sensitive. But then she came to realise that Lauren possessed an intuition too, the ability to know when others were drawing on her, sapping her energy, when to pull back. She had no doubt she would make a brilliant doctor. Of course, her daughter could not be as objective when dealing with Edward.

Amanda was silent, reflecting her uncertainty. Unlike her daughter, she did not possess the same intuition, it had taken her years, until now, to understand that Edward had been insidiously undermining her, ridiculing her, not so much controlling as subtly ruling her. Whatever the outcome of all she was going through was to be, she had learned this.

'Dad says it's too dangerous to come down and see him,' Lauren said, 'what does he mean by that?'

'Well…' Amanda began. 'I don't know what he means. I think he's simply confused at the moment.'

'Mum, is there something I should know about? What with all that's been happening to you, the drug search and everything. I have to ask, is there a connection with what happened to Dad?'

'Is that what your dad said?' suspicion in Amanda's tone.

'Um, not exactly, but yes, kind of.'

So he had.

'No, Lauren,' Amanda reassured her daughter, 'what happened to me was the result of a terrible mix up, you'll see, because I won't let that go, I'll get to the bottom of it. As for your father, believe me, in my twenty-five years as a doctor, I know all about coincidences. And this is all it is, a coincidence. Please, Lauren, don't worry. Promise me.'

The truth was, Amanda didn't know. She didn't know anything anymore.

'But,' Lauren said, 'there was nothing taken, from Dad. He told me. That doesn't make sense, now does it? Mum, I can't help it, I'm worried, for both of you. Is there something you're not telling me?'

'Lauren,' Amanda's voice stiffening, 'I want you to stop worrying about me and your father. Do you hear? We are well able to look after ourselves. This is a coincidence. Do you hear me? That's all.'

Lauren took a slow breath.

'Okay, Mum, if you say so.'

'I do. I say so.'

'Well then, okay, I'll try not to worry.'

'Good. Just concentrate on your studies. I'm going to ring Danny now. I'll talk to you again soon, sweetheart.'

'Okay, Mum.'

'See you soon, darling. Love you.'

'I love you too.'

When she hung up she had the feeling that Lauren had not asked any further questions because she didn't want to know the answers. As if she knew it was time to stand back, to retreat, to leave her parents to deal with their own problems.

She rang Danny, but there was no answer. She held the phone, pondering, then tossed it onto the passenger seat, started the engine, and drove away.

Chapter 33

Before...

Amanda vowed not to eat anymore peanuts. She had already eaten one bowl and was now halfway through another. But it was like trying to take a bath without getting wet. Impossible. But such were her cravings.

They were sitting in the bar of the Templeton Hotel, an old hotel with an old clientele, but one that Edward liked. The barman was old too, in his white tunic and bowtie, referring to Edward –still a student– as Doctor Brody.

Edward never corrected him.

The hotel suited Edward's prissy style perfectly. Amanda always considered that if Ireland were still part of the British Empire, it would have suited Edward just fine too. She could imagine him in a posting to India, sitting beneath the shade of a Karanjatree, being waited on hand and foot by a bevy of servants.

Amanda was desperate. She had a baby in her belly, was prepared to ignore everything that she disliked– even hated– about Edward: that prissiness, his single-mindedness, and ultimately, his narcissism. In the same way that one who is drowning doesn't care if it's a lifebuoy or the floating carcase of a dead dog that offers them something to cling to.

She had not seen him since the Two 4 One night at the student bar. The next morning they had woken up together, badly hung over. But she didn't regret it. Why would she? Edward was a handsome man –very handsome – everyone said so, and with a great body: plenty of girls would give anything to be in her shoes. But she wasn't interested in anything else. To her, it was a moment in time, nothing more. A heart pounding, exhilarating moment for sure, but one, despite this, she did not want to repeat. It would not lead to anything; it certainly would not be her epilogue. Her epilogue, marriage, the rest of her life, did not rest with Edward. No way. She moved on easily, but Edward sulked, took to ringing her, even showing up on her apartment doorstep a couple of times. After a while though he stopped, having gotten the message.

So when Amanda found out she was pregnant, everything changed.

Which was why she had rung him up, why she was in the Templeton Hotel. Why she was prepared to ignore everything that she disliked – even hated – about Edward.

She smiled now, and took his hand in hers, rotating her thumb gently over the back of it. Edward smiled, his shoulders sagging, as he relaxed. He rarely relaxed. He said nothing. She continued rotating her thumb, pushing in close against him.

'Edward,' she began, 'I really missed you, like, really missed you.'

She hated herself for it, for trying to dupe this man, knowing what she was doing, knowing that in her desperation she would do anything, because that's what she was, desperate.

Edward was silent, his expression inscrutable. She could feel his hand turning clammy.

167

'Let's get out of here,' she said, 'what do you say? Go back to your place.'

Edward was on his feet almost immediately. He looked down at her and grinned. 'Well, come on then, before you change your mind.'

Chapter 34

It was just gone five o'clock when Amanda stepped into Pri and Liam's house for the second time that day. She noticed there was no sound, there never was in this house, no TV, no radio, no music, nothing. Apart from the bickering of the two people who lived in it, that is. She thought of that morning again, of Pri, and the man in the bedroom, whose identity she didn't – nor wanted – to know. She still hadn't fully processed what she had seen.

None of my business, she thought again.

As she hung up her coat she looked across the wide hall, could see Pri sitting in the living room, the dull evening sun behind her through the window casting her in half shadow. She had her head bowed, one elbow resting on the armrest, her chin cupped in the palm of her hand, and was very still, she seemed to be sleeping.

Amanda walked over and stood in the doorway, looking in. But something seemed not right. Pri appeared to be so still, *too* still. She took a breath and held it, listening, trying to detect any sound, any subtle movement, a gentle intake and exhale of breath perhaps, something. Instead, she could hear nothing. Her belly tightened.

169

'Pri,' she said softly.

There was no reply.

She walked over to her friend.

'Pri,' she said again, but louder this time.

Still, there was no movement, and no sound. She bent down, feeling increasingly uneasy, peered into her friend's face. A terrible thought struck her, was she dead? She reached for Pri's wrist to check her pulse, but a sudden movement caused her to jump back, with it a loud grinding, guttural sound. She watched as Pri's body jerked again, and with it that same noise, but this time the cough was much softer, Pri merely clearing her throat. She opened her bloodshot eyes and stared at Amanda, looking confused. Amanda felt something touch her foot. She looked down, saw the end of a green glass bottle protruding from beneath the settee. Pri rubbed her hands briskly across her face. 'Oh, I must have fallen asleep... what time is it?'

Amanda checked her watch. She was surprised to see it was just gone half five. She told Pri.

'It's okay, it's okay,' Pri said, in a half mutter.

Amanda knew she was saying this to herself, a reassurance.

Pri looked ahead, silent. Amanda felt she had forgotten she was even there. She sat down next to her on the settee. There was a smell, the lingering sweetness of perfume, mixed in with that of old and new wine and stale sex. Pri seemed stranded in the aftermath of it all, washed up, as the tide went out, leaving her floundering. Again, Amanda found a distraction from her own misery in considering the misery of Pri. What was happening to her friend? She had known her for many years, but how well do you know a person, really know them? Certainly, in turn, Pri had never known very much about her either. Not until today that is, because Amanda had presented an image, as had Pri, just as everybody else. Who knew what really went on in another person's head? And yet, she always thought she knew everything about Pri. It began to make sense now, those times they had met, the hollow eyes, the pasty skin, the distracted mind, not listening to what she said, having to repeat everything. And her endless harping on about Liam. The classic alcoholic, in this case the secret drinker. God, she reminded her of her mother.

'I need a drink,' Pri said, standing awkwardly. 'And how are you? My dear, dear friend. I was thinking of what you told me earlier. How terrible. Really, this world, is it any wonder a person likes the odd drink, to escape...'

Amanda said nothing.

'Anyway, thank you for not objecting,' Pri said, 'for not telling me that drinking doesn't help. Liam's old scratched record.'

'You're a big girl,' Amanda said, 'I'm not going to tell you what to do. By the way, where is he, Liam?'

'Gone to Liverpool. He takes the ferry over once a month. A builders' thingy, on sustainable green living or something. Seemingly he's a bit of an expert. Don't ask me. It means I can, okay, drink a little more than I usually do.'

Pri cut a lonely figure as she shuffled into the kitchen. Amanda heard the clinking of bottles, the sound as one was placed onto the granite worktop, then the plop of the cork being pulled, finally the glug-glug-glug of a glass being filled.

'You want one?' Pri called.

Amanda was about to say no, but then thought, why not?

'Okay, yes I will, thanks.'

Amanda drank quickly, her glass almost empty before she'd realised it, cradling it then in her hands, feeling a little

171

guilty and self-conscious. She looked at Pri, who was staring vacantly ahead, realised she had no reason to feel self-conscious or guilty for having drunk it quickly at all. She thought of her mother again, who at one stage had never left the house in over a year, spent the whole time mostly drinking. She had then gone cold turkey and quit alcohol altogether, for a time that is. Still, even then she couldn't leave the house. Amanda guessed that some type of intervention was required, because it was clear she had wanted to stop drinking, to quit alcohol. In any case, she never got it, the intervention, and returned to drinking, and never stopped. She was dead within a few years.

The alcohol coursed through Amanda's body, leaving a warm, light feeling in its wake. She sat back and sighed, trying not to think of anything, just for this one, brief moment, to have her mind free.

'Well,' Pri said, breaking the silence, 'you're probably wondering why I'm like this, aren't you?'

Again, Amanda thought of her mother. The whole world faded into second place behind her needs. And the selfishness of the active alcoholic was something she came across as a doctor almost every day in her surgery. Thinking of her surgery now, the icy edge of the humiliation she had felt earlier cut through into the eye of the storm, into this brief respite.

'Actually, Pri, I wasn't thinking about that at all,' she said, and added with a touch of scorn that she hadn't quite intended. 'Remember, I have my own problems to contend with?'

Pri's head shot round, her eyes glaring. Amanda waited. In her experience, the problem drinker had three settings: endless romancing of the past, belligerent confrontation with the taking of every second word as a slight, or lastly, a removal from reality coupled with a complete lack of any sense of responsibility, i.e., the so-called happy drunk. There were many variants, but one or more of these were usually at its core. Amanda wondered which setting was Pri's, veering towards the second, the belligerent confrontation. But just then, Pri's expression unexpectedly softened. She placed her glass – empty – onto the floor and took hold of Amanda's hand.

'I'm so, so, sorry, my darling. Now tell me. I insist. What happened with Edward?'

She looked at Amanda with intensity, her blue eyes bobbing about.

Amanda told her.

'The bitch,' she exclaimed.

'What?' Amanda, taken aback, 'what do you mean, the bitch?'

'That woman. Can't you see? What's her name, this Fiona loony tunes person. It has to be.'

'But,' Amanda began. 'How? I mean, Edward was beaten up. Terrible as it is, it happens, he said so himself. As for... okay, maybe... perhaps, I don't know... but not that... I mean, how?'

Pri gave a drunken laugh. 'Oh, sweetie, she could have gotten someone to do it for her of course, paid them, you know. I can't imagine people like that are too hard to come by, if you know where to look that is.'

Amanda sighed. She knew that normally Pri would have kept such observations to herself, conscious of upsetting or worrying her, or of just being plain wrong. But now, uninhibited by alcohol, she had spoken her mind. And now that it was said, Amanda realised, she could be right. Which meant that Edward was, in essence, correct, that it was her fault.

Jess Roy

'Oh, God,' she said, as she felt the alcohol's warmth evaporate, leaving her with the beginnings of a pounding headache.

They had a light meal; Amanda helped Pri prepare pasta with diced ham in a red pesto sauce. Pri's movements were sluggish and exaggerated, as she took utensils and ingredients from drawers and cupboards, like she was in slow motion. Once, Amanda tried to pre-empt her, reaching for a ceramic mixing bowl she knew she was searching for when Pri snapped, 'I can get this myself. What? You think I've had too much to drink, isn't that it?' Amanda stood back with an apology and Pri then smiled, 'Sorry, didn't mean to snap, I can get it. But really, I don't drink that much at all.'

Over the meal Pri rambled on about Liam.

'I love him really,' she said, 'but it's just he's so fucking sensible, you know? I want a man who's, I don't know, vibrant, who… sets me on fire, in that way, you know what I mean, don't you, Amanda?'

'I know what you mean, Pri,' trying to keep the weary boredom from her voice.

'And he doesn't do that, not any longer… I envy you in a way, Amy.'

'You do?'

'Yes. You have your career, a doctor. I never finished college you know? Met Liam in my first week of first year, then got some part-time modelling work, and then I packed it in and left.' She laughed again. 'My parents were soooo angry. But you know, Amy, I'm not a bookish person, I just went to college because that's what everyone else was doing. Liam was besotted with me, and we got married before he even received his degree. Maybe I should have lived a little first.' She laughed. 'I knew I'd never have to worry about money, not so long as I was with Liam. And I never have. My parents changed their minds on everything by the way, once they saw that. But I'm dependent. I'm the bird in the cage. I need him. Suppose in some ways I'm trying to relive my past, doing what I should have done back then, now, or trying to do things differently, but I can't.' She stared past Amanda in a frozen, unblinking stare.

'You're still young,' Amanda offered, careful to keep her voice neutral, not to sound like she was telling Pri what to do. 'I mean,' she continued, 'night classes, something like that, you could...'

Pri's eyes suddenly narrowed, darkening, as they shifted to take her in.

Amanda inwardly groaned, waiting. But Pri raised an eyebrow and gave a cheeky smile. Amanda watched her carefully.

'So,' Pri said, 'does Edward set you on fire in that way? You never told me.'

Amanda was drinking water. She took a long sip.

'Please, Pri, come on...'

Pri giggled.

'Please, Pri, come on,' she mimicked, 'Aw, how cute, Amy's embarrassed. There's no need to be embarrassed with me, Amy, you know that. Come on, tell me, Pri wants to know, everything.'

Amanda got to her feet, pushing her plate away.

'I'm going to bed, Pri, if that's okay. I don't want to talk about this anymore. I'll see you in the morning, okay?'

'I'm sorry,' Pri said suddenly, sounding very sober. Her hand sprung out, grabbing Amanda's wrist. 'Really, Amy, I'm sorry. And selfish. Please talk to me, I want to help. I'm sorry for going on about myself. Tell me about it...' her

175

voice dropped, becoming conspiratorial, hungry, 'tell me more of it, your secret. I want to know.'

Amanda felt Pri's hand start to squeeze, the nails beginning to pinch a little. There was a sense of desperation about her, a thirst, her eyes darkening again, yet her mouth was smiling. Amanda recoiled from the wonky expression, pulling her hand free. She strode across the kitchen.

'Goodnight, Pri.'

When she got into her room, she noticed for the first time that there was a key in the lock. She turned it. She had decided she would not tell Pri anything else. She listened at the door, could hear her downstairs as she wandered about the house, her voice muffled, talking to herself.

She realised in that moment that she didn't know Pri at all.

Chapter 35

Before...

It was late April when Lauren was born, just in time for Amanda to sit her final exams as the new Mrs Amanda Brody. She had the entire summer to stay home and be a fulltime mother before her hospital placement began in September. She harboured worries she might not bond with her child, worried she had made a terrible mistake, that she should have gone to England and had an abortion. So that when the midwife handed her the pink little bundle, and as her heart swelled and overflowed with a love so intense it made her ache, she was utterly relieved. She decided right there and then, that she would put everything behind her. This was her life now, and she was going to make the very most of it.

But no one must ever know her secret...Ever.

Chapter 36

A thought began to formulate in Amanda's head as she lay in bed. Now that she had told Pri she regretted it, regretted having told her anything. How had she been so stupid? Still, she felt she could trust her on this – at least she hoped she could. In any case, there was nothing she could do about it now.

It was too early to try for sleep. So she lay there looking through the window at the growing darkness, the blue grey sky slowly fading into the advancing black of night. Her thought was this: to leave the country. Why not? Go to… Spain? Or Italy? Even Australia? Wherever she wanted. The world was her oyster. She'd be forty six next birthday, not too late to start again. Doctors were in demand all over the world after all, and her record was exemplary. And another thought crossed her mind, one so alien considering what she was going through, but it gave her a warm glow: maybe she might find a new relationship, find love, true love next time round. She entertained the notion, imagined walking along a sun kissed beach with this perfect man, laughing, holding hands, perhaps finding a deserted spot, running up the dunes into it, and…

She giggled aloud, not at the notion of it, but the absurdity. But why was it absurd? And as she thought about it, she couldn't even imagine this perfect mystery man, he appeared more to her a shadow, grey and featureless. She considered this was because she felt she didn't deserve it. It? You can't even say it, can you? Okay, love. She felt she had no right to it, love, from a perfect man, because she felt she wasn't good enough, wasn't worthy. How could she be, she'd never been good enough for the man who'd brought her into this world, who had reared her, who'd been the most important man in her life, despite everything: her father.

She turned onto her side, the warm glow having disappeared, in its place the cold reality of having no home to go to, of lying here, in this room, effectively hiding, because she didn't want to be around Pri any longer. But more than anything, it was not that she was being haunted by her past, of what she had done, her secret, it was that now she was living through it, every waking minute of every day. Her past, that had come back into her present, both merging, a living nightmare.

Clonk. Clonk. Clonk.

An eruption of bright light filled the room.

Amanda stiffened. The distinctive sound she had heard was of the old brass knocker on the front door, the only bow to history in this temple to modernity. The light was the motion-activated security lamp illuminating outside, flooding into the room. She jumped from the bed and crossed to the window. The front door was directly beneath it. She peered out from behind a corner of the curtain and... her hands flew to her mouth, as her body suddenly sagged, trembling at what she saw.

Chapter 37

Amanda listened at the bedroom window as Pri opened the front door. Pri's voice sounded remarkably sober, but Amanda could only just about hear it above the pounding of her heart.

'Yes,' she said.

The only sound then was the beating of that heart as she waited for a reply.

As her fears were realised. Because outside, when she'd looked a moment ago, was a police car.

'Can I speak to Amanda Brody, please,' the voice said. 'Dr Amanda Brody. We believe she's staying here.'

Pri spoke, her voice rising, the words slurring at the edges for the first time.

'Amanda? What's it in connection with, officer?' And added, her voice beginning to slur more now. 'She hasn't gone and killed anybody, has she?'

Pri gave a giggle. Amanda didn't think it was funny, not funny at all.

'Could we speak with her, please? Thank you.'

'Okay, one minute, she's in her room. I'll go and get her.'

Amanda quickly crossed the room and opened the door, went out onto the landing, just as Pri started up the stairs.

'The...' Pri began, stopping, looking up.

Amanda raised her hand and whispered. 'I know. It's the guards.'

Pri took a step back and rested against the banister, crossing her arms, her half sodden eyes silently observing Amanda as she came down the steps.

'I'm sorry,' Amanda said as she passed her, 'I'm sorry about all this, really.'

Pri pursed her lips and nodded her head back towards the door. 'He's very serious about it all,' like it was all part of an amusing adventure.

But it's not, Amanda thought, it's not an amusing adventure, but knew that Pri didn't get it, she didn't get anything at this moment. The three settings of the active alcoholic she used for appraisal, well, she guessed Pri possessed a little bit of each of them.

She ran her hands through her hair and smoothed down her clothes, crossing to the door. The outside light was on a timer and had gone out again, so she couldn't see the policeman until she'd reached the doorway. He seemed to loom up out of the darkness. She knew he was there, but still, it took her by surprise.

She wondered if her startled expression might be misconstrued for something else, guilt perhaps?

'Yes.'

'Doctor Amanda Brody?'

'Yes.'

'Can I come in?'

'Of course.'

He stepped into the hallway. He was middle-aged, with a paunch, but, she noticed more than anything, his eyes, they were kind.

'I'm Garda Gerry Lynn. I debated whether it wasn't too late to call this evening, that maybe I should leave it until morning.'

'Please,' Amanda said, a pleading in her voice, 'what is it?'

'The search of your car, Doctor Brody, what we found?'

An invisible force kicked her in the stomach. It took all her effort not to show it, to stop herself from crumpling to the floor.

'What was it?'

'Unscented talcum powder,' he said, 'that's what it was.'

'Unscented... what? Talcum powder?'

'Talcum powder,' he repeated, 'Yes, completely harmless, and legal. I thought you'd want to know immediately. So I took it upon myself to call, rather than try and ring you, as we were passing.'

The words he'd said sunk in...unscented talcum powder, harmless, legal.

She slumped back against the wall.

'Doctor Brody, are you alright?'

She blinked, her eyes welling up. 'Yes, yes, I'm just so relieved so, you wouldn't believe.' Not drugs, not drugs, not drugs. 'Thank you from the bottom of my heart for coming round, for telling me, it's very kind.'

The policeman pushed his cap back on his head, scratched along the hairline, pushed the cap back into position again.

'But,' Amanda said, speaking her next thought aloud, as if to herself, 'who's responsible, that's what I'd like to know? I mean…'

She fell silent.

'Yes?' the policemen prompted.

Still, she said nothing.

His kind eyes searched hers. 'Would you have any ideas about who might be responsible?'

She shook her head.

'Would you like to make a complaint, officially that is, so we can look into this?'

Again she shook her head.

'No.'

'No? Why not?'

The question took her by surprise.

'Because,' she began, 'I just can't, that's why.'

'Hmmm,' a shadow of suspicion passing behind the kind eyes now for the first time.

Please don't look at me like that, she wanted to scream, really, I'm a good person, this is something I can't talk about, it goes back, way back, to a terrible event.

'Well,' he said, 'it's completely up to you of course.'

She felt he was about to probe further, but he didn't.

'I'll be on my way, Doctor Brody.' He turned and stepped out of the house. The security light activated. He paused, spoke without turning, 'But I'd urge you to consider making a complaint, Doctor Brody. Good night.'

Amanda watched him walk away and slowly closed the door.

'Night cap?' Pri's voice sounded.

Amanda looked to see she was standing on the threshold to the living room, holding up a half empty bottle of wine. 'It'll make you feel better.'

For the first time, Pri was beginning to irritate her, really irritate her. She went to the stairs.

183

'No thanks, Pri, the only thing that'll do is make me feel a lot worse.'

'Ah, come on, one little drinkypoo can't hurt.'

Amanda started up the stairs. 'No thanks, Pri. See you in the morning.' *And maybe you should think of going to bed too.* She reached the top of the stairs and looked down, but Pri had already disappeared back into the living room.

She sat on the bed in her room, feeling some of the tension of the last few days suddenly melt away from her. This news was important, very important.   She did not have to worry about being branded a drug dealer, did not have to face the ordeal of appearing in court, of having her name splashed all over the media, and, most importantly of all, being struck off the medical register. She knew that, and she was glad, grateful for it. But still, this was not over. She knew that. No, this was not over, not over by a long chalk.

Her telephone rang, the sound startling her.

She looked around, having forgotten where she'd placed it, spotted it on the dresser, went and picked it up, looking at the number flashing across the screen. She didn't immediately recognise it, but then it struck. She felt herself go cold. It was Fiona. The cold coiled its way through her. But then the phone fell silent again. Amanda went back and sat on the bed, staring at it. A moment later it pinged an incoming text alert. Her finger trembled as she pressed the button and brought up the message.

'We need to talk,' it said.

The phone fell from her grasp and bounced onto the floor by her feet. She stood and took a step back, rubbing her hands on her clothes, as if trying to clean herself. She took a deep breath, and another, tentatively bent down and picked it up again, took another breath, and began to type a message: 'I don't trust you. After what happened. You frighten me. You were watching. I saw you. It was you who told them, wasn't it? The police. Had to be!'

She sent the message, decided she didn't need to deal with this crazy woman anylonger, was just about to turn off the phone instead, when a text came back almost immediately.

'We need to talk. Told them? Told who what?'

Amanda typed out a reply in a flurry of fingers: 'Don't act so innocent. Like I just said. The police, the guards, that's who.'

Again, a reply came back almost instantaneously: 'I didn't tell the police. I didn't know what was happening. I saw it on YouTube later. None of it made any sense. Still doesn't.'

Amanda considered that's what she would say. Her finger hovered over the power button. Another text pinged in. She looked at it.

'We need to talk. Remember, it was you who contacted me. Think of that. I'll meet you anywhere. I've nothing to do with any of this, please believe me. We are both haunted by that night. You know what I mean. I know you do.'

That night.

To hell with this, she thought, pressed the call button, her pulse quickening, her belly lurching, as the phone at the other end began to ring.

The same raspy, sing along voice as previously answered before the first dial tone had finished ringing. 'Hello, Amanda.'

The sound of it struck a renewed fear in Amanda now. Fiona seemed to sense it.

'There's no point in us talking if you continue to think I had anything to do with what's been happening to you. You should hang up right now if that's what you think and you won't hear from me again – nor do I expect to hear from you. The decision is yours. One way or the other, we need to sort that.'

Amanda said nothing for a moment. Then: 'But, you were watching. I saw you. And no one knew I was meeting you, no one.'

'Yes. Yes. So you think I rang the guards and had them do that to you. On what pretext? Why, Amanda? Why would I do that?'

'You know why.'

'Goodbye, Amanda...'

She was consumed by a sudden panic. 'No,' practically shouting, 'don't. Don't go. Okay. Okay, maybe you didn't, I don't know, I don't know anything. You said that it all went back to that night. As do I...'

'Don't say anything. Not another word. I told you. I don't trust phones. And neither should you.'

'Well what then, for God's sake?'

'Remember you told me once, the place you liked, where you went when you wanted to be alone, where you felt safest, remember?'

Salthill.

'Yes.'

There. I'll meet you there. Tomorrow.'

'What time?'

'The same time as our first shift at St Vincent's? Remember. The time we started?'

They'd started late that day, very late, because the consultant had been delayed. Turned out he had reversed over the family cat in his car when leaving for work. That's why she remembered, why they all did probably.

'Yes, but...' her voice trailed off.

'Look. Do you want to meet or not, Amanda? If not, like I say, don't bother me again, and I won't bother you. We'll end it right here.'

'I remember the time. Yes, I'll meet you, I'll be...'

But the line went dead before she could finish the sentence. Amanda pulled the phone from her ear, wondering if she hadn't just made one of the biggest mistakes of her life.

Chapter 38

S he went to bed, and despite the sounds of doors closing and opening and the mumbling of Pri somewhere as she talked to herself, she drifted off to sleep. But almost immediately her eyes snapped open again. What had woken her? She lay still. There was a sound, like heavy breathing. She turned her head slowly towards it. *Jesus!*

And blinked.

No.

Good God.

No.

Someone was in bed alongside her. She screamed, twisting her body, scrambling to the very edge of the mattress, tottering there, then feeling like she was taking to the air, as if flying, but only for an instant, as she realised she was not flying but instead falling to the floor. She landed with a thud. She screamed again, her arms and legs beginning to flail about on the floorboards, moving her towards the door in wild crab like movements. The diffused light through the curtains cast the room into eerie shadows and pools of black. She knew he was behind her, as she fought against her fear, forcing herself to glance over her shoulder, saw him rising from the bed, starting after her, the stench of his lust scorching the air. She reached the door and her hand clambered up and found the handle, but it was too clammy to grip and turn it properly. Frantically she continued on trying, twisting and pulling on the handle, the latch bolt sliding back but never far enough, hitting the strike plate each time she yanked on it, making a click sound... *click, click, click.*

She opened her mouth to scream, but this time no sound came. He was almost upon her, would soon begin to drag her back to the bed, tie her down, do things to her, violate her. A light reflected on his face. She saw it. He was wearing a mask.

NOOOOO!

Again, her eyes snapped open. But this time it was for real. She was on the floor between the bed and the window, bathed in sweat, her breathing fast and frantic. She looked about the room, but could see nothing. She felt a panic take hold, could feel the outline of the bed next to her.

A nightmare.

That was all.

But was there someone here? In the room? Because it had all seemed so real. In fact, was there someone in her bed? It was dark, and she could see little. The panic deepened as she scrambled to her feet, resting one hand on the mattress, frantically fumbling for the bedside light with the other. She heard a dull thud and knew she had knocked the light over. The panic was almost overpowering now, as she braced for a hand to grasp her wrist and drag her back to the bed.

Ahead of her, on the other side of the bed, a pencil line of white appeared, a rectangle of what she knew now was the light from the landing outside. The pencil line began to widen, becoming an ever increasing wedge as the door

189

opened and the shadowed shape appeared, stooped, with bedraggled hair.

She sank to the floor as she had done in her son's apartment, but she did not cry, instead stared ahead, her chin resting on the bed, waiting for the shape to reveal itself, a silent explosion of light erupting as the light was turned on, dazzling her.

*

It was Pri. She rushed over, sliding down to the floor next to her, holding her gently by the shoulders.

'I heard you scream. It's okay. It's okay. You were having a nightmare?'

Amanda began to cry.

'Yes. Yes. I was,' she said. 'I don't think I can take it any longer, I really don't.'

'It's late. I don't feel so well either. Let's get some sleep. Come on, into bed, I'll stay with you tonight, you won't be alone. Neither of us will.'

Pri helped her into bed and lay beside her, tucking the duvet about them both, the alcohol fumes hot and stale on her breath. Instantly, Pri was snoring. In the darkness, Amanda found the sound comforting, telling her that she was not alone. She was also comforted by the warmth of her friend's body, and the rhythm and sound of her breathing, so that when she went to sleep, she did not wake until the next morning.

I Know Your Secret

Chapter 39

They sat at the kitchen table the next morning, coffees in hands, Pri's complexion a sickly hue in the sharp October sunlight through the bay windows, their eyes bloodshot. Amanda had just told Pri about the meeting arranged with Fiona for later that day. A silence followed, making her wonder if this hadn't been a mistake. Her friend seemed not to have heard, or not to be interested, sitting there, cradling her coffee mug in her hands, merely staring at the table. Amanda was about to give up, to leave and go to her room, maybe go for a walk, anything was better than to have to be here with a hung-over and melancholy Pri. But Pri suddenly looked up.

'I want to go with you,' she said, her voice suddenly not so tired anymore. In fact, it sounded animated.

Amanda was silent, contemplating. Then: 'You do? Why?'

'Because, well... Amanda, she's a bit loo-la, we both agree on that, don't we? What if something happens? Anyway, I find it exciting, an adventure.'

And suddenly Amanda realised that Pri was bored with her life. It all clicked into place as she remembered the comments: *Maybe I should have lived a little first. But I'm dependent. I'm the bird in the cage. I need him.* And as often happens, she knew, when someone realises they need someone, they end up resenting them. She began to understand Pri's attitudes towards Liam now. But Pri was wrong to think that she, Amanda, considered Fiona was, as she put it, 'loo-la'. She didn't. This was a conclusion she had arrived at herself. But she didn't go there now.

'Exciting,' she muttered instead, 'I can do without exciting right now.'

'Yes, of course. But you know what I mean. I could watch, from a distance, keep an eye on you, just in case something goes wrong. Makes sense, doesn't it?'

Amanda had to admit, it did indeed make sense. 'If you're sure,' she said, 'but you can't allow her to see you.'

Pri pursed her lips, seemingly thinking this over.

'Why not? I could be out for a walk, just like anybody else, nothing unusual in that, is there? I've never met this Fiona woman. She doesn't know me. If I'm lurking about she might notice me. I could be invisible in plain sight, that's what they call it, isn't it?'

'Maybe,' Amanda said. 'But... it's a little isolated down there, not a lot of people are about.'

Pri pushed back her chair and slowly stood, holding a hand to her forehead.

'God, I've such a headache. Um, yes, Amanda, that's true, but still, they do go there, it's not off limits, is it?'

Amanda nodded. 'No,' shook her head, 'I suppose it's not. Well, okay then... and Pri?'

'Yes?'

'Thanks, again. It'll be good to have you there, really, to know you're there.'

The crows' feet by Pri's eyes folded as she smiled. Amanda thought her friend was beginning to look prematurely old.

'It's what friends are for,' she said, starting to walk away, 'now, I'm going for a shower.'

They drove in Pri's old Jag and parked in the car park by the Salthill promenade. The time was ten minutes to two. Amanda said she would walk ahead, and it was agreed Pri would follow five minutes later. As Amanda opened the door to get out, Pri said, 'Don't forget, I won't be far away at any time, so try not to worry.'

Amanda nodded, looking at her friend, who appeared much healthier than she had that morning, her eyes clear and her skin ruddy. Amanda considered she was relishing this 'adventure'.

She got out of the car and wrapped her scarf around her neck, nodded in a 'this is it' gesture and began walking along the promenade, away from the city suburb, towards the pebbled shoreline about a half mile away. She glanced out to sea, over the buttress of boulders piled against the promenade, protecting it against the wild Atlantic storms. But now the ocean was quiet and calm, it merely lapped and murmured against the grey rocks. The air was bracing, the light pale and soft, but off in the distance a cobweb of black cloud spread out from the horizon. She walked quickly, she only had ten minutes after all. Reaching the end of the promenade she hurried down the steps by the Blackrock diving tower. Most people ended their walks at this iconic landmark, but others braved on. She braved on, she had to, made her way along a rutted path towards the beach. As she rounded a bend she crossed the dunes of marram grass and onto the shingle shoreline. She started to walk along it, her feet making a crunching sound. Ahead was the shelter, set back from the beach in a clearing within the dunes, ringed by a necklace of sand. With each step the sky began to darken, the ocean turning a gunmetal grey, jarring her mind, the sudden melancholy of this place igniting without warning those memories, of that night, bringing back with it

193

something new, something that previously had been forgotten ….

There was a voice. 'Thank you,' it said, 'no, no, everything's fine, just, y'know, too much to drink, that's all. I've warned her about it, yes I did, doesn't seem to listen to me, it doesn't suit her, told her that an' all' ... 'Well, if you're sure?' ... 'Yes, I'm sure, but thanks anyway, good to know people are watching out for one another, 'cause, you can never tell these days, never know, someone might've spiked her drink'. And then a funnel of cold damp air as the door of The Merchants was opened, and Amanda passed through – half slumped against somebody who smelled of cigarettes and antiseptic, an arm tightly wrapped around her waist as she looked on, a dreamy, detached observer, noting a face floating up from the crowd around her, seemingly smirking at her as she glided past.

She shuddered.

It was the face of Fiona, and she could see it clearly now, as if it was right before her. As the thought struck her, *This is a trap. Get out of here. Oh, God, oh God, please, no...*

She looked around frantically, fear fizzing through her, making her skin literally tingle. Yes, a trap, and she had walked right into it. Her eyes scanned the deserted beach. She could see no one, and there was no sign of Pri. Where the hell was her friend? She was supposed to be keeping an eye on her. But of course, what was that she had said earlier? Yes, she would be 'invisible in clear sight'. That was it. Relax, Amanda told herself, she's probably watching you right now, from somewhere in the dunes, finding this whole caper so 'exciting'.

Or. She may not be here at all.

Amanda stumbled on across the rough ground, a vague sense of wanting, needing, to reach the water's edge. She'd feel safer there, would be able to spot any threat before it had time to manifest, protected on one side by the sea. When she reached it, shadows were creeping in over the ocean and across the landscape, passing over her, taking all colour with them, turning the world monochrome. It was then she felt the first drops of rain on her face, and with it a sudden gust of wind whipping about her, sharp and angry. She had no coat on, so she pulled the scarf tighter around her neck as another gust came, barrelling in off the sea, but this time it did not recede, but remained instead blowing at full force, and with it came a violent downpour, but it was not rain; instead, it was hailstones, as big as marbles. She turned her back against it as the downpour intensified, becoming an onslaught, feeling a thousand barbs on her through the thin fabric of her clothing, stinging her body all over in a furious torment, the wind howling like a beast. She was suddenly consumed by a terrible fear and began running across the shingle, away from the water once more, back towards the dunes. She had only gone a short distance when she stumbled and fell to the ground on the slippery wet surface. She felt something pierce her leg, razor sharp and painful, warm liquid mixing with her cold, damp, flesh. She knew she was bleeding. She looked at her leg and saw a sliver of dirty brown glass protruding from her lower thigh. She knew the glass had gone deep, and by the mere trickle of blood that it was also sealing the wound.   Frantically, she began to clamber to her feet again, careful to leave the glass in place, knowing that to remove it, without knowing the full extent of her injury, was too risky. Although she was a doctor, she was dealing with herself, and so it was impossible for her to know if her femoral artery had been severed or not.

She stooped against the furious wind and downpour, peering ahead, her eyes scanning the dunes. The wind pushed at her back, and she braced herself against it to stop herself from falling over again. She knew that if she fell a second time, she may not be able to get back up. She took a step forward, a hot stab of pain slicing through her thigh. She cried out in pain, but then gasped, as her eyes detected something, a movement in the near distance. She stared, her eyes stinging, her whole body pummelled by the fury of the storm, saw a fleeting glimpse of a figure, blurry within the incessant hail, becoming more distinct as it approached across the beach. Relief and fatigue coursed through her, but her energy was draining, as she began to fall, the shingle rushing to meet her, just in time outstretching her arms, cushioning the impact as she hit the ground.

Thank God, she thought, thank God, it's Pri.

She turned her face up, her mouth tasting of salt and seaweed, taking in the figure standing above her. A figure squat and wide, not tall and petite like Pri. A wave of nausea washed over her as she looked along the short body to the face, a man's face, oddly shaped and strangely oversized, out of all proportion to the rest of his anatomy. He loomed more as a shape, a shadow, than a physical entity, dark, brooding, indistinct, as if one of the very shadows she had witnessed earlier skittering across the landscape had settled to earth. Amanda was overcome by a terrible fear. She turned her head away from the figure, her hands clawing at the ground, as she squirmed her body in a half circle, trying to edge away. But to where? The ocean? She inched her way forward, her back slightly arched, like a sea creature, trapped on land, awkward, desperately seeking to reach the sanctuary of the sea, as the hailstones continued to pound a fusillade against her face. She could see the churning foam as the water crashed to shore. A hopelessness gripped her. What was she doing? What? Heading to her death? In the cold waters of the Atlantic? She glanced over her shoulder. But no one was there! As quickly as it had appeared, the apparition had disappeared again. She stopped moving, was still, gasping for breath.

But then, in the corner of her eye, she saw a movement. She swivelled her eyes to the corners of their sockets. And saw she was wrong. The apparition had not disappeared. No. It was still present, standing on the other side of her, right there, a couple of feet away.

'Please,' she screamed, turning to face it, 'who are you? Why are you doing this to me? Why?'

The shape slithered like a ghostly apparition to her. Amanda wondered if indeed that is what it truly was. An apparition... from that night, returned from the dead perhaps? Back to take her with it to hell.

Again she screamed, louder this time, everything she had and more pushed into that desperate sound, but even so, it was tossed aside and lost to the wind. But she knew it was of no use anyway, there was nothing she could do, she was alone, in this wild but beautiful place. She fell silent, giving in to it all, surrendering, awaiting her fate, sad this place she had always considered her safe harbour, turning out to be nothing more than a treacherous sandbank.

She closed her eyes, and a moment later there was the sensation of being lifted into the air, then of bobbing about, like she was somehow in water, but she could not feel the cold liquid on her body. She opened her eyes, and found herself staring down at the shingle from a height, moving swiftly over it. She tried to wriggle free, but the grip on her was too tight. The hailstones beat against her, the wind howling as before, but now seeming desperate to devour her.

She was carried off, and there was nothing she could do about it. The dim light faded and was gone, and everything became black, just as it had done the first time, on that night.

Chapter 40

She slowly opened her eyes, the lids like great weights, heavy and sluggish, as the ropes cut into her wrists, pulling her arms back, stretching them taut behind her. The bed was hard and cold pressing into her back. She suddenly began to cry, her tears mixing with the water bathing her face. She looked up at the grey ceiling. There was a window open somewhere, the wind blowing through the room in a loud, ominous rumble.

'Amanda?'

She shot her head towards the sound of the voice, her name; saw next to her three dark outlines framed within a black border, a background of murky grey sky. Her leg throbbed, but she ignored it. She began to shiver. A hand pressed down on her forehead and she turned her head furiously against it, trying to shake free from its touch.

'She's burning up,' a voice said, a familiar voice, raspy and sing-a-long.   Where had she heard that voice before?

'I know you,' Amanda spluttered in her delirium. 'I know you. I want to go home, do you hear? I want to go home. What've you done to me? What?'

She felt herself being gently pulled to her feet, and she looked about, at the open bedroom that faced the sea... no, no, not a bedroom. She knew this place. Yes, she did. Where? What was it? Yes, of course. The shelter! But who were these people? She tugged against the hands that held her, trying to break free, to get away. 'No. Leave me. I'm not going with you. I'm not. Leave me. Leave me alone.' A searing pain tore from her leg and up through her body. She screamed.

'C'mon, Amanda, you're safe, we'll take care of you,' the voice gentle and soothing.

'You will?' she said, her voice suddenly softening. 'You will? Really? Untie me then. Take me home. Take me from this place. I can't stay here a moment longer. I can't.'

Chapter 41

An episode from her childhood played out in her mind. She must have been around twelve years old, and had fallen from her bicycle, deeply gashing her knee. She'd been permanently scarred as a result, in the shape of a great big teardrop across her knee. She had limped home, her father watching from the sitting room window as she came down the garden path, waiting for her on the doorstep when she arrived. She remembered the scowl on his face.

'What have you gone and done now?' he demanded, looking at the bike, 'you're not getting another one of those you know, don't let that thought get into your head, you've only had this one a bloody week.'

'I'm sorry,' she said, fighting back the tears, her knee an explosion of pain. 'I'm so sorry, Daddy, I really am, please don't be mad at me.'

'Don't sniffle,' he snapped, 'don't be mad at you? You're completely hopeless you are… I mean, why couldn't I have had a boy?' He shook his head. 'Why oh why? Someone I could be proud of, instead of, instead of…'

His voice trailed off as he turned and went back into the living room, slamming the door shut.

Amanda ran straight to her bedroom, the pain in her heart smothering the physical pain in her knee. She stayed there more or less for three days, until the wound had begun to heal, but she would never forget the words her father had said. The physical wound was never stitched, the ugly scar the result. The emotional wounds, even after all these years, had never even partially healed, were still as raw and tender as ever.

Her eyes were moist and she wiped a hand quickly across them, the images receding. Had she been dreaming? She couldn't be certain. She had a scattered recollection of what had happened on the beach, of falling, a glass shard cutting into her leg. But as for anything afterwards, just as with Dublin, there was little. She felt warm and comfortable though, a bright light bathing the room. She stared across it through a window and could see the tops of trees outside.

The room. What room?

She looked about for the first time, taking it in. A blue curtain was pulled half way around her bed, leaving a vista through the open portion of a beige wall and the window with the trees outside. She heard voices and sounds, familiar sounds. And knew where she was. It was an A&E cubicle at Galway University Hospital. She was dressed in a hospital gown, and a health service regulation pale blue blanket covered the bed, partially folded back to leave the bandaged area of her right leg free. She felt no pain. She tested her leg, raising and lowering it without difficulty, just as a nurse came round the corner of the curtain and smiled.

'Dr Brody, how are you feeling?'

201

Amanda didn't answer, aware of someone standing behind the nurse. Her eyes darted in their direction.

'Yes,' the nurse said, 'someone is here to see you.' The nurse glanced over her shoulder as the two guards entered. A dart of fear struck Amanda, radiating out from her chest, with it a feeling like she had just put her foot out for a step and found it wasn't there, a hollow, disconcerting sensation. One of the police officers she recognised. The one who'd called to Pri's house the night before, but it seemed so long ago now. His name escaped her. His colleague, a young female guard, nodded, but neither guard spoke.

Amanda opened her mouth, but nothing came out. All she could think was, *why are they here?*

The police officers silently observed her.

'My name's Imelda Daly,' the female guard said, community policing, this is my colleague, Gerry Lynn.'

'We met,' Amanda said.

'Really?' Garda Daly's voice lilting a little in surprise.

'Yes, I met Doctor Brody,' Garda Lynn said. 'I went round to tell her last night that the search of her car was negative. How are you, Doctor?'

There was something about his tone that struck Amanda. She remained silent.

'It's okay,' the female guard said, 'if you don't want to talk about it now.'

'Now,' Amanda said, 'talk about it now. Talk about what now? What do you mean?'

She noted the exchange of glances between the two.

'Tell me,' Amanda said. 'Why are you here?'

An expression settled on both their faces similar to Layla's on Tuesday, when Amanda had called to the White Rock to discover another doctor was working in her place.

That look, like they'd just found an overcharge on their Tesco receipt.

'Doctor Brody,' Garda Lynn said, those kind eyes of his boring into hers, 'don't you remember?'

Amanda was silent again, fearful of what was to come. 'Remember what?'

'There's no easy way to say this, but don't you know that you just tried to kill yourself?'

Amanda's mouth dropped open.

'I-I...what?' her voice a strange grumbling sound.

'Yes,' Garda Lynn said, 'we received an anonymous call,' and went on to outline what had happened, a call had been received at Mill Street station in Galway City. 'I'm not certain whether it was male or female,' she continued, 'they said Doctor Amanda Brody had gone to Salthill with the intention of ending her own life, she was heading for a location on the beach just past the Blackrock diving tower, and we were to hurry, before it was too late, she was going to go into the sea. A unit was dispatched immediately.'

'And there wasn't a moment to lose,' Garda Daly chipped in, 'when we got there you were disorientated, bleeding profusely from a leg wound. It looked like the tide had pulled you back to shore. A local man, name of Paddy Ferguson, saw you on the shoreline and went and carried you to safety. You can thank that man that you're alive today, Dr Brody. He saved your life. You were lucky. When we arrived I personally thought it was too late. You weren't moving, we thought you were dead, didn't we, Gerry?' He nodded. 'The ambulance crew brought you round.'

'He found me, this Ferguson man, carried me to safety you say?'

'Yes, if he hadn't you would have drowned on the incoming tide, a high tide by the way, Doctor Brody.'

203

The odd shaped figure, Amanda realised, the sensation she had felt, of being lifted into the air, of bobbling about. It was him, this Paddy Ferguson, as he carried her to safety.

'But,' Amanda said, 'the tide did not pull me back in, because I never went into the water in the first place. I never tried to kill myself, okay?'

Again, the exchange of glances between both officers.

'For God's sake,' Amanda said, looking at each in turn, her voice creeping up an octave, 'I didn't try to kill myself. OK? Please. Believe me. And even if I did, it's not against the law, is it? So, why're you here?'

She knew by their expressions she shouldn't have said that, her comment about suicide not being against the law. She felt certain it entrenched their view that she had been trying to take her own life.

'In actual fact,' the female guard said, Amanda immediately disliking the tone, like she was talking to a child. 'We have to ascertain if you are at risk. It's why we're here.'

'At risk? At risk from who?'

'From yourself, Dr Brody,' Gerry Lynn said. 'That's who.'

'At risk from myself? That's absurd. I'm not at risk from myself. Who decides if I am? You?'

'No,' he said, 'of course we don't. The doctors. And until they do, until they give us their verdict, we have a responsibility, a duty of care. The initial call was made to us, after all.' He smiled. 'We want to do what's right, Dr Brody, can't you see that? We want what's best for you. If you weren't trying to, you know, end your life, what were you doing there on that beach? Tell us, please?'

'And if I don't? What then? You'll arrest me, is it?' Amanda was surprised at her belligerence, and knew it wasn't helping matters.

Garda Daly pursed her lips, hooking a wayward strand of hair dangling in front of her eyes to behind an ear with an index finger. 'Um, yes, Doctor Brody. Actually we can. For your own safety that is. If we deem you to need the appropriate care and if you don't want to receive it. Certainly, yes, under those circumstances, we can arrest you.'

In other words, have her committed to a psychiatric hospital. Amanda dropped her head onto her chest. 'I know how this must sound,' she said softly, 'but I can't. I can't tell you... I just can't.'

Garda Daly sighed. 'We know something's going on,' she said. 'We're not stupid. But if, just say, we were to believe you, that you didn't try to kill...'

'I didn't,' Amanda interjected, 'I didn't try to kill myself.'

'...okay,' the female officer went on, 'then why would someone ring us and tell us that you were? Why would someone go to all that trouble to say it, if it wasn't true? And the same for that call we received that you were carrying drugs in your car? It's stacking up, Doctor Brody. You have to agree. Isn't it? Something here's not right, it's all a bit off.'

Amanda gripped the edges of the blanket and squeezed tight. 'Yes,' her voice compressed, trying to keep it, and herself, measured, 'I have to agree, it is stacking up, and you know what? I can't take it anymore. Okay? I don't know what's going on. I don't. They've tended to my leg. Can I leave? That's what I want to know. Can I?'

'That's not up to us. Of course it's not,' Garda Lynn said. 'That will be a decision for the doctors.'

'Yes, I know, but it seems it's for you to decide if I'm a risk to myself. That's what you said. Well, am I?'

Garda Lynn shook his head, 'No, like I said, that's for the doctors to decide. We just want to be certain you're not going to leave here and make another attempt...'

'I didn't make any attempt.'

'... on your life, Doctor Brody, that's what I'm saying. We're waiting on the resident psychiatrist to come and speak with you, to make the final decision.'

'Doctor Andrew O'Shaughnessy... I know, I've already spoken with him.'

'You have?' Garda Daly asked. 'Where? When? We couldn't find any record of you speaking with him.'

Amanda was about to explain, but instead said nothing. Of course they wouldn't find a record, it had been an informal chat, in her own home, nothing more.

'Why did you speak with him?' Garda Daly asked, studying her much closer now than he had done before. 'What was the reason for it?'

'I-I...' Amanda stuttered, knowing they would ask Dr O'Shaughnessy about it anyway, that there was no point in her trying to hide it. 'I had a bit of a meltdown, okay, that's all.'

That's all? A bit of a meltdown. Like it was an everyday occurrence.

'My family,' she added, 'they were worried about me.'

'I see,' it was Garda Daly, his kind eyes not so kind anymore, and Amanda knew there was no point in her saying another word, not one, because his mind was already made up.

'Where's Pri by the way?' she asked. 'My friend.'

Garda Lynn nodded back over his shoulder. 'Outside in the corridor.'

'I want to see her. Please.'

Daly nodded. 'Okay, I don't see any harm in that. But we'll be right outside, Dr Brody, and we'll be right back again.'

Like, what? she thought, I'm going to try and kill myself right here in this hospital bed? I don't think so. She merely nodded her head, and said nothing.

Chapter 42

Pri entered the cubicle and stood beside Amanda's bed. She'd been sobbing.

'I'm so sorry, Amy, that I wasn't there for you.' Her eyes wandered to the bandaged leg of her friend. 'Oh, Amanda, really, I'm sooo sorry...'

'It's not your fault, and the leg is the least of my worries. Looks much worse than it is, actually. But what happened, Pri? I don't remember much. Tell me.'

Pri looked about for somewhere to sit, but there were no chairs, so she stepped over to the window, leaned against the sill, folding her arms. 'I'm not quite sure myself,' she began, her voice cracking. 'What I know is that I watched you walk away from the car, remember? You went along the promenade, as you said you would. I waited a while, until you were almost at the end, and then I got out myself, to follow. I didn't want to catch you right up, just keep an eye on you, but I'd forgotten how much faster a walker you are than me. I followed, but really, Amy, we both hadn't thought this through, now had we?' She paused, took a breath, before continuing, her voice a little stronger. 'When I got to the dunes the storm just blew up. Jeeze, where did that come from? We should have checked the weather forecast first, shouldn't we? We both know what the weather's like there, how suddenly things can change. And change they did. Anyway, I made my way onto the beach, but I couldn't see you. I panicked, Amy. I hadn't even brought my phone, I'd left it in the bloody car, can you believe that? I started walking along the beach, I knew you couldn't be far away, just couldn't, and then I saw you, off in the distance, but you were too far away... I'm so sorry, Amanda, I really am, that I couldn't stop you from going into the water, that I couldn't get to you in time...' Her voice began to falter again, 'It must have been a cry for help, really, it must. I should have known. Is that why you brought me along? You know? To stop you? Because it was a cry for help? Oh, Amanda.'

'What?' Amanda's tone incredulous, 'a cry for help? You think so too, don't you? You think I was trying to kill myself as well? That's what you're saying, isn't it?'

Pri arched her eyebrows and stepped over to the bed. She rested a hand on Amanda's arm and gently stroked it. 'It's okay, Amanda. Really. I understand. Believe me, I've thought about it a couple of times myself. But I was too caught up in my own stuff to notice. I mean, to really notice, what was happening with my friend, what was happening with you. I was selfish, but I'm not going to be selfish anymore. I'm going to change.'

Amanda tried to keep her voice calm but was unable to. 'I didn't try to kill myself,' she said, the words much louder than she'd intended, adding quickly, lowering it, 'I'm sorry, Pri, but really, I didn't. You know me, if I did, if I was thinking like it, don't you think I would have told you? Of course I would.'

'Is everything alright in there?' A nurse's head appeared around the edge of the curtain.

Amanda nodded.

'Yes, nurse,' Pri added, 'of course. Everything's fine.'

209

'Okay then, keep your voices down, please.'

'The police received a phone call,' Amanda said when the nurse had gone, 'anonymous. Saying I was about to kill myself. I was a fool to have fallen for it a second time.'

'Fiona?'

'Of course. Yes. Fiona. I mean, who else? Has to be her.'

Pri folded the fingers of one hand and peered at her nails.

'I met her,' she said.

Amanda blinked. 'What? She was actually there? You met her?'

'Yes, Amy.' Pri looked up. 'I met her. She was there.'

'I thought that voice was familiar, but I didn't know, thought I was imagining it. I wasn't. Where exactly? I didn't see anybody. The shelter was deserted.'

'It all happened so quickly,' Pri said, 'people were running onto the beach from every direction, police and ambulance. I tell you, I got the shock of my life. She was actually standing right beside me, just down from the dunes, I don't know where she came from, it was like, she was just, well, *there.* She came up to me while all the commotion was going on and asked me if I was with you. What could I say, Amy? I said yes. In hindsight, maybe I shouldn't have let on to that. But I think she knew, I think she'd been watching all along, maybe even saw us arriving in the car, I don't know. But she was watching, had to be. I asked her if she was Fiona, and she simply nodded, then said yes, that she was Fiona, Fiona McBride Crowley.'

Amanda said nothing for a moment, thinking about this information.

'I see. And what then?'

'And then, well, nothing. I left. I was too worried about you. I wanted to be with you, so I started running. That's the last I saw of her.'

Amanda's expression was grim, as she was consumed suddenly by a renewed sense of hopelessness.

'Isn't it time?' Pri said softly, nodding to the corridor, 'to tell them, the police.'

'I told you before. I can't.'

'You can't. Or you won't?'

'I can't. I won't. Both.'

'Why not, for God's sake? This has gone on for long enough.'

'Because if I do, they'll know, *he'll* know. I told you.'

'Would that be so bad, Amy, all things considered?'

Amanda pinched her lips, as if trying to stop herself from speaking.

'Lauren,' her voice so low it was barely audible, 'it would destroy her. I have no doubt. Can't you see that? Well, can't you? I'm doing this for my daughter, I have to protect her.'

Pri cocked her head to one side, looked at her friend. Then her face crumpled as she began to cry softly.

'You poor thing, Amy, you poor, poor thing. How selfish of me. Of course. It's just so terrible, you know, that I can't, I just can't fully comprehend it. It's like I forget about it sometimes, what you told me, I put it out of my mind, like it doesn't exist, simply because I can't deal with it, if that makes sense.'

Oh yes, Amanda thought, that makes sense, perfect sense.

'I'm sorry,' Pri went on. 'How can I...' but her voice trailed off as they entered the cubicle again, taking up position, one either side of the bed. Officers Lynn and Daly.

Chapter 43

Amanda didn't immediately notice Dr Andrew O'Shaughnessy following the two police officers in. But when she did, she knew immediately by his expression that something was not right.

'Can I ask everyone to leave,' he said gravely, looking about at Pri, and then at both police officers, his eyes lingering on them. 'Don't worry. I'll be fine. There's no threat here. Just step out for a moment while I speak to the patient?'

Amanda did not like the sound of this, did not like the sound of this at all: *There's no threat...while I speak to the patient.* What was happening here? She could guess.

'Amanda,' Dr O'Shaughnessy said with that grave tone again when everyone had left the cubicle. He pulled the curtain, sealing them in. In his right hand was a ballpoint pen. He scratched the side of his head with it, a nervous gesture, she felt, rather than one that had the purpose of satisfying an itch. She knew it wasn't like the psychiatrist to be nervous. If it was, he hid it very well.   She waited for him to continue. Dr O'Shaughnessy looked at her for what seemed an eternity before he spoke again.

'I'm sorry, Amanda, but you'll have to spend a little time at Saint   Catherine's. It's in your best interests.'

St Catherine's, what was one time known as the County Mental Infirmary, a dour, sprawling, gothic affair of grey stone, turrets and gargoyles, a couple of miles outside the city. Everyone knew it. Nowadays much of it had changed, the building split into various sections, combining general medicine outpatients' clinics catering to overspill from the University Hospital, as well as an annex of the regional technical college and a Department of Enterprise business incubation centre. Yet a small part still remained as a mental health facility, or the Lock Up ward as it was known, or officially the Regional Mental Health Facility. That's where she was going, the Lock Up.

She fumbled about, pushing herself up in the bed, her hands gripping the side railings.

'Andrew,' she said, her voice surprisingly calm. 'You can't be serious. Please, think about this. You can't. You know me. We spoke about it, remember?'

He smiled, a weak, uncertain smile, the smile he used many times each day no doubt, when faced with difficult situations such as this.

'It's for your own good.'

My own good!

He must really think I'm crazy, she considered, if he thinks I don't know what's for my own good, but yet he seems to think he does. She realised it was no good pleading with him, that indeed, it might make matters worse. Still, she couldn't stop herself from trying.

'But,' she said, 'we spoke about it. Remember? Andrew, we did. You said I was fine, your words, not mine. You said that I was in a 'condition of most robust mental health, with a refreshing lack of reserve in talking truthfully about myself.' I remember it clearly. You said that. You.'

He folded his arms, his tweed jacket suddenly appearing too small for him, the stitch lines along where the arms met the shoulders revealed, as the folds of his neck were squeezed above the collar of his shirt, and his cheeks glowed.

'Yes, yes, I know I did, but circumstances change. You know that yourself, being a medical professional too. Amanda, the truth is, you are a risk – a risk to yourself, and that's my final conclusion. I can't allow you to simply leave this hospital. And for what? For me to wait and hereof what happens to you next? Because something will happen, I have no doubt. No, I can't take that risk. I am responsible for you now, you are my charge. My fear is that you might try it again. And you might succeed next time, in killing yourself. That's a risk I simply can't take. And I won't.'

She took a breath, scarcely believing what she was hearing. 'I tell you,' she began tentatively, 'I didn't... I didn't try to kill myself.' And, noting his expression, added, 'Oh, what's the use?'

'The last time,' he said. 'I was wrong. You fooled me, Amanda.'

'God, I didn't fool you, I didn't fool anyone... except myself maybe, that is.'

'And what does that mean?'

She shook her head. 'Nothing.'

Again, that look she'd been getting a lot of lately.

'I know you're not telling me the truth,' he said. 'Amanda, come on, enough fun and games. It's me you're trying to make a fool of. Because you told me, and you know it. I just want to hear you actually say it, that's all.'

'I told you? I told you what? And you want to hear me actually say what? Andrew, I'm sorry, but what are you talking about now?'

His eyes were still, his expression pensive.

'Please, Amanda, talk to me. Tell me what this is about. Then I can help you.'

'I told you what? *You* tell me.'

'Okay. You told me, about the police, and the search of your car, and your attempt to kill yourself. You told me. Come on now, don't take me for a fool, not for a second time. Please.'

'And how exactly did I tell you?'

He exhaled in a long, low breath, shaking his head, unfolding his arms and reaching into an inside jacket pocket, taking out an envelope.

'You wrote to me. This is it. The letter.' He held it up. Amanda froze.

'You don't remember, do you? Or you're acting like you don't.'

'I don't.'

'You sent this, Amanda, come on.'

The sensation was like a trapdoor opening beneath her and she was tumbling through.

'I didn't send it,' a pleading in her voice that she loathed. 'Look, I know how this must sound. But I didn't send it. I didn't.'

He paused, those same still eyes, that same pensive expression. 'It must be obvious,' he said calmly, in that way that she herself had spoken to very ill patients, 'to even you, Amanda, but you need help.'

'No I bloody don't,' she snapped. 'Okay, okay, I'm sorry. I didn't mean to snap. Just show it to me, please, the letter I mean. Will you?'

He held it just out of reach. 'You won't tear this up or anything, I hope.'

'Andrew, I just want to read it for God's sake.'

He stretched and she took the plain white envelope, just like the one she had found beneath the windscreen of her car. But envelopes such as this were ten a penny. It was addressed, in block letters, to: **DR ANDREW O'SHAUGHNESSY, GALWAY UNIVERSITY HOSPITAL.** She opened it and withdrew the single sheet of paper. The same type of paper too, just as before, thicker than copier paper, but not quite board paper either, somewhere in between, a type of card paper. Her sense of déjà vu was palpable. She opened it and studied the writing. She had the sensation of looking at herself in a mirror for the first time. She never could remember reading her own handwriting, not once, ever, without a recollection of actually having written the words in the first place. But now she had no recollection. None whatsoever. And yet, there it was...

Her handwriting.

'I,' she began, 'I...' and fell silent as nothing came out. She began to read what *she* had written, in her slightly askew, irregular, and typically sloppy doctor's handwriting:

'Dear Andrew – I've been finding things very difficult lately. Very difficult. Indeed. Sometimes I don't know what I'm doing. I mean. My thoughts. I don't know what I'm thinking. It's all. Just. Just. Too much. If you know what I mean. I hope you know what I mean. I mean. I'm sure you can. You are such a good psychiatrist after all. But. My thoughts. They're very erratic. I do things on impulse. I don't know why. Hey, did you hear? You probably did. I was stopped. By the

police. My car was searched. It was all over YouTube. I don't know why. I mean, I don't know why I did it. I really don't. But I was the one who rang the guards. Explain that? Me. Can you believe it? Well, I hardly can. And now... Oh, and another thing. I've left Edward. Yes, poor, poor, Edward. He was assaulted, you know. Somewhere in the city. I might have had something to do with that? Yes, terrible, isn't it? Me. But I might. Nothing more than a feeling. On my part. But still... Look, I never wanted him to be part of this. Part of my insanity. Okay? You see, something happened. To me. Years ago. Something he doesn't know about. No one does. It's ground me down I can tell you. It's left me hopeless. It's left me. It's left me... which is why I've decided to end it all. I can't take it anymore... Andrew, I want to tell you. But I don't want my family to know. Please. Well, I do, but not until it's finished. Until it's too late. Until I'm free. And they can't stop me. Oh God, I want to be free, I really, really, do. And, by consequence. So will they. My family. They will be Free too.'

Amanda put the letter down, stared at it, then picked it up again, folded it carefully, placed it back in its envelope and handed it to Andrew.

'There, you can have it back, no problem,' and, with a slight smile, 'I doubted myself for a minute there. I mean, so much has been happening, I really, actually did, doubt myself. The handwriting is very convincing. But it's not mine. And I'd never write anything like that, too flowery, and that punctuation? No, it's not me. It's someone else, doing this to me. Andrew, I think it's rather obvious, and you're falling right into the trap.'

217

'A trap,' he said, 'you see it like that? A trap? What trap?'

She knew she had to be careful, every word was being scrutinised.

'It doesn't matter. You don't believe me. Let's just leave it at that. Anything I say will be too much.'

He gave a slight shrug. 'Fine, we can do that, for now... but we'll talk about this later. About everything. I'll give you plenty of time, Amanda, there's no rush. Now, if you'll excuse me a moment.'

He left, but this time, pulled the curtains behind him.

Amanda rested her head back against the pillow, closing her eyes. A short while later she heard footsteps again, this time approaching unusually slow and ponderous, stopping right outside the closed curtains. She looked up as a hand appeared, pulling the curtain aside: a male hand, she assumed it was Andrew O'Shaughnessy. He pushed through into the cubicle.

But it wasn't Dr O'Shaughnessy. Her belly lurched when she saw who was standing there.

Her husband smiled. She noted Edward was leaning on something. She recognised it then as the old blackthorn walking stick that had been lying around the house for ages. It had been a gift from somebody or other years ago, she couldn't remember who. The last she had seen of it was at the back of the very cluttered garage.

'I needed something to help me get about. They were going to give me a walking stick at the hospital, but then I remembered we had this. Perfect.' He smiled again, and his expression was warm. He nodded towards her, 'And you might need something too, eh? But the doctors say your leg should be fine in a day or two. And you're not in any pain, are you, darling?'

Darling. She shook her head, thinking of that word. When had he last called her that? 'No, I'm not,' she muttered.

He limped over to the bedside and stood above her, resting his weight awkwardly on the stick. A dressing covered a corner of his forehead, and purple and yellow bruising streaked his face. Amanda felt a wave of pity for him, and guilt too that in some way she had not only caused this, but had abandoned him. It pushed everything else aside. She looked around.

'I don't think there's a chair in here. I can ring for the nurse, she'll get you one. Will I do that?'

She was about to raise her hand for the call button.

'No, there's no need,' he said. 'I won't be long. I just called to say whatever is happening between us we can get through, together.' He smiled, and his eyes held a tenderness she couldn't remember having ever seen before. 'I haven't always been nice to you, Amanda, I know that. I can be moody, and yes, condescending. I can be difficult to live with. I'm sorry. Since you left I realised how much you mean to me. Look, when this is all over, when you finish your, well, your...'

'Treatment, is that the word you're searching for?'

'I didn't want to use that word, Amanda, I didn't think it appropriate, or that you'd like it.'

She didn't like it.

'But afterwards,' he said brightly, 'when the whatever you want to call it is finished, you come back home and I'll take a week off. We can start all over again. I'll take care of you. Let me do that. What do you say? We can use this horrible experience to give ourselves some space; we can start over again, Amanda.'

219

His words were delivered with a tenderness that matched the dreamy look in his eyes. She could never remember him speaking to her like this before. She had no doubt of his sincerity or conviction, and probably because of this she knew she could not be with him, she could never be with him again. Not unless she did something. Not unless she told him the truth.

'Edward.'

'Yes, Amanda?'

All sound seemed to cease in that moment, background noises, of voices, of rushing footsteps, gurneys and medicine trolleys, occasional cries of pain, all gone. And in that moment their eyes locked together.

She stared at him. Could she visit her torture upon him? Did she want to destroy him too? Did she want that? Wasn't it better to leave him be, as he was, ignorant of the facts? What would be the purpose in telling him anyway? Now, after all this time? She understood that a part of her loved Edward, always had, always would, and that that part of her did not want to hurt him.

'I was just going to say... thank you. For coming here. For saying what you said. But I don't want to talk about anything else, not now.'

He said nothing, as the hospital noises burst back into life, and she realised they'd never gone away, she'd merely tuned them out. Something passed behind his eyes, a mixture of sadness and pain she considered. But then he smiled.

'Of course, we don't have to talk about it now... By the way, I haven't mentioned it to the kids, the current situation that is, your well, you know...'

She nodded. 'I know. Thank you.'

'We'll keep it from them.'

She nodded. 'I agree. Thank you.'

The fact that he was not going to press her on anything, as the old Edward would have done, that alone, was a sign that maybe he really had changed. And she was relieved the children were being kept out of it. Her husband had everyone's best interests at heart.

'I only want what's best for you, Amanda, truly.' He brushed a hand gently against her cheek and smiled. 'Now, I'd better be going, Andrew told me not to stay too long.'

She nodded and watched as he left the cubicle, feeling a warmth spread through her, before reality crashed back again and with it the sense of hopelessness stronger than ever. She knew it would never work with Edward. Never. Not unless she told him the truth, that his daughter, Lauren, wasn't his daughter at all.

And that, she could never do.

A nurse came in almost as soon as Edward had gone.

'Just to let you know, Amanda,' she said, 'you'll be remaining here until the morning. Someone will be with you at all times, so don't worry.'

'I'm not worried,' Amanda said. 'I feel fine.'

'Yes, of course,' the tone patronising Amanda considered. 'You don't have your own bathroom facilities,' the nurse added. 'As you know, the loo is right outside.'

'I've already been. I'm able to hobble to it myself.'

'Well, if you need to go, before the special comes on duty, just press the call button.'

A special: term for a nurse or assistant assigned to a patient requiring round the clock observation.

The nurse turned, about to leave again.

'But,' Amanda said, 'I don't need anyone, I don't need a special. I just told you. I can manage by myself.'

'Of course. But I wasn't talking about that.'

'You weren't? What were you talking about?'

'The cubicle door, Doctor Brody, it will be locked.'

The nurse was gone before the full impact of those words sunk in. Amanda heard a short snapping sound. She knew it was the bolt sliding across inside the door lock.

She felt an urge to scream, took a deep breath, opening her mouth, her vocal chords constricting, poised to send out a piercing, desperate sound. But at the last moment she snapped her mouth shut again, fighting back against the rising panic, and the fear that made her feel hollow inside, like she might break and fragment into a thousand pieces. This was the closest she had come to completely losing it, abandoning herself to a swirling vortex where she might be lost forever should she fall in, and even if she did re-emerge, she would never be the same again. It wouldn't take much for her to break, she knew that. She really was skirting the edges right now –the edges of a nervous breakdown.

She thought of Lauren, dear sweet Lauren, who cared about everyone else more than she cared about herself, and Danny, her surprisingly responsible, caring, beautiful son.

She couldn't allow this to happen. She wouldn't allow it to.

She clamped a corner of her lip between her teeth and bit down, felt the hard, sharp incisor pressing against the skin, the pain wrenching her back into the present, onto the correct side of sanity. She flopped her head back against the pillow, staring up at the ceiling.

She could get through this.

She would get through this.

She *had* to get through this.

Chapter 44

Amanda knew that A&E beds were always at a premium. And yet they had allowed her to remain here, not only in A&E, but in an A&E cubicle, of which no hospital had very many. She wondered if they would move her onto a ward later? Possibly. She concentrated on this, and other practical questions, successfully halting her mind from wandering to where it wanted to go, to a place of hopeless fatalism.

She'd had an omelette and salad for supper – surprisingly good – and sometime later that evening, just after darkness had fallen on the world outside the window, the orderly came round again pushing a tea trolley and poured her a cup from a great big urn. After this she was alone, the sounds of the A&E department outside a constant backdrop. She didn't know where her phone was, and her not having it compounded her sense of isolation.

The main light in the room was off, in its place a night light along the wall gave off a weak, yellow glow, as the moon crept high in a clear sky outside the window, the tops of the trees spindly against the washed sky, appearing like hands as they moved about in the breeze, as if about to tap on the window. She dozed after that, which is the best that can be hoped for in a hospital, and her last images were of those spindly hands outside the window before she slumbered.

She dreamt. Of running across an open field. It was a scorching hot day, yet she was dressed in a long woollen skirt and turtleneck jumper. Someone was chasing her, but each time she looked over her shoulder to see who it was, no one was there. She reached the other side and tried to jump a wide ditch. She fell short, managed to gain a grip as she slid down, her legs scrambling wildly for footing and then finding it as she began to clamber up again. She hauled herself over the top and ran on, through a tunnel of tall bramble, at the end a corner, and then another, and yet another, before she realised what this was: a maze. She was becoming increasingly frantic, the tall bramble squeezing in on either side of her. She knew she should turn around and go back, yet she seemed unable to, just couldn't stop running, as the bramble continued to press in, now beginning to tear at her clothes, at her flesh. But she persevered, pushing forward, until the space was too narrow to move, and she became trapped like a fly in a web, the light dwindling all around her and then everything was pitch black. Behind her she could hear the footsteps of her pursuer, slow and steady, louder and louder until they stopped, right behind her. There was a hot, heavy breath on her shoulder, and with it a smell, of alcohol and sweat – male sweat. But at that moment she was free, the thick tangle of bramble was gone, had simply disappeared. She bolted forward, scarcely believing it, lunging into the darkness. But only for a short distance, before she was viciously yanked back, the binds cutting into her flesh, a dead weight pressing down, that stench of alcohol and sweat intensifying, making her gag, threatening to smother her.

224

Her eyelids parted and she was awake again, back in the A&E cubicle, her body bathed in sweat, her breathing frantic, the bed sheets sticky against her skin.

She heard something, what she thought was the sound of someone speaking. It came again. And she knew. It was the sound of someone speaking. She strained her ear to hear what was being said.

'How are you, Amanda?'

She turned her head, but there was no one there.

'How are you, Amanda?' the voice repeated.

She looked again, in the other direction this time, and now could discern a shape moving about a short distance away. It approached her, and stopped next to the bed. Amanda felt angry at the special for creeping around like this. Didn't she know it would alarm her? At the very least, she should have introduced herself.

But Amanda said nothing about this, instead answered, 'I'm fine.'

'Good, because we have a lot to do.'

'We have a lot to... what do you mean?'

Amanda felt goose bumps forming on her skin. Something was not right here. Not right at all. And the voice was familiar.

A beam of light sliced through the air, a pencil torch, swinging wildly for a moment before settling in a pool of white onto the centre of the bed. Amanda was numb, her body, her mind, everything, she was unable to even blink. And then, in a sudden flurry of movement, she raised an arm, fumbling about for the call button. And just as suddenly, a hand clamped onto her wrist, a small hand, but surprisingly strong, and cold.

'Don't,' Fiona commanded. 'Don't.'

The torch light had shifted, shining onto a portion of the face; Amanda could see ribs of pale grey hair draped across the forehead. For the first time in a long, long time, twenty five years or more, she was looking into the face of Fiona. She noted, even in the partial light, that same anxious expression, but the face gaunt now, the cheeks sunken, the flesh lined like crumpled paper.

Amanda felt her body slacken, sinking into the mattress, as the cubicle door opened, and she turned her eyes to see someone enter.

'Turn on the light,' Fiona snapped.

The harsh florescent ceiling light flickered into life.

Amanda stared at the person who had just come in, her eyes bulging. It took a second for her to process the image, so inconceivable was it.

'What are you doing here?' she spluttered.

'Hi, Amanda,' Pri said.

I Know Your Secret

Chapter 45

Threatening stimulus to the brain, if extreme enough, can sometimes result in what is known as the Matrix Effect. Amanda was experiencing this right now. Everything slowing down, as she looked on, an observer, Fiona leaning towards her, placing a finger against her lips, her expression a silent communication. Amanda gave a slow nod of her head, an exaggerated, sluggish, movement, and stayed silent.

'Trust me?' Fiona said, her voice an echo from somewhere far off, though she was standing right in front of her.

Amanda shook her head, not in reply, but in an attempt to free it from what felt like an invisible shroud draped around it. A glass of water was held to her lips, and she drank from it greedily, almost emptying the glass. She felt a little better.

Pri spoke quickly. 'Amanda. Listen. We were speaking. Fiona and I. I believe her. You've got to believe her too. That's why I'm here. We came to get you... Amanda, have you heard me? We've come to get you. Before they take you to St. Catherine's.'

Amanda raised a finger and pointed at Fiona. 'You've done this to me. You.' The words seemed out of synch with her lips, following on a split second behind, trailing back, cluttering her mind. She shook her head again, as if trying to shake them free.

'I've done nothing to you, Amanda,' Fiona said.

'But...' the word emerged from her lips and slithered away. She didn't want to clutter her mind again, so said nothing more.

'My life was destroyed that night too,' Fiona said. 'We're in this together. And we're close, Amanda, so close...'

Amanda raised her eyebrows in a question.

'To the end, Amanda. I feel it. That's why I came. Because it's come back. It's come back for you. And maybe I'm next, I don't know. So I, we, need to find out, we need to know who is doing this. We may never get another chance.'

Amanda blinked.

'Us,' she said, the word settling for the first time in unison with the movement of her lips, 'what do you mean, us?'

'That night,' Fiona said, 'it happened to me too. We never spoke about it, did we? That night. Isn't that crazy? We were both raped, Amanda. Yes, me too, and we tried to act as if nothing had happened. We tried to bury it, but we couldn't, and we can't, we never will. Amanda, we don't have much time. Come with us.' She looked to Pri, then back to Amanda. 'Will you?'

'How did you get in here?' Amanda asked softly.

'Does it matter? I know the procedure, I worked in the system for long enough. They think I'm your special. The real special will be here shortly. I need an answer.'

Amanda said nothing, a part of her retreating, too overwhelmed to know what to do.

'You trust me, don't you?' It was Pri.

Amanda nodded.

'Right then, so you really need to trust me now.'

Amanda nodded.

'Not a sound then.'

Pri kicked the bed brake off and tugged on the end as Fiona went behind the headboard and pushed. Together they began wheeling the bed from the room.

It's quite normal for beds to be wheeled through A&E departments, patients are continuously being conveyed to wards and other departments. No one took any notice. Pri's Jag was parked just outside the boom barrier to the ambulance bay. There, they helped Amanda from the bed and into the Jag, pushing the bed to the side and out of the way.

Amanda peered from the rear window as the Jag sped from the hospital. Fiona was sitting beside her. She remembered suddenly back to a time before that night, a time of laughter, fun and adventure, before it all came crashing down. A particular episode, forgotten until this moment.

'God, he's cute isn't he? So gorgeous,' Fiona was giggling like a schoolgirl.

'He's not so bad I suppose,' Amanda said.

'Is that all you can say?'

'Okay. He's more than cute. He's beautiful. He's Rudolph Valentino incarnate. God, what am I saying? The man is…' she lowered her voice, a little embarrassed, 'sex on legs, okay?'

Jess Roy

They were lying sprawled on the sofa, Amanda's head on the armrest. It was 5 a.m. and they had just come in. Fiona giggled again.

'El Dorado,' she said, 'That's some club. Oh yes.'

And it was. A pulsating, grinding audio and visual extravaganza, the number one play pit for the A-listers of Dublin city, the bankers, the media luvvies,... everybody who was anybody, the big fish in a small pond.

'Edward,' Fiona said, and Amanda's ear's pricked up.

'What about him?'

Fiona's voice had taken on a slushy tone that Amanda had never noticed before.

'Okay, be like that, you know what I mean girl.'

'Know what?'

Fiona sat up, looking at Amanda intently.

'Did I ever tell you?' she asked.

It was Amanda's turn to giggle now.

'Tell me what? That you like girls?'

Fiona's eyes blazed.

'Is that what you think? Seriously? Like, is it?'

Amanda took a breath.

'Is there any more wine?'

'No. There's not.'

'Okay... what's the question again?'

'You just said, do I like girls. You asked that. Why? Do I look like a dyke to you?'

Amanda gave another giggle.

'Come on. I was only messin'. Don't get so serious. I know you don't like girls.'

Fiona's face was hard, expressionless.

'Really, come on,' Amanda said, 'I was only joking.'

And then Fiona burst out laughing.

'Fooled ya. You thought I was serious. Ha!' She fell silent. 'Maybe I do like girls.' Fiona placed her hand on Amanda's. 'Maybe I like you…'

Amanda laughed.

'Woo hoo,' she said, and puckered her lips playfully, closing her eyes, 'gis'a kiss then.'

Which Fiona proceeded to do, Amanda feeling her lips press against hers. She turned her head away.

'Okay, okay,' her eyes snapping open, 'this's gone far enough.'

Fiona burst out laughing again, pointing. 'Look at you. Would ya get a grip, girl, I'm only winding you up. Jeeze, and you thought I was the uptight one.'

But Amanda wasn't sure about that, not sure at all.

'I know,' Fiona said, 'let's go out and get something to eat. Someplace must be open.'

'It's five o'clock in the morning. We need to get some sleep. What's got into you? I've never seen you like this before. Did you take something at that club I don't know about? Did you?'

A guilty look crossed Fiona's face. She giggled, got up and started wobbling towards her bedroom. She opened the door and turned.

'Maybe,' she said, taking a step backwards, closing the door slowly, looking at Amanda all the time, 'maybe Fiona's been a naughty girl.' She laughed again, and the door closed, the sound of her laughter echoing from the other side.

Amanda squeezed her eyes shut, turning off the memory. She didn't trust Fiona, and never had.

Chapter 46

S he listened to the drone of the powerful engine, felt every pitch and roll as the car took bends and corners at high speed. Amanda was sweating again, her whole body stiff and tense. She fumbled for the window button on the door console and pressed it, felt the cool air flood in. The road noise was a flat, constant background monotone. Pri was talking rapidly, and Amanda tried to concentrate on what she was saying... 'We went to the shelter and spent over an hour there talking...Fiona told me everything, about what happened to her that night...She had nothing to do with this, Amy, and I believe her...'

'Where're we going?' Amanda asked.

'To a house I own,' Fiona answered. 'Outside Limerick city. No one will find us there.'

'Pri,' Amanda said, staring ahead, 'what if you're wrong? What if this's a trap?'

Pri looked back at her in the rear-view mirror, the headlights of a passing car making her look like she was peering through a letter box. Her eyes were bright, *alive,* more alive than Amanda could remember ever having seen them before. This was still an adventure to her, Amanda knew, a break from the monotony of her stay-at-home boring life and her husband. But she saw too in that fleeting moment a flicker of doubt, because Pri hadn't fully thought this through. Neither had Amanda of course, but the difference was Amanda didn't have a choice.

Amanda turned back to the open window again, felt the cold air on her face, closing her eyes, taking a deep breath, doing her potato sack routine. But it was too late. Everything was too late.

There was no going back now.

She must have slept. When she opened her eyes again she saw a high, red brick wall running along the side of the road outside her window. She looked to the other side and there was a row of terraced houses. As they continued, the houses gave way to fields crossed diagonally by a line of huge electricity pylons. On her side of the road the high stone wall continued however, and up ahead she could see a gap appear in it. As they approached, Fiona pointed to it and told Pri to slow down. 'Turn in there,' she said.

The car swung through the gap, a rough track stretching ahead in a long gently sweeping curve, disappearing into a thicket of trees.

They continued on, and in the middle of the thicket of trees was a clearing, and in the middle of the clearing was a small, red brick cottage. Darkness was coming down now, but within the trees, it had already settled. The cottage was little more than a dark outline squatting before them, the lattice of the brickwork visible by the lighter tone of the mortar. Pri drove along the side of the cottage and turned the Jag in a wide circle until it was pointing back the way they had come. She cut the engine.

The silence was sudden and disconcerting. Amanda stared through the windscreen, through the gap in the trees, at the remaining daylight outside, the track they had just come down disappearing off into the distance.

'No one knows about this place,' Fiona said, and something about her tone struck Amanda with apprehension and fear. She suddenly felt there was no escape, like she was never going to get out of here... alive, that is. And worse still, a part of her didn't care.

Pri opened the driver's door and was about to get out.

'Wait,' Fiona said. 'Listen.'

Amanda held her breath, not daring to move. She thought she had heard something. She listened, but could hear nothing, nothing at all. She looked at Fiona beside her, but could only make out her outline in the thick, syrupy light.

'Okay,' Fiona said, 'I thought I heard something, that's all. Let's go. Come on, let's get our stuff and go inside.' She opened her door and climbed out. Amanda followed. Fiona fumbled for the key at the front door, Amanda's eyes adjusting to the darkness. She could see scaffolding fixed to a gable wall at one end, and the sash windows along the front of the cottage were sandpapered down to bare wood in preparation for painting. Building debris lay scattered about on the muddy ground by both sides of the door. Amanda heard the lock slide back as Fiona turned the key. She pushed the door open and stepped into the inky blackness of the cottage. But Amanda didn't move. She heard the clip of Fiona's shoes on the floor, a stone floor by the sounds of it.

Pri came from behind and stood next to her.

'Go on, Amy, get inside,' she said.

'Are you sure about this?' Amanda whispered. 'I mean. Think about it.'

Pri nudged her, a little too roughly, Amanda thought. 'It's okay' she said, 'go on. Get inside.'

Amanda stepped into the house and Pri followed. The door closed behind her and a light came on.

'I'm sorry, Amy,' Pri said, catching her look, 'if I was a little rough just now, but we needed to get inside.'

234

The air was cold inside the cottage, and there was a musty smell, a mixture of damp and wood. They were standing in a short hallway, and ahead of them Fiona was standing in a room. Pri led the way in. It was a combined living room cum kitchen, furnished in retro style, lots of pine wood, a couple of worn fabric sofas and a couch, an old fashioned range cooker, bare rafter ceiling. It took a lot of money to have a place look this simple.

'Thank God I have the inside finished,' Fiona said, moving to a back door and sliding a heavy bolt across it. 'At least we should be safe until...' She walked back across the room, passed Amanda and Pri, went along the hall to the front door and did the same there, sliding the bolt across, the sound a metallic whip crack, carrying a sense of ill will with it, and so too, a latent violence.

Sounds that brought Amanda back to that night, back to that room, and to that bed. She could smell that mixture of alcohol and sweat again, male sweat, overpowering, consuming her, as Fiona turned, and smiled. But something about that smile struck fear in Amanda. She took an involuntary step back, as if trying to escape. But there was no escape. Not now. They were all locked in this house together.

Chapter 47

'Are you afraid?' Fiona asked. 'Uncomfortable? Of me?' Amanda said nothing.

'Understandable if you are,' Fiona added. 'We have a lot to talk about, Amanda. Let's get a fire going.'

They sat around the open fire a little later, mugs of steaming tea in their hands. Fiona had to go back outside to fetch a bucket of logs. When she came back in she pulled the curtain tighter about one of the windows because the light could be seen from outside. Amanda's wrists suddenly hurt, and she ran a hand over them, feeling what she thought were welts, and with it a numbness, but when she looked, there was nothing there. Slowly, the numbness receded, and she pushed forward in her seat, feeling the welcoming heat of the flames on her face.

'You want me to make myself scarce?' Pri asked, as if sensing the solemnity of the moment between both women.

'No, Pri,' Amanda said. 'I want you here.'

Pri nodded.

Amanda sipped the piping hot tea and cradled the mug in both hands. She detected the faint aroma of body wash, and remembered that Fiona had always liked gels, soaps and bubble baths. The bathroom in their apartment had always been full of them.

For some moments no one spoke, the only sound the crackling of the logs in the open hearth.

'It's not unusual,' Fiona said then, her voice very low, like a baritone, as if a different person was speaking. Her expression had altered too, distant, removed. Amanda knew in that moment that this was how she had dealt with everything, by removing herself from it. 'I mean, in my professional career I've dealt with countless similar cases. I coined a phrase for it, nescius, from the Latin, pronounced *ness-shoes,* for unconscious, or not aware, in this case an unconscious violation. Probably, knowing what I do now, by the symptoms that I certainly exhibited, and I presume you too, Amanda, my...drinks, were spiked with Rohypnol.'

'I know that,' Amanda said, 'or something similar.'

'No. I'm certain that's the one,' Fiona said. 'By the way, you know that that drug has never been approved for medical use in the U.S.?'

'No,' Amanda said, shaking her head. 'I didn't. Look, wait... you mean, it happened to you too? Is that what you're saying?'

Fiona nodded. 'Yes. Couldn't you guess, at the time I mean?'

'No,' Amanda said. 'I couldn't.' She could hear an anger creeping into her voice.

'Because we never spoke about it,' Fiona said softly. 'Remember?'

A part of Amanda wanted to get up and leave, not to have to deal with this, because, even after all this time, and after all that had happened recently, a part of her still wanted to forget about it, just pretend that it had never happened.

'But,' Amanda began, 'I have a recollection, of passing you that night, it's never left my mind, you looked at me, and you seemed...' her voice trailed off.

'I seemed out of it,' Fiona said, 'is that what you're trying to say?'

Amanda nodded.

'Because I was out of it. I just told you. My drink was spiked too.'

Amanda thought about that.

'And,' she said, her voice dropping to almost a whisper, 'what about the rest of it?'

'What about the rest of it? Yes, the rest of it. Let's call it what it is, Amanda: rape. It happened to me too. I told you. I was raped.'

Amanda fell silent.

'I never stopped to consider it might have happened to you as well,' she said after a moment. 'And that we never talked about it. Can you believe it? I was too caught up in my own shame to even begin to think about what might have happened to you. I didn't even want to see you in fact, because you reminded me. I just wanted to forget.'

'Yes,' Fiona said, 'I know. But you had nothing to be ashamed of, and neither did I. We were victims. We were not responsible. But like many victims, we didn't see it that way. Did you think it was somehow your fault?'

'Yes,' Amanda said, 'sometimes I did.' And, her voice rising. 'But it wasn't my fault. I know that now. But, over the years, when I was alone sometimes, feeling particularly low, I'd think about it, and think about it, until it would consume me, with no release, no one to talk to about it, to share it with, and then, during those times, well then, I

could believe anything, yes, that it was my fault, and yes...'
her voice dropped, 'that I even deserved it.'

'But it's not,' Fiona snapped, 'you understand that now,
don't you?'

Amanda nodded.

'I want you to say it,' Fiona said. 'Don't just nod your
head. I want you to say it, "It's not my fault". Go on.'

Amanda noted the fire in Fiona's eyes.

'It's not,' she began, but fell silent, feeling the anger
building in her again, rolling through her, a snow ball,
getting bigger and bigger, as she suddenly shouted. *'It's not
my fault. No! It's not. I didn't deserve it. It's not my fault!'*

Fiona smiled.

'Good,' she said, 'that's what I wanted to hear.'

'But,' Amanda began, 'but...' Once more she fell silent

Because even now, that instinct, that need to keep
everything quiet, hidden, was overpowering. She closed her
mouth again.

'I told her,' Pri said, 'I told her, Amy, that you got
pregnant.'

Amanda stared at her friend and thought, of course you
did, because you never could keep a secret. But her anger
had evaporated. No, instead, she was relieved. As she
thought again, but with a stab of guilt this time, that not
once, not once, had she ever considered the affect that night
might have had on Fiona. But she did now, and Fiona
seemed to sense it. They both looked at one another.

'After that night,' Fiona began, 'I became honest with
myself... in around-about way. But first I went through a
process, a craving to belong, to be accepted. Every night I
would wake up consumed by guilt and self-loathing, and
that's always the barometer to me of what matters in my life
at any one moment, what I have to deal with, what I *must*

deal with, even if I'm trying to deny it myself, to avoid it. But that need to belong, to be accepted, to be...' she raised her hands and used a couple of fingers to apostrophise, 'normal, to blend in.' She lowered her hands again. 'I got married. His name was Alex Crowley, the last man I ever had a relationship with, before I became honest with myself that is. The marriage was a disaster. Poor man. When I told him a couple of months later that I was leaving, I could see the relief on his face. He subsequently married again, to a woman who this time appreciated him, because he really was a lovely man. He has three lovely children now, and we still keep in touch. Anyway, I kept his name, it helped me fit in, took suspicion from me I felt, the fact that I'd been married, it removed the need for explanation, and gave me that sense of belonging I craved. And it forced me to become honest; I stopped trying to fool myself, and everybody else, which I'd been doing all along. I said to myself, 'To hell with it.' So I became true to my own sexuality, and it was a liberation, I can tell you. Ireland back then was such a different place, wasn't it, Amanda? You know what I mean, don't you?'

Amanda nodded, thinking back to the stifling religiosity that controlled every aspect of life back then. Even now, in an age of relative enlightenment, when the prime minister of the country himself was gay for God's sake, it was hard to believe that back then, having a child out of wedlock, or being gay, meant being socially shunned, being an outcast, ostracised by everybody, even your own family. She thought of her own parents, and had no doubt that's how they would have treated her had they known. Indeed, those were cruel times for anyone who in anyway was an outsider.

'But,' Fiona continued, 'if I may put it like this, I always, well, leaned the other way, didn't I, Amanda? You picked up on it, right?'

Amanda thought back again to that night, when they had come home from the club, and Fiona had kissed her. She nodded.

'I tell you this for a reason,' Fiona said. 'Because I lived with a partner for a number of years. We eventually split. She had been married, to a man of course, and had one child, a son, Shane. I have to say, those years I spent with her were the happiest of my life. But it didn't work out. Anyway, when the relationship finished, I was broken hearted, not so much for what had been lost between myself and Angela, that was her name by the way, but with Shane, her son. He was three years old, she was pregnant when we met, so I was always there, and then she cut me clean out of their lives. It was heartbreaking. I always wanted a child. I thought I was so close to him, I had to pinch myself that he wasn't really my child. Can you imagine how that feels? I mean, really?'

Amanda nodded. She knew how that felt.

'Yes,' Fiona said knowingly, 'I know you can. It's so, so... visceral, like having your heart ripped out. I never forgot him, how could I? Some years later, he was a teenager by then, and I had lost all contact, a person was referred to me by Social Services. It was him. He never made the connection. How could he? But it was him, Shane.' Fiona paused, her eyes misting over. 'I should never have allowed it, I really shouldn't, because it was a conflict of interest, it was never going to be possible for me to be impartial. But I was so delighted to be able to spend time with him, and I looked forward to seeing him once a week, every week. I never revealed the connection to him, I couldn't. He had a lot of issues, and I was very concerned, it obscured my professional judgement. He took his own life, and I was struck off because I was deemed, correctly, not to have acted professionally. I enabled his deviant behaviour, his drug taking, other things too, allowed him to do what he wanted, rather than doing what was right, giving him what he needed. There is a crucial difference. But at the time I couldn't see it, I chose the easier option, because I didn't want to challenge, to upset him, told myself it would be alright, he would be alright. Unbelievable, really, for a mental health professional to do such a thing. In other words, I fooled myself. They said I caused his death. In any case, I lost my career. Why do I tell you this? Because that boy had been raped too, his drink had been spiked, it had happened to him just as it happened me, to us. But he couldn't deal with it. It set up a rage in me. It was obvious I was angry, I was angry with everyone, friends, relatives, assistants at the supermarket, everybody, you name it. Until eventually, people would have nothing to do with me, can't say I blame them. I was angry towards you too, Amanda, when I heard from you, until I realised why you were contacting me, and it gave me something for the first time in years. It gave me hope. If I could try and understand what happened that night, then I might find peace, we both might.'

A log in the fire crackled, throwing up a shower of sparks that fell against the fire guard and extinguished.

A sudden, loud, shrill voice could be heard, *'Go on, Go on, Go on.'* Amanda snapped her head towards it, saw Pri pick up her mobile phone from the table. She couldn't help but smile, it was just another of her wacky ring-tones. Pri placed a hand over the phone, muffling the sound, not answering it. She turned to Amanda. 'It's Lauren, she's been ringing me, this is the third call. She wants to talk to you. You OK to take it?'

Amanda stretched out her hand. 'Yes, Pri, thanks.'

Pri handed her the phone.

Amanda cleared her throat, took a breath, and pressed the answer button.

'Lauren, sweethe...'

'Mum!' Lauren cut her off, her tone urgent. 'Where are you for God's sake. I couldn't get hold of you on your mobile. What's happening, Mum? Tell me.'

Amanda wondered, did her daughter know about the hospital? Had Edward, after all, or somebody else, told her?

'Everything is fine, Lauren,' hoping her voice did not portray the lie.

'Where are you?'

'I told you. I'm with Pri.'

'But I rang Pri's landline. Liam answered. He doesn't know where anybody is, Mother.'

'Oh, well, um, that's because I had to... you know I slipped, your dad told you that. I needed to get my leg looked at, but everything's fine, Lauren, honestly.'

Lauren fell silent. Amanda crossed her fingers.

'Well, if you're sure,' Lauren said.

'I'm sure.'

The line crackled with static.

'Please, Lauren, everything is fine... I need to go, it's getting late, talk to you tomorrow, okay? Goodnight sweetheart.'

She finished the call before Lauren could reply, sat holding the phone, thinking of her daughter, who was now thinking and worrying about her. How was all this going to end? And, more importantly, when?

Suddenly, the lights flickered and went out, throwing the room into darkness save for the glow from the open fire. The three women silently looked to one another, the flames dancing over them, catching their startled expressions, like images in a gothic painting. There was a sound, so soft it could have been a breath of wind. But it wasn't –it was a noise, from outside; it seemed to have come from the other side of the front door. They waited, but nothing followed. Amanda exhaled the breath she'd been holding, relaxing her tight shoulders, turning her gaze from the door. Just then, something flickered at the very edge of her vision. She returned her gaze, staring, saw that Fiona had forgotten to slide the bolt back into place after bringing in the wood.

Or had she? Could she have done this on purpose? To make the task easier for whoever it was outside to enter.

She saw it again, what had attracted her attention, and blinked. Was she seeing things? Then it came again, and now there was no doubt. She was not seeing things.

The handle was turning.

I Know Your Secret

Chapter 48

As the door opened, Amanda felt an icy blast of wind blow in. For a moment it seemed that no one was there, but then she saw something, a movement, sudden, indistinct, featureless, a ghostly apparition, an orb of bright light, it seemed to float into the cottage and move along the wall from the door.

She stiffened, the light was so bright, she raised a hand, shading her eyes against it. Then she understood what it was, it was the light of a powerful torch, and it was pointed directly at her, into her eyes, dazzling her. She was about to turn her head away, but the light shifted, settling on Pri. Who bowed her head away from it, looking at the floor, wrapping her arms tightly about herself, as if trying to become smaller, to hide, to disappear. The light shifted again, onto Fiona now, who continued to sit straight-backed in her chair, staring ahead, unflinching, defiant.

And Amanda knew she had gotten this wrong. Very wrong. Fiona had nothing to do with anything.

She closed her eyes, but quickly opened them again because, like Pri, she had sought escape, had sought to disappear, to block everything out, this living nightmare.

But she knew this was impossible. It was not going to go away.

Oh Christ.

She began to shake, as everything from the last twenty-five years, all her fear, anxiety, stress, that entire cesspit, came to the fore now, threatening to drown her. She could feel herself slipping into it, her grip along the edges of reality tentative and fading. She knew it would be so easy to just let go and drift off.

No. No. No. Hold on. You must. You need. To be strong.

The light suddenly shifted away from them, and Amanda could see the shape for a brief moment as it moved back to the door and kicked it shut. It was a tall, wide silhouette, of a man most certainly, the movements slow but yet fluid, confident.

And then the shape was gone, hidden again behind the beam of light, that widened now, taking in the three women sitting in a half circle in front of a roaring fire, like a spotlight in a macabre play. The dancing flames of the fire gave brief glimpses of him as he came and stood next to it, revealing more detail, and one in particular. That his face was covered by a mask, cling-wrapping the ears and nose, buttressing the lips, cob webbing the eyes behind a fine mesh.

Amanda's body began to spasm at the sight of it, her belly contracting like a concertina, tighter and tighter, as she tried vainly to stop what was about to happen, but it was no use, the liquid coming, forming a puddle on the chair between her legs, warm and strangely comforting, before dripping onto the floor, the sound loud and out of all proportion to the source, *plop, plop, plop.*

Her hands moved, pressing down onto the corners of the chair, as she tried to stand. She had to get out of here. Just had to. She began to rise, and just as she was almost on her feet, her injured leg buckled and she stumbled forward, began to fall onto the cold, stone floor, stretching her arms out at the last moment, her hands cushioning the impact. There was a silence then, a thick, heavy silence that seemed to catch in her throat, like she wanted to spit it out. The firelight flickered on a pair of shoes a little way in front of her, fawn leather, a crows' feet of black crease lines across the middle. Something about those shoes seemed vaguely familiar, but she forgot about them as her mouth opened and omitted a low croaking noise. She turned her eyes up, peering at the shape towering above her, as she heard a voice, realised it was her own, as she asked, 'Who are you?'

Her question was greeted with silence, and she repeated it, louder this time, 'Who are you?' as she began to crawl forward, wincing with the pain. She suddenly reached out with a speed that would have surprised her if she'd even been conscious of it. But she wasn't. All she was aware of was the gritty texture of the fabric of the trousers he, this person, was wearing, between her fingers as she grabbed it. Her breathing seemed to pulse through the air.

'Tell me?' she screamed, summoning all her energy. 'Who are you? And why... why have you come back? Tell me.'

Something moved, the dancing flames revealing an abstract of flesh that she knew then to be his hand. A noise, similar to that of the buzzing she had heard all those years ago, but this time softer, not an electric razor, more like a zipper. She stared, discerning in the soupy light that he wore an overall, and that he had unzipped the front to roughly his navel, his hand disappearing inside, emerging again clutching a large plastic bottle, a Coke bottle, the label removed. He twisted the cap off and discarded it; she heard it tinkle across the floor. One of the fawn leather shoes moved, swinging back into the darkness, before emerging again – at speed, heading straight for her face. She gasped,

247

and jerked her head to the side just in time, felt the wash of air on her skin as it passed.

For a moment she was unable to move, frozen to the spot, but then realised he had not sought to kick her, he was merely stepping by. She lay her head down, pressing her cheek against the cold floor, watching as he approached Pri, holding the bottle out to her. Now the light was sufficient for her to see something else, and this was a coil of rope hanging from his belt. And she knew, just knew, with a sickening clarity, what that was intended for. She calculated that she was being ignored – merely for now –only because she was injured and probably too because she had pissed herself. Amanda was certain of something else also, that none of this would be enough to save her.

An inexplicable sense of calmness started to spread through her, with it a feeling of detachment, she could feel the regular beat of her heart through her chest against the floor – it was almost hypnotic. She was calm, because in this moment she didn't care what happened to her, because there was something she sought, and she would do whatever it took to achieve it: Revenge.

She used the darkness to conceal herself just as he had done. There wasn't a lot of time. He started to nudge the bottle against Pri's closed mouth, some of the contents spilling down her chin. It would not be long before Pri succumbed and was forced to drink some or all of the contents.

Amanda crawled across the floor, biting her lip against the pain in her leg, hidden within the darkness lying beyond the pool of torch light. The fire was ahead of her, mere feet away, and soon its light would cast itself onto her too. But for now she was safe. She continued, as a tentative plan began to form in her mind, feeling the growing heat on her body as she approached the flames.   The heat became intense as she stopped in front of the fire, glancing back, knowing that if he turned now he would see her. Pri's head was yanked back, the bottle pressed so tightly against her lips that she could not even move her head. It would not be long now before those lips parted. A rage began to burn in Amanda as intense as the fire now clawing at her skin. She looked ahead again, squinting against the heat, saw the fire shovel with its wooden handle leaning against the wall by the hearth. Her plan became complete. She quickly reached out and gripped the shovel handle, stretching up her other hand, gripping the edge of the stone mantle above. She began to pull herself up, the heat mercifully moving from her face onto her clothes that acted as a temporary shield, and pushed the shovel into the flames. At that moment he spoke, a gruff command, repeating it over and over, 'Open your mouth. Open your mouth. Open your mouth...' his voice masking the sound of the shovel.

She pulled it from the flames loaded with burning logs. But it was too heavy to lift with only one hand. She took her other from the mantle and used both to hoist it into the air. Her heart pounded like a drum, and she expected at any moment to feel his hand on her shoulder, flinging her back from the fire, across the floor. She began to turn awkwardly, her raging endorphins masking the pain in her legs, convinced she would find him standing behind, waiting for her. But he was not, too preoccupied dealing with Pri. Amanda knew at any moment Pri would be forced to give in.

She hobbled up behind him, seeing nothing but the broad outline of his back, there was nothing else that existed in the world but that. Closer and closer she came, the heat and smoke from the logs shrouding and stinging her face, forcing her to partially close her eyes, her vision like looking through blades of grass at twilight. She was almost there, his bulk filling her limited vision. He suddenly leaned forward, growling, 'Take this, bitch, take it,' the movement

249

causing his overall to billow. It was just what she needed. She paused, calculating, gaining a crucial sense of perspective, because she would only get one attempt at this. She stepped to the left, onto her injured leg, forcing herself to ignore the pain, and then one step ahead, on her good leg, into the pool of torch light. She could see that he held it in the same hand as the bottle, the light concentrated onto Pri's face. All his attention was on her, with evidently no concern that his two other captives posed him any danger. Amanda swung the shovel, keeping the motion fast but measured. Immediately she felt it impact his chest, and she felt the teeth of the partially open overall zipper along the edge of her palm, before she flipped the shovel handle up, the burning logs sliding off inside the overall, that, because it was sealed from midway down, trapped them inside around his crotch area.

His roars sent shock waves through the air. Amanda opened her eyes wide to see him scampering like a wounded animal towards the door, trailing smoke and flames, still clutching the torch and bottle, the room illuminated in the spasmodic jerky light. He pulled the door open, and Amanda immediately felt the merciful wash of cold air over her. He flew out into the night with a feral howling sound, dropping the torch, slapping at his crotch area, sparks and smoke billowing up into the night.

And then he was gone, the horrible howling sound fading to silence. If it hadn't been so deathly serious, it might have been funny.

Amanda flopped down into the empty chair next to her, and looked at Pri in the wedge of light from the torch lying on the ground by the door. Without a word her friend reached down and pulled out a mobile phone from her handbag lying on the floor next to her. A light illuminated on it as she brought it to life, capturing the mixture of fear and shock on her face. Amanda watched as she stabbed a

button three times, a voice answering almost immediately:
'999, what's your emergency?'

As Pri began to speak, Amanda looked past her, the rest
of the room in darkness. 'Fiona, where are you?' she said.

She strained to hear any answer while Pri continued
talking frantically into the phone. But there was none. The
air then filled with an ear splitting boom, one she
recognised immediately as the sound of a firearm being
discharged – a shotgun probably – somewhere close by
outside. And then a voice sounded, high pitched and
desperate. It was Fiona's, as she screamed one word:
'Help.'

Chapter 49

Pri took the phone from her ear as her mouth dropped open. She stared at Amanda, who had started to push herself back up from the chair.

'Don't,' Pri said, her voice quivering.

'Don't? We – I – have to. Fiona...she's in trouble.'

Pri reached out and grabbed Amanda's wrist. 'Don't. We can't... go out there. We can't. We wait. That's what we do. The police are on their way.'

'No,' Amanda said, pulling her hand away. 'Not this time. This time I fight back. This time it's different.' She stood. The pain was not so acute this time, instead her leg felt hot, the wound viscous. She knew she probably had an infection. Pri wrapped her arms tightly around herself again, squeezing, dropped her head onto her chest: *Everything just go away and leave me alone.*

Amanda knew how that felt, and thought, *But this time I can fight back. I can. And I will.*

She dragged the chair round to in front of her and leaned on it, used it as support to hobble to the open doorway. When she reached it she looked out, the moon high in the sky, the ground coated in a glistening frost. What should be a pretty picture postcard was instead a poster to that horror movie she was living through.

Her eyes searched through the moonlight-diluted darkness. She detected the faint aroma of cordite and burning flesh on the air.

Her eye caught something glint by the gable wall to her left, and she turned towards it. It was the reflection of moonlight on the steel chamber of a shotgun. She gasped. A body was lying on the ground a short distance in front of it.

'My God,' Amanda said, hobbling out into the night as quickly as she could.   She discarded the chair and instead used the wall for support.

Fiona turned lazily and watched her approach, shifting the shotgun. Amanda stopped.

'I didn't kill him,' Fiona said, her voice surprisingly calm, 'just winged him on the shoulder. But he hit his head on the way down, so I'm not so sure of anything anymore.'

Amanda eyed the shotgun warily, and breathed a sigh of relief when Fiona snapped it open and cradled it across her arms.

'Where'd you get that?'

'I've had it years.'

Amanda turned her gaze onto the body lying face down and said nothing.   There it was, the source of everything, the evil that had torn her life asunder, the moonlight burnishing the mask, with that sprinkling of fine dust or whatever it was. Now she would find out. But more than anything, she would know who was beneath it.

She suddenly felt like throwing up, and swallowed quickly a couple of times, forcing the bile back down her throat.

'Maybe he's dead,' she said softly, 'look how still he is.'

'Or pretending to be,' Fiona added.

'I doubt it. The pain would be too intense, he couldn't lie still like that, and he's burned... down there, 'cept the way he's lying, on his belly, will have put it out.'

'Do I care?' Fiona said. 'I hope he burns in hell, the bastard...here, take this shotgun will you?'

'Why?'

'Because I want to use that rope hanging there from his waist to tie his legs together. Just in case. Not taking any chances with him, not now, not when we're this close.'

Amanda made her way along the wall until she was next to Fiona, who replaced the spent cartridge with a fresh one and snapped the shotgun shut, and handed it to her. It was lighter than she expected. Fiona helped her press the butt stock against the wall, so that she could balance against it and aim at the same time. Amanda watched as Fiona began walking over to the body, feeling the outline of the trigger against her finger, hoping she had the courage to pull it if required. Fiona took a couple of paces before she paused, glancing back at Amanda. She looked very uncertain all of a sudden.

In the distance there was the sound of sirens, barely audible, but growing louder with each passing second. Amanda felt suddenly overcome by a fear that this opportunity would be lost. That she might never know who lay behind the mask. And she couldn't take that risk. She had to find out.

'Fiona,' she called, 'wait, come here, help me,' her tone authoritative, in control, her medical professional's voice. Fiona seemed reassured by it, her expression softening as she turned and started back.

'Take it you,' Amanda said, nodding towards the shotgun. Fiona did not object. When she reached her she took it without a word. 'Now,' Amanda said, 'put your arm around me, support me, and help me over there.'

They crossed to the body, the sound of the sirens much louder now. Amanda knew she had to be quick. The body was completely, deathly still. Perhaps he really was dead?

'We don't need to worry about tying him up,' Amanda said. 'Just help me down.'

'Help you down?'

'Onto my knees, come on...'

When Amanda was on the ground Fiona raised the shotgun to her shoulder and aimed it at the body, staring along the barrel. Amanda had no doubt that she would pull the trigger without hesitation – at the least provocation. She lay on her belly and pulled herself forward, feeling a trickle of moisture run down the back of her neck, her hands turning clammy. But her determination did not waver, even as she reached out a hand and saw that it was shaking.

Time seemed to slow down again. But she knew. She had to do this. She held her hand over the mask before lowering it, running her fingers along the gritty surface. What she thought was a coating of tiny particles of some sort, dust maybe, was, in fact, finely textured rubber. She hooked a couple of fingers beneath it, but immediately pulled them back again when she touched the flesh, wrinkly and brittle like it had been left in water too long. So he was dead.

She swallowed, gritting herself, a part of her wanting to crawl back to Fiona and not have to do this, wanting to return to the house and wait for the police, have them deal with it. But her fingers seemed to move of their own accord, squeezing under the mask again.

The sounds of sirens were ear splitting, and she could see headlights in the distance, blue flashing lights bouncing through the air along the track to the cottage.

She took a breath, and pulled.

Chapter 50

'My God,' her voice hushed, like escaping steam. 'It can't be.' She turned her head, before looking back again. Just to make sure.

Amanda could not believe it.

Yet.

There it was. In front of her. The proof.

How was it possible? It wasn't. It couldn't be. But it was. Because she was seeing it with her own eyes, she was staring at it. That face. *His* face. That benign, gentle face, that gentle soul, lifeless now. But he wasn't gentle or benign. He was none of those things. She reached out and touched his skin, making sure that this was real, that he was real, desperately needing to reassure herself of it. And he was, it was, it was all real.

How dare he? How dare the bastard? Fool me. Fool everybody. Her anger continued to build, reaching such a climax that it threatened to devour her, that she couldn't take it any longer. She grabbed a fist full of her hair in each hand and started to scream, releasing just enough of twenty-five years of pent up rage that it was sufficient to shore her up, to hold her together, was just enough to stop her from falling apart.

Because of this it took her a moment to realise.

Jesus!

That his eyes were open, and he was staring up at her. She instantly fell silent, as if morbidly mesmerised. She felt a pressure on her hand, and looked to see his hand resting on hers. She yelped and tugged on it, but his grip instantly tightened, as his lips parted into a twisted smile, and in a rumbling whisper he spoke her name, *'Amanda.'*

She screamed again now and did not stop, the sound briefly drowned out by what seemed like a huge explosion, loud enough to make her ears ring. It was that of gunpowder igniting, hurling out its load of buckshot from the barrel of the shotgun in Fiona's hand. On her right side, Amanda felt a sensation like hot sparks against her flesh as she watched Andrew O'Shaughnessy's face rupture, spouting a geyser of blood and skin and god knows what else, some of it raining down on her, vile and sticky. She screamed harder than ever, and with one final, desperate tug, yanked her hand free from his death grasp, and plopped onto her back, falling silent, staring at the sky, at the moon...thinking how beautiful it was, reassuring herself, in this moment, just for this moment, how damn beautiful it was, giving her hope.

She became aware of the sirens again, and an engine growling, of the scraping of tyres on gravel as a vehicle skidded to a halt metres behind her, headlights turning night into day. She pushed herself up onto her side, stared ahead in the harsh, glaring light, heard the pounding of feet rushing towards her, and voices, among them Fiona's, all shouting at the same time: 'Jesus, she's got a shotgun'.... 'I shot him'... 'Shot who? ... 'Him' ... 'Give me that' ... 'Sorry, sorry'.... 'What the fuck happened here?'

To Amanda it was merely background noise, chaff.

She was aware of someone leaning over her. She looked up to see a policeman unclipping a radio mouthpiece from his jacket. It made a squawking sound as he raised it to his lips, and then he began speaking into it rapidly, requesting an ambulance and other units to attend. He quickly pulled on latex gloves when he'd finished and squatted down beside O'Shaughnessy. The geyser had stopped, in its place was what resembled a thick red stew, white fragments of bone and one intact eye floating on the surface of it.

The policeman looked at her briefly – he was scarcely more than a teenager – as he stood. He turned away, began to get violently sick.

Chapter 51

The clock on the mantelpiece read 12:15 a.m..
Amanda, Pri and Fiona were sitting by the window
next to the front door of the cottage. The curtains
had been pulled and the door was open. The lights were on,
someone had discovered that the main switch in the
electricity service box had been turned to off.   Outside
there were lights all ablaze too, and the generators providing
the power for these gave off a constant humming noise.
Officers were coming and going, consulting with another
who was sitting at the kitchen table, a string of epaulettes on
his shoulder, clearly he was the one in charge. Amanda
could not stop glancing over at this heavily built, bald
headed man, and each time she did she found his gaze was
already upon her.

The realisation began to dawn: they were being treated –
all of them – as suspects.

The clock read 1:25 when this officer finally
approached, stood before them with hands on his hips,
silently observing them for a time before he spoke.

'Inspector Myles McDonald, ladies. If you would be so
kind as to tell me what went on here tonight?'

259

'It's a long story,' Fiona said.

'Then shorten it,' he snapped. 'Who shot the victim, Andrew O'Shaughnessy - *Doctor* Andrew O'Shaughnessy? Who?'

'Me.'

He stared at Fiona.

'Did you now? Torture him too, or was that a group effort?'

'Torture,' the three women said in shocked unison.

'His balls were like used coals from a charcoal grill.'

'He wasn't tortured,' Amanda blurted, 'it was an act of self-defence. He was going to drug us. Rape us. You saw the mask. And the bottle, it's somewhere around here. He wanted us to drink from it... analyse the contents, you'll see.'

'An act of self-defence,' he repeated. 'By who? You?'

'Yes, by me.'

He raised an eyebrow. 'Yes, I'm beginning to see. Indeed, it must be a long story. It always is. One that we're not going to make any sense of tonight I can tell. You'll be all coming to the station, all of you, pending interviews in the morning.'

'You mean we're being arrested?' it was Pri, who up to now had been very subdued and silent, so much so that Amanda was certain she was in a state of shock. She looked at her, but thought that by her voice and clear eyed expression that probably she wasn't. Pri glanced furtively back to her, then to Fiona, and Amanda could see something pass behind her eyes. 'Well, *I've* done nothing wrong,' she said slyly.

Amanda's mind whirled. Pri was trying to distance herself from them, at a time when they all needed to stick together?

'What do you mean by that?' the inspector asked, his voice rising. 'That *you've* done nothing wrong? By

260

inference I take it to mean that these two,' nodding his head, 'have. What exactly do you mean, please?'

Pri said nothing, dropped her head onto her chest in that way of hers that she'd been doing a lot of lately.

'I don't know,' she muttered. 'I'm just saying. I did nothing wrong. That's all.'

The inspector was about to say something when an officer suddenly rushed into the room and over to him. He spoke in a voice so low that Amanda couldn't hear. Then this officer turned. Amanda recognised him. It was Broderick, who had interviewed her along with Kinsella at the station in Limerick. Amanda had a feeling that, as far as he was concerned, connections were continuing to build up. The look on his face said it all as he turned to her: *Villain.*

'So,' Inspector McDonald said, looking directly at Amanda too, 'you didn't mention any of what this officer has just informed me of, did you now? Thought we wouldn't find out, did you? Thought we wouldn't enquire? Silly. You, Doctor Amanda Brody, are a runner from protected custody at the University Hospital in Galway, specifically psychiatric services. You were to be committed, Doctor Brody, weren't you, for your own good? And, I can see now, for the good of others too. Well, they're not getting you back until we talk to you first, and I don't care how mad you are.'

She stared at him, stung by the comment, pressing herself against the wall, as if trying to escape through it, from this place, from him. In all her professional life she'd always understood the importance of empathy, no matter what the circumstances. It shocked her that a policeman – a senior policeman – could display such a lack of these same qualities now.

'I'll remember that,' she said, her eyes blazing. 'I won't forget it, I promise you that. And neither will you. I'll make sure of that. You're making a big mistake.' She looked to Pri and Fiona. 'Because we're the victims here. Us.'

'Yes of course,' he said, condescension dripping from his tone, 'you would say that, wouldn't you? Now, Broderick, take them away, for God's sake. I'm getting a headache.'

But Broderick hesitated.

'Where will I take her?' He pointed at Amanda. 'There's a signed committal order for St Catherine's for her. If she's...'

'Yes, I know, mad, then we can't lock her up at the station. Yes, yes, I know. Take her to St Catherine's then. Makes no difference to me, we still interview her in the morning, only we now do it there. Take the other two to the station, arrest them on suspicion.'

'You can't...' Fiona started.

'I can,' he cut her off. 'And I just have. You've a history too, my lady, don't you? Yes, I know all about it.'

'Who signed the committal order?' Amanda demanded.

'None of your business,' the senior officer retorted.

'O'Shaughnessy, wasn't it? Jesus, don't you get it? Well, don't you?'

'Get them out of here, Broderick,' he snarled. 'I told you. I'm getting a headache.'

Chapter 52

Broderick sat in the back of the patrol car alongside her. He said nothing on the half hour drive to St Catherine's. The hospital was in darkness when they arrived, no exterior lights, no lights along the driveway either. Nothing, except, that is, for a single bulb glowing above the heavy wooden main door. They drew up outside and the driver went and rang the bell. When the door opened a tall, hulking man, dressed in a white tunic and trousers was standing there. The officer spoke with him, gesturing towards the car. The man, a nurse Amanda presumed, nodded, then emerged and they both approached. Broderick got out and went round and opened her door.

'Out you get,' he said.

She shifted, slowly positioning her good leg out of the car.

'Can someone help me?'

The nurse immediately came and assisted her gently from the car.

'This way, please,' he said, 'we have a room ready, Dr Brody.'

She felt his hand on her back, and with his other hand he indicated to the door. 'This way, please,' he repeated.

She heard the officers getting back into their car behind her. But only when she'd passed through the doorway into St Catherine's and the thick heavy door had begun to close, did the patrol car pull away.

She'd been to St Catherine's a couple of times in the past. Now, with most of the lights off and shafts of moonlight coming through the high, narrow, arched, windows, it seemed to exude its gothic soul, its true self, so that she hardly recognised it.

The nurse seemed to read her thoughts

'Yes,' he said, 'it's very quiet at night here. Our patients sleep best when the whole building is silent and in darkness. They're very sensitive to any light or noise.'

She nodded, noticing his name tag, "Kevin".

'Oh, I almost forgot,' he said, stepping away towards the reception desk that was nothing more than a shadowed outline, returning with a crutch, holding it out to her. 'You'll need this.'

She took it, relieved to finally have something to lean on, slid her arm in and gripped the handle.

'Let's get you to your room,' Kevin said, the sounds as they moved towards the elevator in a corner echoing in the empty foyer. They took it to the third floor, got off into a long corridor with numbered doors on either side. They stopped outside 243 and Kevin used a key card to open it.

'I left a nightshirt and a few things on the bed for you,' he said, 'slippers too, and fresh towels in the bathroom. Anything else, you let me know.' He turned on the lights, and Amanda squinted against the sudden brightness. When her eyes had adjusted she saw that the room was not too dissimilar to any to be found in any mid-scale, branded, High Street hotel chain.

'It's not what you thought, is it?' he said.

And it wasn't, but more especially for the bars across the window.

She didn't answer.

He walked to the window and held the cord dangling from a corner and pulled the slats shut.

'Your leg,' he said, turning. 'Is it giving you pain? You need me to have a look at it?'

He lowered his gaze, and his eyes seemed to linger on her chest area, before slowly moving down, over her body, to her leg.

'No,' she said. 'I don't,' starting to feel uncomfortable.

'Are you sure?' a curdling to his voice, as he stepped closer. She could smell his stale breath. 'Because I think you need a good seeing to, Dr Brody, I really do.' He ran his tongue slowly between his lips.

She gripped the handle of her crutch tighter, feeling an invisible kick to her stomach, a mixture of fear and shock. 'I want you to leave this room. Now.'

He smiled, revealing small, yellow, crooked teeth.

'Of course, Doctor Brody, anything you say. But he made no effort to leave, instead reached into a pocket of his tunic and took from it a small vial of pills. He opened it and took out two, offered them to her between two chubby fingers.   'Here, take these.'

She peered at them. 'What?'

'They'll help you sleep, stop you thinking about things, they've been prescribed, Dr Brody.'

'No. I don't want them.' Amanda felt so tired she would not need anything to help her sleep. But that was not why she wasn't taking them. She would take nothing this man offered her.

'You have to. They've been prescribed, Dr Brody, I just said.'

'By who?'

He sighed. 'The chief psychiatrist, that's who. When the committal order was signed. Any other questions?'

'Oh, Doctor O'Shaughnessy, that's who you mean.'

'Yes, of course, Doctor O'Shaughnessy.'

Amanda edged backward. He was speaking like he didn't know O'Shaughnessy was dead. Or maybe he didn't care. In any case, she wasn't going to tell him. She really wanted to sit down. But she wouldn't, not until he had left. She was motionless, then reached out a hand. He smiled.

'That's it. Good girl.' He placed the pills onto her palm. 'Now, down the hatch.'

But Amanda turned her hand over so that the tablets dropped to the floor.   She quickly squashed them beneath the end of her crutch.

'If you don't leave now,' she hissed, 'I'll scream, and I'll wake this whole fucking place up. You have five seconds, one... two...'

He raised the palms of both hands into the air, smiling again, displaying those horrible teeth once more, his eyes rummaging over her, like she was stock in a market, making no attempt to hide his leering. Amanda felt violated, crossing an arm tightly over her chest.

He turned and loped over to the door in a slow, cocky, gait, stepped out into the corridor, turned. 'Feisty, Dr Brody, aren't you? Just the way I like them.'

The door banged shut, and Amanda felt the energy evaporating from her body, leaving her on the verge of collapse. She just managed to hobble to the bed, stretching out her hands, grabbing a corner and pulling herself onto it. She lay there, holding the crutch across her front like a sword. The words he'd said repeated in her head. She thought of his leering too. He was a predator, no doubt, as was O'Shaughnessy, such creatures always sought each other out, no matter where they were. But in here, amongst their helpless victims, gathered like sheep in a pen, they had their pick of easy prey.

Her eyes felt heavy, so heavy, and she fought against the urge to close them, knowing that to do so meant she would fall asleep, and then she would be vulnerable.

'I must not sleep,' she muttered, 'I dare not, not here, in this place, I must...' But she could no longer resist, her eye closing, clamping shut, and instantly she was taken down into a deep, dreamless void.

Chapter 53

'When we went to church, hey ding dooram day, when we went to church, me being young, when we went to church, he left me in the lurch, maids when you're young, never wed an old man...'

The voice was so sweet that Amanda thought she must be dreaming. She liked that voice, and the ballad was familiar, the mighty Dubliners had made it popular years ago, a bawdy, rousing, funny, song. But then another song entered her head, and she heard the chorus shouted out as it had been that night, when her voice was one of those half singing, half shouting along, *'Alice, who the fuck is Alice.'*

She opened her eyes. Daylight was flooding into the room. She looked down, saw that she was still lying on her back, the blanket half pulled around her, the crutch still lying across her front. Reassured, she glanced about the room, saw an over-bed tray next to her, a tray with a bowl, a teapot, cup and saucer on top.

'Sleeping beauty has awoken, just in time for her porridge.'

The voice came from somewhere close by, but Amanda couldn't see anyone. She turned her head both ways,

straining her eyes to see behind her. The woman stepped
forward, as if from the wall, into Amanda's field of vision.

'Hello,' she said.

'Hello.'

The woman pointed. 'I was just taking down the name,
removing it.

From the wall. Of the last person in here.' She glanced at
something in her hand. 'Mary, that was her name. Mary,
Mary quite contrary. You're not contrary, are you? I don't
know your name. They told me, but I forgot. That's why we
have name tags on the wall, so people don't forget you see.
Do you like porridge? I hope you do, it's all we have.'

Amanda observed her. The woman wore a pale yellow
smock with white trim, an embroidered patch on the front
that said, 'Ursula, Special Catering Assistant.' She was
small and thin, the body of a child, but the weathered face
of an old woman, sunken cheeks and thin, flat hair.

'You come in last night?' she asked.

Amanda nodded. She needed to use the bathroom.

'You met Kevin then,' Ursula pointed a finger and
laughed, displaying her gums and a few teeth, lopsided like
gravestones in an old graveyard. 'He's alright, but I much
prefer Tommy. Tommy's nicer. He says he might marry me,
if I'm good that is, and if I do everything he says.'

Ursula laughed, and began pressing the fingers of one
hand into her groin area, as she sang in that sweet voice of
hers that did not belong in a place like this... *Maids when
you're young, never wed an old man...*'

She continued singing, stepping towards the door.

'Ursula,' Amanda called, and she stopped, smiling,
angling her head in curiosity as she looked at her. 'What
about Doctor O'Shaughnessy, Ursula, what's he like?'

Her smile disappeared. She shook her head, pursing her lips, and didn't speak.

'Tell me, Ursula, what was he like? You know he died last night, don't you?'

Ursula blinked, but her expression remained, like she couldn't process this information.

'Yes, Ursula. Dr O'Shaughnessy. He's dead.'

'Dead?'

Amanda nodded.

'Ghostface, dead?'

'Ghostface?'

'Yes. His nickname, silly. 'Cause of the mask he wore.'

Amanda shuddered. 'Mask? He wore a mask?'

'Yes. Scary. He's dead? Really? Ghostface?'

'Yes.'

Ursula laughed suddenly, stopped again just as quickly. And then that sound came once more, of her sweet voice singing, as she left the room, and Amanda could hear it in the corridor outside, slowly fading until it was gone, as she closed her eyes again.

*

It took her a moment to make sense of anything. Of the voices around her, of the memories from the night before. She tried to open her eyes... but was unable to. Was she trapped in this nightmare now? Forever? A fear consumed her, that she would never be able to open them again. *Maybe I'm dead? Or maybe these people think I'm dead. Maybe I'm in a coffin, and maybe they are the congregation gathered round my grave. But I'm not dead. I'm here. I'm breathing. I'm not dead. I just can't open my damn eyes, that's all. Look at me, look, I'm breathing.*

She felt a hand on hers, soft, gentle, and another on her forehead, brushing across it, and over her hair. 'Amanda, how are you?' a voice just as gentle asked. 'You seem agitated, Amanda. Is everything all right in there? Are you awake? Your eyes are flickering.'

And just like that, as if determining that it was safe now, her eyes opened, and she was staring into the face of a woman, a woman in a white tunic just as he, *him,* Kevin, had worn. Amanda jerked her head back into the pillow at the sight of it. She was wrong, she wasn't safe.

'No,' she said, 'no, go away...'

'Don't be alarmed, Amanda, everything's alright. My name's Jill O'Leary, head nurse... You do know where you are, don't you?'

Amanda nodded, and took a gulp of air, looked about. She'd been sleeping.

'Of course,' she said. 'I'm in the bloody loony bin.'

'We prefer to call it a psychiatric facility, Amanda.'

'Yes. Of course you do.'

The nurse peered down, her gaze searching.

'You've been through a lot. It will take time. Now, I want to look at your leg, and you must then shower. You agree, Amanda?'

'What about him? The one who works nights.' Amanda could scarcely bring herself to say his name. 'Kevin. I don't want him near me, I don't want him touching me – ever. Do you hear me?'

'And did he?' Jill asked, no surprise or shock in her tone, merely a sense of resignation.

'You know about him, don't you?'

The head nurse didn't answer.

'Yes, you do. And O'Shaughnessy. You know about him too. What is it, the dirty little secret? Brushed under the carpet. I thought those days were over. You should be ashamed of yourself.'

'I tried,' the nurse said. 'I really did. It's not what you think, Amanda, just trust me on that, will you?'

'And what does that mean?'

'So, this is our patient,' a male voice suddenly sounded, and Amanda looked to see a young man dressed in a grey suit, white shirt and red tie, enter the room, come and stand by her bed. 'Dr Talbot, Dr O'Shaughnessy's registrar.' He gave a weak smile, as he added. 'How are you, Amanda?'

'As well as might be expected.'

'The police are anxious to speak with you, but I wanted to get to you first.' He glanced to the head nurse. 'We both did. Is that alright?'

'You both did?'

He looked over his shoulder, like he was checking that nobody was standing there. 'I've been going over your notes. This may be a lot to take in, as events are happening so quickly, and I hope it doesn't all overwhelm you.' He fell silent.

'Why should it? There's nothing wrong with me, apart from the injury to this leg.' She tapped a finger against her head. 'In here, I mean.'

He smiled again. 'Yes, I have no doubt.'

'You don't? Then why am I here?'

'Let's get you sitting up first.'

When she was sitting up and comfortable, the head nurse standing on one side of the bed, Dr Talbot the other, he began.

'I need to be quick. Long story short, as I say, I've been going over your notes, all of them.' He glanced to the head nurse. 'In the absence of Dr O'Shaughnessy, after the tragic events of last night, I am in charge now. Yes, I've been over your notes, Dr Brody, and your medical history too. I've looked at everything carefully. I really can't understand, no I can't...'

He fell silent.

'Can't understand what?' Amanda prompted.

'Just as you say, there's nothing wrong with you. So what the hell are you doing here?'

'Is there anything you want to add?' Garda Broderick asked after he'd filled three foolscap sheets of paper with his neat cursive script. She had hesitated just a moment too long so that he looked up, his eyes narrowing ever so slightly, '...well, is there?'

She shook her head emphatically, compensating for her hesitancy. Reassured, he smiled, replaced his pen back into the loop on the arm of his fleece and folded the statement carefully.

No, she had not lied, she had just not told him the whole truth.

'What about Fiona?' she asked as he got to his feet, 'did you get a statement from her?'

'Yes. I did.'

She noted the way that he looked at her had changed: his eyes no longer held dislike or accusation, instead – and she wasn't sure she liked this either, but she much preferred it – they held pity.

He stood still, holding her gaze. And in that moment, Amanda was certain that Fiona had told the policeman everything, her own complete story. And she felt certain too, that he knew that she had not.

'There's something else,' Broderick said, his tone lowering.

'Yes.' Here it comes, she thought.

273

'She has quite the CCTV set-up there, at the cottage. We were surprised at how elaborate it was, and the fact that she had it in the first place.'

'Really?' Amanda said, unable to hide her surprise, not surprised at this news, but surprise that Broderick wasn't pressing the matter of her statement – not for now in any case. As for Fiona having CCTV, that wasn't a surprise, not in the slightest, and not because she'd already mentioned it, she hadn't, but because it was just the sort of thing she'd expect her to have.

'And it provides evidence,' Broderick went on. 'It captures Dr O'Shaughnessy very well... suffice to say it provides a clear sequence of events.' He paused. 'I'd like to apologise, Dr Brody. I got this one wrong. I'm sorry, if you can accept my apology. I have no doubt O'Shaughnessy is behind all this.'

A thought crossed Amanda's mind. Were his words a genuine act of contrition or rather the application of a coating of Teflon in the hope that nothing adverse would stick to him? She liked to think, and hoped, it was the former.

She nodded. 'And I accept your apology, of course. You were only doing your job after all. But I wonder why he went to all the effort that he went to?'

She felt an involuntary shudder ripple through her body at what could have happened. But why had he left notes on her car, hacked into her computer, and all the rest of it? There were much easier, simpler, yes, more crass methods for him to achieve what he wanted: God forbid, he could have hit her on the head and simply bundled her into a car.

Broderick squeezed his lower lip between an index finger and thumb, staring at the floor, thinking. He remained like that for what seemed ages, but in reality was less than a minute.

'It kind of makes perfect sense to me,' he said finally, looking up. 'Because it's all about risk, that's how predators operate. If the risks were to remain the same, it gets boring for them. They need to feel that rush, like they did the first time, but they've got to work harder and harder to get that same high. I would say we will find as this investigation continues a pattern of incremental deviant activity that had been building over many years. But, of course, he's dead, we can't ask him, so we may never know. And, Dr Brody, sometimes the thought processes of the criminal never make sense, perhaps we'd never have known anyway.'

It was just after lunch when the young woman came into Amanda's room, dressed in a smart navy blue skirt suit and holding a clipboard. Her name was Marie and she was a senior official with the Health Service. She was friendly and efficient and spent some time taking all the details that Amanda could remember from her experiences in St Catherine's and everything she knew about Dr O'Shaughnessy.

When she was finished she stood and said, 'Our investigation is only beginning, and we will be in touch with you again soon. I've contacted your family. Your husband asked if it was okay for him to come and collect you later today. I said I was sure it would be, but he said to ask, that you'd understand why. He also said to tell you that things can change for the better when we least expect them, and that you'd understand that too.'

Amanda felt light headed and slightly dizzy, like she had been spinning on a carousel and just been tossed off it. She thought of Edward, and felt a sudden tenderness for her husband, with it a sense of guilt, from somewhere deep

275

within, burrowed into her very core. Because he had nothing to do with this, it was she who was the keeper of secrets, and she didn't know how she was going to deal with it. But she wasn't going to deal with it now.

'Yes, of course, tell him. And tell him I can't wait to see him. Tell him everything's going to be alright. Tell him I can't wait to get home again too. Tell him that I lo...' she fell silent, dropping her eyes, smiling, feeling like a teenager again. 'That'll be enough, I think, thank you.'

She felt hot tears welling in her eyes: *Please, let it be possible? To get a second chance. To be able to get it right the second time round. Please. Please. Please.*

'Oh, another thing,' the official said. She reached into a pocket of her jacket and took something out. 'I'm sure you'll want this back, I had it sent down.'

It was her mobile phone.

Amanda took it, feeling as if her freedom was being handed back to her. For the first time, she felt the horror movie was coming to an end.

Chapter 54

In a strange way it was like old times, old *old* times, before the rot had really set in. She'd felt a physical jolt when Edward had walked into the room, realising she was so relieved at seeing him again. Smiling, she noticed his shirt collar was open and his tie knot pulled down a couple of inches, the cuffs of his shirt open too and folded back. She'd never known him to be so casual in his formal clothes before. It was like he was making a statement – this is the new me, Amanda, no more stuffy old Edward from now on. 'Darling,' he'd said, kissing her on the lips, and whispering, 'Thank you for coming home, everything's going to be alright now, we're going to be alright, you'll see.'

Again, she felt hope, real hope. She thought of her beautiful children, and considered how lucky she was to have a family to call her own, which was all she had ever wanted. And then she thought of Emily O'Shaughnessy. She'd never really liked the woman, but had felt a profound sense of sadness for her, wondering how she was going to deal with knowing the truth about her husband. As for her own husband, Edward, she was grateful that they had been offered a second chance, and that some good might come from this ordeal, by renewing their relationship, making it

277

deep and strong. Her thinking had completely changed. She was going to work hard at making it work; she would give it everything she had, and more.

Edward didn't ask questions on the drive home, probably because he knew she didn't have any answers, no one really did, not yet. The big Volvo ate up the miles, and Amanda found a wonderful sense of belonging, of true contentment, just from being with her husband, of sitting next to him. However, he made her jump when he'd suddenly slapped a hand on the steering wheel. 'That bastard,' his face turning crimson, 'that absolute bastard.' She placed a hand on his thigh and squeezed gently. 'I know, darling, I know, but it's over now.' He had glanced over to her. 'But why, Amanda, why?' She was glad when he turned back to watch the road, she didn't want him watching her expression when he'd asked that question.

For the remainder of the journey they didn't talk much, and Amanda was grateful, content to sit quietly next to Edward, who, she sensed, was just happy to be with her too. Now, being with each other seemed to be enough for both of them.

When the car turned into the driveway of their home she saw them standing by the front door.

'Oh my God,' she squealed in delight, 'I didn't know they were here.'

Lauren and Danny rushed forward to greet her as she got out of the car, gently embracing her. They were joined by Edward, and together she felt like she was the centre of the universe, their universe, her family's, the centre of their unbridled love.

There was a delicious smell of cooking when they went inside. She knew that smell, it was lamb casserole. It was the favourite dish of the one person who could make it to the standard of a Michelin star chef – but without all the fuss.

'Yes,' Lauren said, 'we asked Bridie to come in, although it's not her day. She was delighted, and wishes you the best, said she hopes her casserole tastes as good as it ever did, and she'll drop by to see you soon.'

After they'd eaten, Lauren fussed over her, made her comfortable on the sofa in the drawing room, resting her legs on a stool with a cushion on top.

'What?' she said, straightening, 'you're looking at me odd, Mum. Something you want to tell me?'

'Am I, darling? I didn't realise. No, of course not, sweetheart, how could I ever look at you oddly?' She reached out and took Lauren's hands in hers. 'You are the best daughter anyone could ever wish for. Truly, Lauren, you are, and I love you so much.'

'Aw, Mum,' Lauren reached down again and embraced her mother. Then both of them started to cry. She whispered. 'You've been through a lot. You can talk to me, you know you can. About anything.'

'Hey, that's my line,' Amanda said, 'I'm the one who says you can talk to me about anything.'

They both laughed.

'Right,' Lauren said, 'let me go and clear the dishes,'

'Darling, I don't want to start this again, but you really should be at college instead of down here clearing away dishes.'

'Mum, it was my choice. Do you realise how worried we were about you? I had to come down, we both did, Danny and I.'

'I know, darling, I know.' But in truth, she had no idea what it was like for them. To have their mother missing as she'd been. A thought occurred to her. 'How did you find out, darling? Who told you?'

'I work in the health service, Mum, okay. Don't you know... no, you probably don't. The Red Alert System, it's just come in, if a patient goes missing from any health care facility, it's flagged on the system. I nearly choked when I saw your name pop up on the computer screen at the hospital. My mother.'

'Really?'

'Yes, really.'

Amanda glanced to Danny. He was sitting in a corner of the room, his legs crossed, staring ahead, seemingly preoccupied with his thoughts. Edward was a short distance away, standing in front of the bookcase, his finger trailing over the titles, looking for something. She could tell by their demeanours that something had happened – had they had a row? Edward turned suddenly and caught her eye, smiled. He came over, sat down on the sofa, rested his hand on hers. She glanced to Danny, then back to her husband. Edward shrugged, and whispered. 'He's in a mood. It's a lot for the boy to take in, bless him.'

Amanda felt her belly tighten. She didn't like this comment. She felt it was a gentle reminder that this was all her fault. She thought about that. Well, it was, wasn't it? Yes, of course it was, he was only speaking the truth, and the truth hurt. She knew that very well.

Amanda smiled, feeling the cloak of guilt beginning to settle on her once again, deciding she would talk with her son the first opportunity she got. Still, it was not enough to dampen her relief that this nightmare was over. She thought of Fiona and Pri, she must contact them, but again, not right now. Her feelings towards Pri had changed. Because she could not forget that comment she'd made to Inspector McDonald, *'Well, I've done nothing wrong.'* It really meant she was prepared to throw them under the bus to save her own skin. Was that understandable? No, Amanda decided, it wasn't.

A little later, she thought some distraction was needed. She knew just the thing. Something that they all enjoyed.

'Danny, go get the Trivial Pursuit. Go on, good lad, you'll enjoy it, we all will...'

Her son threw a petulant look, one she hadn't seen in a long time, one she'd thought he'd left behind in his sulky teenage years. But now, here it was, back again. Still, he got up and went to fetch the game.

Yes, she would really have to have a talk with her son.

They played the game, but it was quickly apparent to Amanda that beneath her surface layer of relief and ebullience, the reality remained. She could hear it in her husband's tone at times during the game, the old Edward attempting to push through, before being nudged back again behind an apologetic smile.

At least he was trying, she thought.

She began to wonder if she was starting to fool herself once more. Was her husband really capable of change? And there was something definitely not right between himself and Danny. Her son could hardly take it upon himself to even look his father in the eyes. Could it be that Danny was refusing to accept that his father was trying to change, was even capable of it?

She would have to get to the bottom of it, and soon.

Chapter 55

When Amanda awoke the next morning, she couldn't believe it. She blinked and looked again. Yes, it was true. The green electronic display on the bedside clock really did say 8:15a.m.. She'd had a full night's sleep. And she could feel the benefit of it, her mind fresh and alert like a spring lamb. She pulled back the duvet and stood. Her leg hardly hurt, and the movement was a fluid and easy one. She looked at the crumpled bed, she hadn't even been disturbed by Edward getting up and leaving for work. She took a breath, crossed the room and pulled back the curtains. The sky outside was clear except for some roving wisps of white cloud, the pale sun tucked into a corner.

She went downstairs to find Danny sitting at the kitchen table with what she thought was a mug of tea before him. As she passed she could see the mug was empty.

'Sit down, Mum. You want a cup of tea? Let me put the kettle on. I'll do it. Would you like me to cook something, eggs on toast, you like that, ya?' He stood, pointed to a chair. 'Sit there.' He smiled, but there was no mistaking the worry in his eyes.

'Okay, Danny, just the toast then, thanks. Where's Lauren?'

'She had to nip into town to collect something or other from somebody, something to do with her course.'

'At this hour?'

He shrugged.

'Seems I'm the only sloth around here then this morning, everyone is so busy.'

'Not really, Mum. I'm not up to much, am I?'

'Well, at least you're up, Danny, which would be, as we both remember, quite an achievement in itself not so long ago, wouldn't it? And Danny?'

He was at the sink now, his back to her, holding the spout of the electric kettle into the flow of water. 'Yes, Mum?'

'You're a good boy. I want to thank you. The way you acted when I went to visit in Dublin. I'm proud of you, and I'm sorry, too, okay, for everything... and embarrassed as well.'

He switched on the kettle and popped two slices of bread into the toaster. 'There's no need, Mum,' he said, turning, 'I know all about being embarrassed. Don't be. Promise me you won't.'

She nodded. 'I'll do my best.'

After she'd eaten and pushed the empty plate away she took a sip from her tea. Danny was still at the sink, leaning against it, observing her, his arms folded.

'Okay, Danny, what is it? Spit it out. Tell me. I know something's wrong.'

He didn't answer, instead picked at something on the front of his hoodie.

'Daaaany? Come on I said. Tell me.'

He stopped picking. 'It's nothing, Mum, honest.'

283

'I don't believe you.'

He walked over and sat next to her, said nothing.

'You've been sitting here waiting for me, haven't you?' she said. 'How long has that cup been empty? Tell me. Tell me what's going on.'

'Mum, I can't, okay. I want to tell you, but I can't.'

'No, Danny, I think you do want to tell me. And you can. Don't be ridiculous.'

He took a deep breath, intertwining his hands, squeezing them tight. Amanda could see the flesh turning white.

'It's Dad,' he said, his voice almost a whisper.

Amanda nodded, and waited. When it seemed he wasn't going to continue, she opened her mouth to speak, but before she could, Danny blurted, 'He's having an affair, Mum. Dad.'

Although his diction was crystal clear, and she had heard what he had said, still, she couldn't possibly have heard correctly. Could she? That what? Stuffy old Edward was having an affair?

I don't think so.

Her son seemed to be able read her mind. 'I'm sorry Mum. But he is.'

Those two words "He is", had the effect of destroying her doubt, blowing it to smithereens. She turned them over in her mind: He is. Her husband, Edward, was having an affair. He is.

The room suddenly lurched, she reached out and held onto the table with both hands to steady herself. She closed her eyes and swallowed a couple of times. How did she not know? How did she not suspect? Surely she would have noticed? Surely she would have noticed something? And he had the cheek to question her, asking if she was the one having an affair on the drive to Dublin. She had thrown it right back at him and she remembered his righteous reaction, with his comment, "I don't want to be cuckolded." Clever Edward, she'd no idea.

'How long?' she asked, opening her eyes again.

Danny shrugged, and in that moment she saw her son as a child again, lost and unsure of himself. She took his hand in hers.

'Danny. How are *you* with this?'

'I'm alright with it, Mum. Shit happens.'

She wondered if that were true or merely bravado.

'Really, I am,' like he was reading her mind again. 'It's you I'm worried about. I wasn't going to tell you, I agonised about it for ages. But I had to. I did the right thing... didn't I, Mum?'

'Of course, sweetheart, you did.' She squeezed his hand, then added gently. 'How long've you known?'

Another shrug. 'A while, Mum, ever since... well, I don't know, few weeks ago, last time I was down, remember?'

Last time he was down. It was a Thursday; couple of weeks back, something like that. He'd made a long weekend of it. She'd collected him from the bus station with his two bags of dirty laundry, and didn't really see him again until it was time to drive him back to the station on Sunday evening.

'How...?' she began, but the words seemed to become stuck in her throat. She coughed. '...did you exactly find out?'

He was motionless for a moment, then reached into the back pocket of his jeans and took out his phone, scrolled across the screen a couple of times, and handed it to her.

'It may be painful,' he said. 'But this is it.'

'No, it's not painful. Not as such.' She took the phone. 'It's more like shocked surprise, and it's wearing off quicker than I'd have thought possible... Did you mention this to anybody? Lauren?'

'Course not, Mum, and especially not Lauren, you know how close she is to Dad.'

Amanda nodded. 'Thank you, Danny.'

She looked at the phone, on it a frozen image of Edward standing in front of a grey door. She thought the door looked familiar. The play button icon told her the photo was part of a video. She pressed it, and the image came to life, Edward, swivelling back and forth on the balls of his feet, a habit of his when he was nervous about anything... or so too, when he was excited. She watched as he placed his hands into his pockets and looked about, then took them out again. She knew now what it was, he was both nervous and excited. The camera briefly took in a bare trellis fixed to the wall just down from the door.

With a start, she knew something else now too. Nothing had ever grown on that trellis. The contract gardener had tried, but clematis had never taken hold on it and had died back. The gardener had taken them all away again and was to come back with something else. But as yet he never had, they were still waiting. By the 'they' she meant the White Rock Private Clinic. Because that's where it was, this trellis, more specifically by a grey door at the rear of the building, once used for taking out medical waste but little used now since new guidelines meant an annex had to be built to house the waste instead. That's why she had not recognised it initially. But she did now.

She brought the phone closer, intrigued, hunching her shoulders, waiting...

It seemed forever before the door was opened. But when it was, the woman standing there looked as excited and nervous as Edward, glancing over her shoulder, then up and down the path running along either side. The audacity, Amanda thought, the place where I work. But she knew that was part of it, the excitement, the thrill. The woman stretched out her arms and took hold of Edward's hands, pulled him into her, and they both kissed passionately, one of Edward's hands moving up immediately, crawling inside the woman's blouse.

'Ugh,' Amanda said, looking briefly away, but when she looked back, she was just in time to see both of them disappear inside the building and the door close.

'Her,' she exclaimed, the sense of betrayal cutting like a knife. She looked at Danny.

He nodded. She knew that he knew what she was thinking.

'Layla's like what, twenty three? A couple of years older than you, Danny, that's all.'

Danny nodded again.

'How did you get this?'

He looked away, uncomfortable, crimson creeping up his cheeks.

'I,' he began, 'went into see you.'

'But you hardly ever come to the Clinic. I don't remember seeing you recently.'

The crimson grew deeper.

'I know, Mum. I came down on Thursday so I would be able to call into the White Rock on the Friday. I wanted to meet... I wanted to meet Layla, okay? I wanted...to see her, to ask her out. Silly, ya, I know. I was letting on to be dropping into see you, if anyone asked. I used to think she was cool, Layla.'

'You don't even know her, Danny.'

'OK, she looked cool so. But I don't want to know her now. Anyway, that's why I was on my way into The White

Rock. It was a Friday morning. But then I thought I saw
Dad, and wondered what the hell he was doing there? I saw
him, or thought I saw him, walking quickly along the side
of the building, so I hurried to catch up. And then I
definitely knew it was him, he was hanging around outside
that door, and he looked nervous, you know the way he
does, going back and forward on each foot. I thought to
myself something's not right here. So, instead of going up
to him, I just hung back, and you know how bloody self-
righteous he is, ya? I said to myself, I'm not going to miss
this, what are you up to, bro? This is my chance to get you.
So I took out my phone and started recording. Just did.
Didn't know what he was up to. Deep down I suppose, I
don't trust Dad, never have. That's how I got it, Mum.'

The absolute bastard, Amanda thought, to put their child
in this position.   She thought of the other evening, when
she had begged Edward to come to bed with her, and now it
was her turn to turn crimson. He's energetic, she thought.

'You don't need to feel embarrassed,' she said, 'it's
perfectly natural to like someone. Layla is very attractive
after all. Danny, this is not good for you. We are your
parents; you shouldn't have to deal with this. Really, you
shouldn't.'

He grinned. 'I'm cool about it, Mum, just embarrassed to
have to tell you, that's all. But it all worked out, for me I
mean. Because if I had hooked up with her, Layla I mean' –
Amanda was beginning to hate that name – 'then I'd never
have hooked up with Sally, see. And I've got a real, deep,
connection with Sal, I really do, and we understand each
other so well. In fact, I think I'm in love Mum, I really do. I
think she's the one.'

Amanda cupped her son's face between her hands and
saw an innocence in his eyes she had not seen in a long

while and which surprised and delighted her at the same time. She kissed his forehead.

'Good,' Amanda said, 'enjoy it,' but couldn't help think, while it lasts.

Chapter 56

Amanda dialled Fiona's number on the landline in her bedroom and listened as it rang on the other end. She counted ten rings before she pulled the phone from her ear, about to hang-up, but just then a tinny voice wafted from the earpiece, 'Hello.'

Amanda quickly pressed it to her ear again.

'Hello. Fiona. It's me. Amanda.'

'Oh, I didn't recognise the number. To tell the truth, I wasn't going to answer.'

'I rang to find out how you were, that's all.'

'That's good of you,' a tone to her words that made Amanda wonder if she wasn't being sarcastic?

'Where are you, Fiona?'

'Home, they drove me, the police.'

'How're you feeling?'

There was an intake of breath. 'I don't like you asking that question.'

Amanda was silent, the only sound the static on the line.

'Don't you?' she said then. 'Sorry, Fiona, perhaps this was a mistake? Maybe I shouldn't have rung?'

'No. That's okay. It's just when you ask how I feel, I mean, how am I supposed to feel? How am I supposed to answer that? I myself have asked that question of countless patients down through the years. Every single one in fact. I don't like being asked that question myself. Just don't. Have you heard from the police? I haven't.'

'No.'

'You know I had CCTV?'

'I know now. The police told me.'

'Christ, if I hadn't, I shudder to think... but I'll tell you something.'

'Yes?'

'I'm glad I blew that bastard's head almost clean off his shoulders. I'm glad I killed him. It's liberated me. I don't feel any remorse. None.'

Amanda was taken by surprise. She herself hadn't come to terms with O'Shaughnessy's death. She wasn't even thinking about it, in fact, it was as if her brain had shut down around it, refusing to go there. She knew it was a natural form of defence, to stop her from being completely overwrought. Because this was Lauren's father, after all, and there was no escaping that fact. In that moment she realised she had been doing it all her life, too timid, fearful, always hiding among the shadows, too afraid to come out into the open, just wishing for things to go away. A frightened little mouse. Which played right into Edward's hands, having her like that, so he could do what he wanted...but what exactly did he want? To have an affair for a start, that was clear. God knows what else he'd been up to down through the years. She hadn't a clue. None. She'd been too preoccupied with appeasing him, with trying to pacify his moods, with taking whatever he threw at her, with being ground down beneath his boot thinking she

291

didn't deserve any better, that whatever it was, it had to be her fault. She'd wasted so much of her bloody life doing this. She suddenly wanted to cry.

'Are you still there?'

Amanda swallowed. 'Yes. Yes. I'm still here.' She closed her eyes, pushing back against the tears. 'I admire you, Fiona, I really do. I didn't know it until now, but I do. Look, to tell the truth, I thought you were mad.'

There was a sudden sound on the phone, so loud Amanda winced and quickly pulled it from her ear. She realised what it was, the sound of Fiona laughing. She put the phone back to her ear as the sound faded.

'Thought I was mad?' Fiona said. 'Well, what a surprise – not. I come across it quite a lot. You see, after the death of Shane, I stopping pretending, because I realised – well, I knew it all along but was too desperate to fit in that I just went along with everything – that we are all pretenders, all actors on a stage, hiding behind our flimsy masks of expressions. And some are better actors than others. But under our veneer of respectability we are mere savages, Amanda, our brains the same as those of our ancestors who thought the world was flat and that it was a good idea to offer human sacrifices to the gods, or any one of a thousand other abhorrent things they got up to. Oh, the same brains too that not so long ago sat around a conference table politely drinking coffee and organising the mass extermination of millions of people in concentration camps. We, you and I, are of the same species, with the same brains, nothing has changed, except now we pretend to act so civilised. But no one knows what goes on inside our heads, what *really* goes on inside there. Well, I decided not to pretend any longer, I'd had enough. It doesn't make me any better a human being, whatever that means, just a more honest one – to myself that is. And I can live with myself a little easier now. There, that's the end of the sermon I didn't intend to make. Tell me, have you spoken to your friend, Pri, today?'

'No.'

'Hhmm, your tone was a little pointed there.'

'Was it?'

'Yes.'

'It's like what you say, some are better actors than others.'

'Yes,' Fiona said, 'they are, and sometimes the mask slips, doesn't it?'

Amanda nodded, that remark of Pri's playing over in her mind once again, *'Well, I've done nothing wrong.'*

'I've got to go, Amanda, we'll talk again.'

'I'd like that.'

'Goodbye.'

'Goodbye, Fiona.'

Amanda remained sitting on the edge of the bed for a long while after she'd finished speaking with Fiona, the receiver pressed against her chin, thinking. Then she stood, not needing any support, her leg strong enough with just a little tingle of pain, that's all. She walked slowly around the bed onto Edward's side, replaced the receiver into its cradle on the dresser there. Before, she would stretch across the bed to do this. She crossed to the window, turned and leaned against the sill, looking about the room as if for the first time. In some ways she was looking at it for the first time, the way she was seeing it now.

This was a prison cell, she decided. Despite the deep pile floral carpet – Amanda didn't like carpets, she much preferred wooden flooring – and the €80 per roll wallpaper, the gilt edged prints on the wall, and by square footage, the size larger than many six figure single bedroom apartments that she could think of. But to her, this is what it was, a prison cell. She hadn't realised it before. But she did now, and it had taken Fiona, with all her talk about brains and flat earths to come to this conclusion. Why? Because yes, while she could come and go freely– she had an en-suite for God's sake – she couldn't, not really, come and go freely. She was living in her very own Truman Show, brain-washed, a prisoner of Edward, prepared, up until last evening, to fool herself yet again that everything was good between them both. She glanced at the phone.

For instance, how many times had she used that? Not without it being handed to her first by Edward that is. Never. That was the answer. How many times had she actually gone round to his side of the bed to pick it up? Again. Never. Not once. She lived on *this* side of the bed, rose each morning and walked the same path to the en-suite on *this* side of the room, then back again, the same path to the wardrobe, using the left door only – never the right, or heaven forbid, both of them – selected what she needed, and closed it again, rejoined the path back to the bed where she stood on a piece of carpet probably on closer inspection to be found worn by her endless treading. Is this how animals survive in a zoo? *I never realised before, but that is what I am – or was – an animal in a zoo.*

Her eyes wandered to his side of the bed again, before diverting to straight ahead, staring at the picture of a Clydesdale horse on the wall opposite. She could feel a tightness in her belly, but her eyes wandered back again, taking in Edward's pillow – an orthopaedic one that he had ordered specially from a hospital supplier–and the dresser. The exact same dresser as on her side of the bed, white with gold-coloured handles.

She couldn't take her eyes from it. The more she stared at it, the more she wondered... what was in there? She was suddenly curious, so very, very curious, like an explorer who had discovered the outcrop to a new world.

But still, she was afraid, too conditioned to act in a certain way, to go there. All her married life she had never encroached on Edward's half of anything. There was fifty percent of her husband that she knew nothing about.

The dresser.

The fucking dresser.

It intrigued her.

It felt like a no fly zone surrounded it. What would happen if she were to go over and just open a drawer? Instant vaporisation?

Her belly tightened and her breathing, short and shallow, made a clicking noise at the back of her throat.

No.

She couldn't do that.

She mustn't do that.

No.

She thought of Fiona, liberated after shooting a man to death.

Yes, I fucking can.

Amanda strode over to the dresser, grabbed the handle and pulled it open.

Foolish. That was the first emotion she felt. Why was she even doing this? To find evidence of what, his affair? She didn't think she cared enough. The second emotion was surprise, because the drawer was relatively messy– by Edward's standards at least that is: block of cling wrapped sticky notes carrying the logo of a pharmacy company on it, no doubt given to Edward by some salesman or other, a couple of telephone chargers, paperback novel of some description, various pens, couple of loose buttons... the usual detritus to be found in any drawer in any house anywhere in the country. She was about to close the drawer again when she noticed something lying at the bottom, white so that it appeared to be a part of the actual bottom itself, but shorter so she could see the gap between the side of the drawer and the edge, so knew it wasn't... it was something else. She pushed aside the telephone chargers and sticky notes, took hold of a corner and pulled. It was a sheet of paper, and it came out easily. If it had been light paper it would have torn, but it wasn't. It was heavy, like card paper.

Her mind reverberated with conflicting thoughts... So what? It's only paper... *Yes, of course it's like that paper, isn't it?... No, it's not like it, it* is *the same paper...So? Paper like that is ten a penny, means nothing... Yes, yes, silly. I am being silly... Means nothing.*

She held it up by a corner edge, and wondered what to do? Should she crumple it and throw it away, burn it in the fire? But perhaps it was of some importance, you never knew with Edward – no, impossible, it was only a piece of paper, there were others just like it in the drawer. She stepped back, turning from the bed, her other hand coming up, about to concertina it between them. A ray of cold winter light through the window caught the paper and it seemed to glow, highlighting a faint trail of imprints that twisted across it, clearly the outline of words. She angled the paper, but the light reflected directly onto it so that the outlines disappeared. She walked round to her side of the bed, sat down and opened her bedside locker, rummaged through it and found a pencil, placed the paper onto the dresser top, deftly began running the pencil across the page, holding the lead flat, shading it in quickly and evenly from

296

top to bottom. She purposefully did not concentrate on the white, worm like outlines that appeared until the whole page was completely shaded in. Then she held it before her.

But she already knew. *Just knew.* What it would say.

She looked.

She felt the breath being literally sucked out of her body as she stared, placing a hand onto her chest, above her heart, gasping for breath. With it came a heaviness in her upper chest, getting heavier, like a big rock was sitting inside there – *Jesus, I'm getting a heart attack.* Then the heaviness began to recede as she started to breath normally again. It was her body's reaction to the shock of what she was seeing.

A pen had pressed the outline of the words through a sheet of paper that had rested on top of the paper she was now holding. Those same four words. Fifteen letters in total, combining into four words, combining into one sickening belly punch:

I KNOW YOUR SECRET

Chapter 57

Amanda lay down and curled her body on the bed, an arm over her face, shutting out the light, retreating into the darkness, a cave, that she wanted to swallow her up, from which she never cared if she emerged again. Her body did not seem like it belonged to her, but was separate, a hollow vessel, and one she was merely hiding within now. Her mind crackled and sparked, short circuiting, and nothing was making sense. Not only that, but her life did not make sense.   The lights, she decided, would never come up on this movie, the credits would never roll "The End." This horror movie would continue forever.

Her arm began to feel heavy after a time. Heavy like back then, during the opening scene to the movie, the camera panning to reveal a woman tethered to a bed, the woman: her. She could hear music, a building crescendo of screeching violins and pounding drums, as she opened her eyes and peered ahead to see a masked figure approach, with the head of a goat – or was it a mask? – and hoofed feet – or were they boots? With an enormous penis, erect and quivering, like it was scenting the air, as it came to within inches of her face. She writhed about on the bed and screamed. She could hear footsteps advancing. *No, no, no, not again...*

'Mum. Mum. Are you alright? Mum.'

Her eyes sprang open and she was looking into a face. She stared, trying to make sense of it, and then eventually, she did.

'Danny. Oh, Danny, I must have dropped off. I was having a nightmare.'

She could see the concern on his face and in that moment all she wanted was to reassure him.

She pushed herself up onto an elbow and slid her feet onto the floor.

'What...?' she asked.

Danny was pointing.

She stood and looked to the bed, saw the sheet of paper lying on it. She reached down and took it up, folded it quickly, folded it again, wrapped her hand around it.

'Oh, nothing. Just a bit of doodling, that's all.'

She knew he didn't believe her.

'You're white as a sheet, Mum. This reminds me of last week, when you came to Dublin to me. Mum, for God's sake. I should never have told you... about Dad? I shouldn't.'

She forced a laugh. 'Of course you should have told me. I'm glad you did. It was the right thing to do. I just fell asleep now, that's all. I'm fine, Danny, really. Go down and put the kettle on, good lad. Make me a cup of tea... Lauren back yet?'

'No.'

'Okay then, I'll be down in a minute. Off you go. Please. And Danny...?'

'Yes, Mum.'

'I'll look after this. With your father, I mean. You're not to...'

'Say anything about it. Of course not. I won't.'

He left the room without another word.

The shrill sound of the telephone suddenly sounded. Amanda waited, hoping Danny would pick up downstairs. When he didn't, she leaned across the bed and grabbed it. 'Yes.'

Silence.

'Yes,' she repeated.

Again, silence, then a voice, a female voice, sounding a little hoarse.

'Amanda?'

'Yes.'

'It's me.'

'Oh,' Amanda felt a hot flare of anxiety in her belly, recognising the voice now. 'Emily, hello.'

'My husband is dead, Amanda.'

She said nothing, her mind suddenly blank. She had not expected this, to get a phone call from Andrew O'Shaughnessy's wife, now widow.

'You were there when he was shot, weren't you? What happened?'

'W-well, I don't really want to speak about it, Emily. I don't think it's appropriate. Perhaps you should speak to the po...'

'Who shot him, Amanda? Was it you?'

'No. Of course not.'

'Who then? And why? Tell me!' Emily's voice had risen.

'I can't talk, Emily, I'm sorry, not now.'

'You bitch,' Andrew O'Shaughnessy's widow suddenly shouted. 'He's my husband. And now he's dead. They're saying horrible things about him. I've heard. Horrible lies. Tell me. You bitch. Tell me.'

Amanda pulled the phone from her ear and terminated the call, her heart pounding, and tossed it onto the bed. She was shaking, and sat down heavily onto the bed again, buried her face in her hands. Then she thought that Emily would ring back, so picked up the phone, held her finger ready to terminate the call if she did. She waited, but the phone didn't ring. She replaced it back onto its cradle and left the room, went down the stairs, crossed the foyer towards the kitchen as the front door swung open and Lauren bounded in.

'Hi, Mum. I didn't think I'd be so long. Hey, everything alright? You don't look so good.'

'I'm fine,' Amanda said with a nod.

'Good,' Lauren said, 'because I've got some amazing news.'

They were sitting drinking tea at the kitchen island. Lauren had bought fresh scones from the bakery, but Amanda's remained untouched. When Lauren told them she had won her faculty's gold medal for a thesis on DNA and Genomes, Amanda's heart swelled with delight and pride, smothering the other, negative emotions. But as Lauren continued to speak, the negative emotions regained control, and cold fear gripped Amanda and began to squeeze, tighter and tighter. She dropped her head, stared into her mug of tea...

'I had taken dad's DNA,' Lauren went on. 'By the way, he didn't want to give it to me, so I said nothing, just took it from his coffee mug. And guess what? We share a unique code. It's too technical to get into here, but it's called an ASR Strand. So, thanks Dad. It means I could write a thesis on it, no one else in my class could. And it got me that gold medal.'

Amanda stared into her tea, absentmindedly picked up the tea spoon and began stirring it. As it swirled around, so too did her mind, her thoughts trailing behind. She stirred quicker and quicker, trying to keep ahead, trying to stop her thoughts from catching up. Tea spilled over the top of the cup as she suddenly looked up.

'But it can't be?' She could hear the pleading in her voice. 'It just can't be.'

Her children looked at her silently.

Amanda spread her arms. 'I mean... I mean... Just can't be right, just can't. You're wrong, Lauren, sorry, but you have to be.'

Lauren's eyebrows arched and Amanda caught the exchange of glances between her and her brother.

'Mother, why do you think it's not possible?'

Amanda shook her head a couple of times then stopped, as the truth struck the bedrock of her consciousness, because there was nowhere else to go. It settled there, and Amanda stared at it. Stared at the truth. The horrible, appalling, inconceivable, truth. That Edward *was* Lauren's father. He was the masked monster who had raped her, not O'Shaughnessy.

Edward.

Her husband.

The room began to close in on her. She became aware of someone standing in the doorway, heard a voice. 'Thought I'd surprise you all and come home early. Not every day that my kids are at home, that I have all my family together.'

'Dad,' Lauren said with delight.

Amanda was vaguely aware of her daughter getting up and rushing over to her father, hugging him. 'Dad, I've got some great news, listen to this... '

Amanda mumbled that she needed some fresh air, left the kitchen and went into the drawing room, opened the French windows and stepped out into the garden. She took a breath, and sensed someone standing behind her. She turned. It was Danny.

'No,' she said softly. 'I want to be left alone. I just need to be alone. A few moments, that's all, Danny. Please.'

He looked at her with that same concern she had seen earlier. It broke her heart that she was putting him through this. Danny smiled, nodded. As he walked away, she vowed that whatever happened, she had to protect her children, she had to do what was best for them.

She walked out into the garden, feeling the cool air on her skin. From high in a tree she could hear the sharp, raspy chatter of magpies. She went to the wicker egg chair and pulled it towards her. The metal clasp on top that secured it to the hanging rope acted like a miniature funhouse mirror, giving her reflection a tiny head, long spidery legs and a Humpy Dumpty belly. She sat into the chair and heard his footsteps on the cold grass as he walked round in front and faced her.

For the first time in her life, as she looked at him, she felt she was seeing the real Edward.

Chapter 58

There was a look in his eyes, the layers he had been hiding behind stripped away, leaving two hard, lifeless, cold orbs staring at her. Strangely, she was not afraid, now that the beast had slunk out from the shadows and was in the open.

'My children are in there,' she said, 'that is all I care about. If you leave now, and have nothing again to do with me, I might consider leaving things as they are. But first I want an answer: Why?'

His hands were in his pockets, as he very subtly began rocking back and forth on the balls of his feet. He stopped moving as a gust of wind blew, and opened his mouth, just as the magpies chattered again; making it appear the sound was coming from him. Edward, she saw, was laughing. She became afraid now, turned her head to glance back at the house, but knew that unless she swivelled the egg chair she wouldn't be able to see it. Her fear suddenly stopped her from doing this, from turning her back on Edward.

'Why you ask. I want you gone, Amanda, that's why. From here, from this house, from my life… God, why do you think? It may seem like a lot of trouble to have gone through. But not really, it's surprisingly easy to hack into a computer, and writing notes, leaving them on your car was nothing, neither was the phone call to the Gardaí, oh, and the malarkey on the beach with your suicide letter... mere semantics. Except hitting myself with a shoe to support my story that I was mugged. That might have been a bit over the top, granted. But even so I took pleasure from it all, because it meant I was getting back at you, at you, Amanda, for making such a fool out of me.'

'What?' Amanda said, astonished. 'Making a fool out of *you?*'

Edward was silent for a moment.

'Of course,' he said then. 'Because you never mentioned it, did you? That Lauren wasn't my daughter – which is what you thought. You said nothing about it, you took me for a fool, you married me for convenience. How dare you!'

Amanda shook her head, incredulous. He was blaming her for what had happened, what had happened to her, it was all *her* fault.

'It didn't work out the way I quite wanted it to,' he said smugly, 'but it came close. Then again, nothing's perfect is it? It's time for a change, Amanda, really, for both of us. But I'm not leaving. You are. It's the least you can do, and I know you'll do it, now you know what I'm capable of.'

'You bastard,' she hissed. 'I know about Layla, by the way.'

Her body had slouched, her voice meek. She was cowering from him. Amanda forced herself to look up. She saw that his eyes held surprise.

'How do you know that, Amanda? Tell me.'

She pursed her lips. So, she had a little power after all.

He stepped closer, snarled, 'Well. Fucking tell me.'

She pursed her lips tighter, saw his fists clench, the knuckles turning ivory. It would be best if she left. He could have the house, if it meant that much to him. She wanted peace, her life back. Yes, she would leave; he could take the trophy of his triumph and mount it over the fireplace for himself and bloody Layla to look at. The poor, stupid girl.

'Mum, everything alright out there?' It was Danny, calling from the house.

Edward looked back, his hands relaxing.

'Yes, Danny,' she shouted, 'go inside, everything's fine.' And to Edward, as he turned to look at her again. 'It doesn't matter who. You were seen.'

'Was I now?' the tone contemplative. 'Was I now indeed?' He stroked his chin.

Amanda knew she had surprised him. And she guessed by the way he stroked his chin, like a bad poker player, that it had gotten to him, giving him pause for concern. As if reading her thoughts he dropped his arm to his side.

'You sick fucker,' Amanda hissed.

But Edward only smiled, regaining his composure. 'You enjoyed it though, didn't you? Oh, yes you did.'

'You sick, sick, fucker.' Amanda pushed herself off the chair to her feet. 'You'll go to prison for this. That'll wipe the smile off your face.'

His smile only widened, goading her. 'How do you work that out?'

She was about to speak, formulating the words in her mind, words that she suddenly realised would make no sense, would only reinforce what Edward was already trying to prove, that she was crazy. Because she had nothing, no evidence, merely the ramblings of what some might consider as a deluded mind to go on. And that would not be enough.

She dropped her eyes to the ground in defeat.

'I thought so,' he said. 'Anyway, it was all Andrew's idea, his sexual peccadilloes. My friend had some very specific, if extreme, tastes...'

'Is that what you call it?' cutting him off, forcing herself not to shout. 'Peccadilloes? Tastes? His fault. To hell with you.'

'I went along with it that one time, that's all. With you. That one time.'

'You sick bastard. You mean I should feel honoured? I don't believe a word out of your mouth. Not a word.'

'I wanted you. I did what was required to get you. I got you pregnant. Surprisingly easy once I worked out dates. You wouldn't have been interested in me otherwise. This way, I was your knight in shining armour; I saved you from being ostracised, from disgrace and exile, from losing your career. Come on, you have to admit, it all worked out in the end. Well, didn't it? Until now, that is.'

That smile of his was beginning to infuriate her. She thought of what O'Shaughnessy had said: *I can safely say, Amanda, you are in a condition of most robust mental health, with a refreshing lack of reserve in talking truthfully about yourself. I'll tell Edward if I may, he will be greatly reassured.* She could only assume this was some sort of bluff, a red herring, designed so that when his true, final verdict did come, it would be less likely to draw suspicion.

'I want a divorce, Amanda. An *uncontested* divorce. And at the first opportunity, I want you out of this house. We can say we drifted apart, we got tired of pretending, and we couldn't pretend any longer that things were good between us. It happens. The children will get over it, especially if we continue to pretend we are the best of friends...after all, if nothing else, the two of us are great actors, are we not?'

She looked up, into those cold, lifeless hard orbs of his. 'Really? It's all for this? You sought to destroy me just for this? Just so you could have an uncontested divorce? This bloody house?' That smile was still on his face, she wanted to rip it off him.

'Trust me,' he said, 'people have done an awful lot more for an awful lot less. And, as I told you, you deceived me. I didn't like that. In any case, I thought the effort was more than appropriate...it's quite substantial, the assets I mean.'

'An uncontested divorce,' she repeated. 'Why didn't you simply just ask me for it if that's what you wanted?'

He laughed, and it was gone again just as quickly, the condescending smile all that remained.

'Amanda, darling, because you simply would have said no. Come on now. Don't be silly. You know you would.'

She was silent. He was correct of course. And how deviously clever, wanting to make it look like it was her fault. If he didn't get what he wanted, this uncontested divorce, it would all start again, the drip, drip, drip of mental torture. She had no doubt about that. Her husband really was a devious, manipulative bastard.

'Mum. Dad.'

It was Lauren, a timbre in her voice that instantly made Amanda even more alert. She turned, saw her daughter standing in the open French windows.

'Yes, sweetheart.'

'There's a couple of policemen here, a detective Broderick.'

Amanda could see from the corner of her eye Edward look at her, his smile one of triumph: *I have won.*

'I'll be right there, Lauren. Tell them I won't be a minute.'

'No, Mum. They're not here for you. They want to speak to Dad.'

Amanda saw the smile instantly disappear from Edward's face.

She followed her husband into the house, surprised when she saw a uniformed officer reach out and grab his wrist the instant he stepped through the French windows. As she glanced ahead she saw, standing in the centre of the room, detective Broderick, his expression stern. When she looked back to her husband, she saw that Edward's hands were gathered together before him – in handcuffs. She was glad her children were not in the room to witness this.

The police officer standing next to him was a young woman which Amanda thought appropriate. She listened as the officer spoke: 'Edward Brody, you are under arrest on suspicion of kidnap, rape and false imprisonment. You are not obliged to say anything unless you wish to do so, but whatever you say will be taken down in writing and may be given in evidence. Do you understand?'

Edward didn't speak. Amanda saw his eyes slide to the corners of their sockets, nostrils flaring with arrogance, scarcely believing what was happening.

'Do you fucking understand, Dr Brody?' the officer grunted, her tone and demeanour out of character with her petite appearance.

Edward was stung by the comment, by the lack of respect. He narrowed his eyes, looking at her. 'That's impossible,' he said, 'you're making a terrible mistake. And how dare you speak to me like that.'

'Ya, ya, you can save that for the judge,' she retorted.

'We searched the home of Dr Andrew O'Shaughnessy,' Broderick chipped in, 'we found videos, diaries, even a handwritten book manuscript. The man was a meticulous

Jess Roy

note taker and chronicler of events. The sick pervert.
Enough to put you away for a very long time, Dr Brody.'

For the first time in his life, Amanda's husband was
speechless.

I Know Your Secret

Chapter 59

Eighteen Months Later

The TV studio was hot, very hot, beneath the rows of
lights suspended from the ceiling. Amanda was just
about to reach for the glass of water on the table
between her and host Brian Sullivan, when he spoke to
camera and she quickly pulled back her hand.

'Good evening, and welcome to tonight's episode of *The
Topic*. My guest is Doctor Amanda Ryan, whose book
Living a Nightmare has become a global bestselling
phenomenon. Welcome, Doctor Ryan, and what can I say?
What a book.'

'Thank you, Brian, and thanks for having me.'

'Um, I still can't get my head around all of this though. I
mean, I'm going to jump right in here, but your husband...'

'Ex-husband, Brian. We've divorced. Which is ironic
because it's what he wanted, just not the way he wanted it.
That's why I go by my maiden name now, which is Ryan of
course.'

'Oh, of course, Doctor Ryan. Yes of course. Apologies.'

Amanda gave a wry smile and nodded.

Jess Roy

'As I was saying,' he continued, 'I still can't get my head around all that's happened. Quite unbelievable. I mean, this sort of thing happens in movies, doesn't it? Not in real life. But that's not true, because it happened to you, didn't it, Doctor Ryan? It actually happened to you.'

Brian Sullivan looked at her in that way of his she'd seen countless times on the ratings topping TV show, faux concern she'd always called it, except now she wasn't so sure, he seemed genuine enough.

'Thing is, what happened to me, is… I'm not going to say it's common, but it does happen, and more than you'd think. I've had countless letters from readers who've had similar experiences.'

'Really?' Brian Sullivan leant back in his chair and pressed a finger against his cheek. 'Countless letters. Really? You mean women who have married the men who have done such a thing to them…'

'No, I'm not saying that. No. Most women don't marry their abuser. In that sense I am unique, yes, but I didn't know that the man who'd drugged and raped me all those years ago was the man I'd been married to for more than a quarter of a century. What I mean is that women are drugged and raped, more than you'd ever think. Most don't even report it. I didn't. Which I am ashamed to admit to now, by the way. I'm lucky to live in a democracy with a rule of law. In some countries in the world they don't have that, and women in such places have little or no rights. In that sense, I would urge anyone who has been abused to report it to the police, no ifs or buts, do it.'

Brian Sullivan nodded. 'Yes, shocking, utterly shocking, and people should report it, male or female.'

'As I say, I didn't report what happened to me. I was trying to protect my daughter, I didn't want her knowing

anything about it. It was wrong. I should have reported it.
But as I say in the book, I also felt dirty and sullied. I was
ashamed. I just wanted to put the whole affair behind me.'

'Until you found that note on your car, isn't that right?
That's when it all started.'

Amanda nodded. She suddenly felt like she might cough,
reached for the glass of water and took a long swallow.

'Yes,' she said, putting the glass back onto the table.
'And what my ex-husband started was eventually his
undoing, and also the demise of his co-conspirator, Andrew
O'Shaughnessy.'

'And the reason,' Brian Sullivan said, his voice rising
with each word, adding tension, 'was that your ex-husband
was having an affair and wanted a divorce. Isn't that it?'

'Yes,' Amanda said.

'With your secretary,' his voice almost high pitched,
'who was over twenty years younger than him.'

'Yes,' Amanda said again. 'In some ways I feel sorry for
her. She's living in New Zealand now, I believe. Anyway
crazy, all of it, I know. He wanted an uncontested divorce,
to hold onto the assets, all the assets – that was important to
him. So he set up this elaborate plan to have me declared
mentally unstable. It almost worked. I came close to it, for a
time, I will admit, because I was in a terribly dark, hopeless
place, all alone. I was really close to the edge on occasions I
can tell you, close to crossing over to the other side.'

'And that's where Andrew O'Shaughnessy came in, isn't
it?' The TV host looked directly into the camera. 'For the
benefit of viewers who may not know, members of staff at
St Catherine's Mental Health facility have been suspended
and currently under investigation. An investigation is also
underway to try and establish the number of victims
O'Shaughnessy abused.' Looking away from the camera,

back to Amanda, 'And that just might be possible, isn't that right, Doctor Ryan? Because it appears he kept records. In fact, the level of meticulous detail reflects a clinical approach, he carefully planned things – one of the reasons, I suspect, he managed to get away with it for so long.'

'Yes,' Amanda agreed, 'and clearly he was an extremely cruel and manipulative individual, his victims in the main vulnerable women at the lowest points in their lives, women who had been incarcerated into the mental health system and had no voice whatsoever. And then there were the others, women like me, who were drugged and effectively kidnapped and raped, but I suspect few of us want to be reminded of what happened to us. The women in the care of the psychiatric services, in the care of the State you have to remember, sought help, safety and protection, but instead, well, as we are beginning to find out, were exploited in the cruellest possible way by that man. As, I would have been exploited once again too, I have no doubt, if I had remained committed to St Catherine's for any longer that was the case.'

Brian Sullivan shook his head gravely. 'I can only say the title of your book sums it all up, Doctor Ryan, doesn't it? *Living a Nightmare.*' He fell silent, allowed it to percolate a moment for effect, then: 'Andrew O'Shaughnessy was shot dead by Fiona McBride Crowley...by the way, our researchers contacted her, to at the very least try and obtain a comment for tonight's show, ideally have her appear, but she refused, and refuses, to talk to us. Are you still in contact with her?'

Amanda shrugged. 'Yes. On and off.'

'And she was acquitted of all charges?'

'Yes, indeed she was. It was determined, quite rightly in my view, to be a clear case of self-defence.'

I Know Your Secret

A look crossed Brian Sullivan's face. Was he going to probe further into that night? It had been agreed beforehand that her appearance on the show would be brief, the conversation a mere sketched outline of her story. This was her publisher's idea, who had agreed the terms, seeking merely to whet the public's appetite, that they might actually go out and buy the book. Which suited Amanda fine, because she didn't want to be on this show at all. The book was written as a means of cathartic release for herself but, as she was beginning to realise, from a publisher's perspective, marketing was as important as the writing. So she was going along with it.

But if he had been considering this, he had changed his mind. 'And as a result of the way you were treated by some members of the force, the Garda Commissioner has publicly stated that procedures are to be overhauled. That's quite an achievement, Dr Ryan.'

'Yes, it is,' she agreed, 'I'm quite proud of that, to be honest.'

'And what of your friend, Pri?' he asked.

Amanda pursed her lips, shaking her head slowly. 'Things are different now. No, we're not so friendly anymore. And that's all I'd like to say on that.'

Again, the faux look of concern crossed his face, and this time it looked anything but genuine.

'Your kids, Doctor Ryan, this can't have been easy on them. How are they bearing up?'

Amanda smiled warmly. 'They're in the audience, you can ask them yourself if you like?'

'Oh, really,' shading his eyes with a hand, in faux surprise again, because he already knew they were there.

Jess Roy

A camera on a remotely operated boom swooped down from the ceiling and picked out Danny and Lauren easily. Amanda saw their faces appear on a monitor.

'Hi... Danny and Lauren, isn't it?' Brian Sullivan said.

They both nodded.

'This can't have been easy, guys.'

They looked at one another, uncertain, before Lauren looked ahead to the presenter again.

'No,' she said, 'it hasn't.'

Amanda wanted to get up, go down to her kids, and hold them close.

'But especially for you, isn't that right, Lauren?' Brian Sullivan asked.

Lauren stared ahead blankly for a moment.

'For both of us,' she said then, glancing to her brother, smiling warmly at him, 'but you're correct, especially for me. It was a lot to take in, your father,' pausing, taking a breath, before continuing with resolve, 'a father you're particularly close to, drugged and raped your mother. I mean, if that doesn't...' her voice trailed off. 'But I've received help from an excellent therapist and I'm coming out the other end. Because I have my life to lead, and I can't lead it if I allow this to drag me back. I can't allow it too. I know my mother loves me dearly, and that's all that matters at the moment.'

'And your father?' Brian Sullivan said. 'You keep in contact?'

Amanda watched her daughter's pained expression and wanted to go to her, to protect her, but knew she couldn't.

'No,' Lauren said, 'neither of us do. I don't think I, we, either of us, can ever forgive him... but still, he is my father. I don't know what the future holds, maybe in time, a lot of time, but not now.'

I Know Your Secret

'Andrew O'Shaughnessy was a friend of the family too, wasn't he?'

Amanda's head swung towards the presenter. She hadn't expected that question to be asked of her children. None of that had been discussed beforehand.

'Yes,' it was Danny, a note of defiance in his tone. 'And I feel sorry for them, really, his family. But what else can I say? What can anyone say? We're all victims.'

'Indeed,' Brian Sullivan said, turning back to Amanda, 'there is nothing anyone can say. You've returned to work, Doctor Ryan?'

'No,' she said, 'I haven't. And I won't. I'm taking early retirement. There's a big world out there, and I want to see as much of it as I can. This is my time to live, to explore.'

A faux laugh and a wave of the hand. 'Early retirement. Surely not, you look much too young for early retirement.'

Amanda could not help but give a curt nod. The truth was, Brian Sullivan, in his well-cut suit and clipped diction, his dyed hair and made up face, was beginning to irritate her. She wanted this interview finished with. The TV host, attuned to the nuances of guests from over a quarter century of presenting, immediately sensed it. His smile widened, as he looked to the audience and swept his arm towards Amanda.

'Doctor Amanda Ryan, ladies and gentlemen, and her book *Living a Nightmare*. It's out now. And I can't recommend it highly enough.'

A large screen hanging from the ceiling announced 'Ad Break', a clock beneath running down the seconds from two minutes.

A voice through an intercom announced, 'Anyone need the bathroom, do so now. Thank you.'

Jess Roy

'That wasn't so bad, was it?' Brian Sullivan said to her with a lingering look.

'No, it wasn't,' she lied.

'I don't bite, do I, Doctor Ryan?'

'No, you certainly don't bite.'

'Okay then, see you in the Green Room in a little while? We can have a glass of Champagne maybe.'

Amanda stood. 'Unfortunately, I can't. I have an arrangement to meet a friend. But thank you again, for everything.'

The TV host did not reply, his attention taken up by his schedule card and the next guest who was walking onto the set, a small young man, dressed in jeans, boots and sweatshirt.

'Ted Breen, up and coming country star, how are you? Pleasure to meet you, sir, take a seat.'

Amanda stepped away and a head-phoned assistant pointed towards a door at the back of the studio, smiling as she passed. Brian Sullivan said nothing, like he had already forgotten her. Danny and Lauren met her by the door. It led out to the rear car park, and was the one she had come through earlier.

They group hugged.

'You were brilliant,' Lauren said.

'Yes, Mum, brillo,' added Danny.

Amanda pulled back, resting a hand on the back of each of her children's shoulders, looking at them both in turn.

'I'm so proud of you, you've dealt with this amazingly.' Her eyes lingered on Lauren. 'Especially you, Lauren.'

'I have Fiona to thank for that. She's been amazing, Mum, really.'

Yes, Fiona had been amazing. When Amanda had told her she was appearing on the nation's number one talk show, she'd been very specific: she did not want it mentioned that she was counselling her daughter. 'Keep it vague, just say we stay in touch occasionally, and leave it at that.'

And Amanda had. Fiona, after all, had been struck off the Medical Register.

'What are you two up to now?' Amanda asked.

'We're catching a late night movie,' Danny said, 'actually, it's kind of a double date.'

'No it's not,' Lauren said, 'I said I liked him, your friend Eamon, that's all, and I agreed to go with you to the movie because I want to see it. That's it.'

'Ya, ya, whatever,' Danny said with a laugh, 'but we need to get going, or we'll be late.'

Amanda smiled as Danny pushed the door and they all stepped out into the night.

'I've a taxi coming in a couple of minutes, I can give you a lift,' Amanda said, tightening her scarf around her neck. The night was cold.

'No thanks,' Danny replied, 'it's right by here.'

She watched her children walking across the car park towards the security barrier, speaking briefly with the security officer, and then making their way out onto the busy roadway. She felt that sense of overwhelming love again, doing her best to ignore the small barb of guilt that was beginning to scratch in a corner of her consciousness, trying to get a firmer hold on her, that somehow, maybe, she could have done all this differently. She took a breath, upturning the sack of potatoes in her mind, watching them roll away, emptying the bag completely.

There, that's better.

The headlights swung into the car park and a moment later the taxi pulled up next to her.

Jess Roy

'Doctor Amanda Ryan?' the driver asked, 'for Lambert's on the Green?'

'That's me,' she said, pulling the door open and getting in. Now, she was beginning to feel nervous.

I Know Your Secret

Chapter 60

S he was the first to arrive. The maître d' showed her to the discreet table in a dark wood-panelled alcove along a side wall. The restaurant was long and narrow, and she could glimpse through the window the tops of people hurrying by, couples mostly, and gaggles of young men and women at this time of evening. She checked the time, just gone 10:15 p.m. She'd hoped they wouldn't be late: the maître d' had gently but insistently informed her that orders ceased at 10:30 sharp.

It was almost that time when they rushed in together. The maître d' didn't need to check their booking; they were the last diners of the day. He led them immediately to the table as Amanda stood and embraced each in turn. A waiter appeared and handed them menus, continuing to hover, pen prominently poised above his pad.

'We'd better order, or we'll end up having to go to a fast-food joint,' Amanda said.

They hastily did, and when their pre-dinner cocktails arrived and they began to sip and relax, Amanda spoke.

'I was beginning to think you weren't going to show.'

'We got stuck in traffic, sorry.'

Amanda gave Fiona a warm smile.

'That's alright.'

'The truth is,' said the other woman, 'Fiona had to coax me somewhat.

I didn't think I could come, that anyone would want to be around me, least of all you two.' Emily O'Shaughnessy's tone was, just like her expression, pained.

'Enough,' it was Fiona, tapping a fish fork on her glass theatrically, 'I need to say something.'

Amanda and Emily turned silently to look at her.

'This is our first time gathering together,' Fiona went on, 'and hopefully it won't be our last. But please, can we look towards the rising sun as it were, to a new day, for us all, and make a pact?'

'A pact?' Amanda said.

'Yes, a pact,' Fiona said, placing one hand onto the centre of the table, 'come on, join me, lay your hands on top of mine.' They did, and Fiona continued, 'Because we vow to live from this moment forward in the understanding that we carry no shame, and that although we are victims, we refuse to act as such, because we are now free, empowered in the knowledge that we can live our lives without the censure of our fiercest critic – ourselves. But we will not squander this freedom, continuously looking over our shoulders to the past, but we decide here and now to leave it behind and set our eyes only to the future, to the promises it holds. A toast, ladies. To us.'

They picked up their glasses.

'To us,' Fiona repeated.

'To us,' they said in unison.

The End

Acknowledgements

Firstly, I would like to thank you, dear reader, for taking a chance on me in purchasing this book. It humbles me that someone would pay their hard earned cash for something I essentially wrote at my kitchen table. I sincerely hope you enjoyed it. If this is the case, I'd really appreciate if you could leave a favourable review on Amazon and Goodreads, because positive reviews are the wings that allow books to fly. If you didn't like it, allow me to activate my neuralyzer and wipe away all memory of having read I Know Your Secret, lol.

Moving on. I would like to say a big thank you to Jim Ody, founder of Question Mark Press, what I would describe as a writers' publishing co-op, and without whom I simply would not have been able to do this.

Thank you too to my fellow QMP authors, M.L. Rayner, Jane Badrock, E.J. Wood, Michelle Kidd, Zóe Lee O'Farrell, and L.B. Stimson. Thank-you all for your support. Thank you to Shelagh Corker, Sue Scott and Andrea Neal for their invaluable editing, and to Elli Toney for an excellent cover. I'd also like to thank Valerie Dickinson for her continued encouragement and support. To my wife, Eileen, the first person to read my work and who disproves the maxim you should never seek the opinion of friends and family with your writing. Eileen can be my toughest critic, but always seems to be spot on in her observations.

Finally, I'd like to finish by raising a virtual glass beneath a virtual banner, the words on it in flashing neon lights: THANK YOU.

I Know Your Secret is essentially a work of fiction, but key facts are based on real life events, taken from a variety of sources, rather than from one single experience or episode. Under my real name, Michael Scanlon, I've written three crime novels, all published by Bookouture. However, in writing this book, I considered it a good idea to use a short, snappy, pseudonym, in keeping it with the style of writing of the book, and also to separate it from my crime novels. Hence Jess Roy was born. I've been writing all my life, but only became published in 2019. Help in my publishing journey came from an unexpected source. In 2014 I became gravely ill with a mystery illness while on holiday in Spain. I nearly died. During those dark years of slow recovery I filled my time by reading and writing copiously. Married to Eileen, we have one beautiful daughter, Sarah. We live in the West of Ireland, which is damp and grey in winter but becomes an explosion of colour in summer.

Question Mark Press

To find out more go to:
www.questionmarkpress.com

Question Mark Horror

A new series of YA Horror books. One series by a handful of authors.

Are you ready?

1 – Camp Death
2 – Ouija

Printed in Great Britain
by Amazon

70929202R00196